Curiosity Killed
the Cat Sitter

Curiosity Killed the Cat Sitter

The First Dixie Hemingway Mystery

Blaize Clement

THORNDIKE
CHIVERS

This Large Print edition is published by Thorndike Press®, Waterville, Maine USA and by BBC Audiobooks Ltd, Bath, England.

Published in 2006 in the U.S. by arrangement with St. Martin's Press, LLC.

Published in 2006 in the U.K. by arrangement with the author.

U.S. Hardcover ISBN   0-7862-8402-1   (Mystery)
U.K. Hardcover ISBN 10 1 4056 3761 7   (Chivers Large Print)
U.K. Hardcover ISBN 13 978 1 405 63761 9
U.K. Softcover ISBN 10 1 4056 3762 5   (Camden Large Print)
U.K. Softcover ISBN 13 978 1 405 63762 6

The text of this Large Print edition is unabridged.
Other aspects of the book may vary from the original edition.

Set in 16 pt. Plantin by Christina S. Huff.

Printed in the United States on permanent paper.

British Library Cataloguing-in-Publication Data available

Library of Congress Cataloging-in-Publication Data

Clement, Blaize.
    Curiosity killed the cat sitter : the first Dixie Hemingway
mystery / by Blaize Clement.
        p. cm. — (Thorndike Press large print mystery)
    ISBN 0-7862-8402-1 (lg. print : hc : alk. paper)
    1. Women detectives — Florida — Sarasota — Fiction.
2. Sarasota (Fla.) — Fiction.   3. Pet sitting — Fiction.
4. Cats — Fiction.   5. Large type books.   I. Title.
II. Thorndike Press large print mystery series.
PS3603.L463C87 2006b
    813'.6—dc22   2005034402

Curiosity Killed the Cat Sitter

Acknowledgments

My greatest thanks to the "Thursday Group" — Susana Gonzalez, Kate Holmes, Greg Jorgensen, and Clark Lauren — who listened to scenes from this novel as it took shape, and who are unfailingly kind even when I write trash.

Also to Pamela Strom and Dr. Everett Shocket for law-enforcement and medical information.

To Florida licensed trauma cleaner Bill Sullivan for explaining how crime scenes are sanitized. To professional pet-sitter Virginia Wilson for insider information. To Lora Garrett, crime-scene technician with the Sarasota County Sheriff's Department, for information on who does what in forensic investigation. To Dr. Reinhard Motte, Miami–Dade County associate medical examiner, who gave me some unpleasant facts involving death and pets. To Mary V. Welk, ER nurse and author, who cut to the nitty-gritty and told me how my victim would look.

And most of all, thanks to my dream team: Marcia Markland, who is such a warm and generous person that she should be in an editors' hall of fame; Diana Szu, Marcia's patient and efficient assistant; Annelise Robey, who was brave enough to become my agent, and Don Cleary, who handles all the legal stuff with wit and style.

1

It was about 3:30 Thursday afternoon when I stopped by Marilee Doerring's house to pick up a new key. I have keys to all my clients' houses. I carry them on a big round ring like a French chatelaine. If a robber broke into my apartment, it wouldn't be to rip off my Patsy Cline CDs, it would be for my key ring.

I'm Dixie Hemingway, no relation to you know who. I'm a pet-sitter. I live on Siesta Key in Sarasota, Florida, and so do all my clients. Until three years ago, when the world crashed around me, I was a deputy with the Sarasota County Sheriff's Department. Now I take care of animals. I go to their homes while their owners are away and feed them and groom them and play with them. They don't ask a lot of questions or expect much from me, and I don't have to interact with people any more than I choose to. At least most of the time. On this particular afternoon, I was about to become a lot more involved with a lot more people than I wanted to be.

Siesta Key is an eight-mile barrier island connected to the mainland by two bridges. The Gulf of Mexico laps at the west side, and Sarasota Bay and the Intracoastal Waterway are on the east. Inside the key itself, there are fifty miles of canals, so we have almost as many boats and boat docks as we have seabirds, which is a bunch. You name it, we've got it. Terns, plovers, gulls, egrets, herons, cranes, spoonbills, storks, ibis, and pelicans all happily scoop up their favorite entrées on our beaches and in our backyards. Offshore, manatees and dolphins play in the warm water.

Counting part-time residents, the key is home to about 24,000 suntanned people. Except for "the season," when snowbirds come down and inflict their money on us, and spring break, when college students get drunk and pee on the hibiscus, Siesta Key is a quiet, laid-back place. On the map, it looks like an alligator's head with an extremely long and skinny nose. Siesta Village and Roberts Bay form the head, with Crescent Beach where eyes would be. The nose is just wide enough for one street — Midnight Pass Road — with private lanes and tourist lodgings on each side, along with occasional undeveloped wooded areas.

Marilee's cat was a silver-blue Abyssinian named Ghost. Awful name, sweet cat. I had taken care of him several times before, and the only thing different about this time was that Marilee had called the night before to tell me she'd had her locks changed, so I would have to pick up a new key before she left town. She lived on the bay side of Midnight Pass Road, about midway between Turtle Beach and the south bridge. Her street was curvy, lushly tree-lined and short, the house a low-slung stucco with a red barrel-tile roof and deep recessed arches over doors and windows, the kind of Mexican-Mediterranean hybrid that Floridians love. Dwarf schefflerias and pittisporum and hollies made swirling patterns of ground cover in the front yard, interspersed with clumps of red geraniums and bird of paradise plants. The front door undoubtedly had once hung on a cathedral in some South American country, and the doorbell was a deep-bonging thing that sounded like it might have come from the same cathedral. As I waited, I could hear the faint sound of classical piano music from next door.

Marilee opened the door a cautious slit and peered out at me. Later, I would wonder about that, but at the time it didn't seem unusual for a cat owner. A cat can be

11

taking a nap on its hundred-dollar kitty pillow or watching a television program especially designed for its feline pleasure, but let somebody open an outside door the narrowest bit, and it will go streaking out like it's escaping a torture chamber.

Marilee was stunningly beautiful, with glossy black hair tumbling over her shoulders in the kind of casual disarray that takes a lot of work. It framed an oval face with skin like a cosmetic commercial, only hers wasn't airbrushed, it was really that perfect. Her eyes were dark violet blue, with thick black lashes, and her mouth had the kind of moist expectancy that automatically makes you think of sex. I could smell expensive perfume, the kind I've only worn by rubbing a strip from a magazine on my wrist. She was wearing a short pink terry-cloth robe that cost more than my entire wardrobe, including the winter coat I have salted away in mothballs in case I ever travel north. Her legs were long and slim, tanned enough to look healthy but not so dark as to look like she tarted herself up in a tanning booth.

At first she looked surprised to see me, then in that breathy voice of hers, said, "Oh, you've come for the key! I was just about to jump in the shower. Hold on, I'll get it."

She closed the door and I imagined her

bare feet sprinting over Mexican tile. Next door, the music stopped and a moment later the garage door opened and a white Jeep Cherokee backed out and headed toward Midnight Pass Road. As it made the turn, I could see the driver was a young man, no more than a teenager, which surprised me. Somehow I never think of teenagers listening to classical music, which shows what a lowbrow I am.

Marilee opened the door again, wider this time, and stretched her arm out with a loop of red silk ribbon dangling from a finger. A shiny new door key hung on the ribbon like a gold pendant on a necklace.

Feeling a bit like the upstairs maid, I held out my hand and let her drop it into my palm. I said, "Don't forget to leave me a number where I can reach you, and the date and time you'll return."

I should have whipped out my notebook and made her give me the number right then. But she knew the routine, and I already had all the pertinent information in my files — her vet's name and number, the dates of Ghost's immunization shots, his medical history, his favorite foods and toys and where they were located, and his favorite hiding place in case he decided to play Where's Ghost?

I told her to have a safe journey and not to worry about Ghost, and went on my merry way. I never saw Marilee again, at least not alive.

My alarm went off at 4:00 the next morning, and I got right up. One thing you can say for me, I wake up well. I sleep in underpants, so all I had to do was pull on khaki cargo shorts and a T and lace up my Keds. I brushed my teeth, splashed water on my face, pulled my hair into a ponytail, and I was ready. Animals don't expect you to dress up for them. I could go naked for all they care. By 4:15, I was halfway to my first stop. The sky was just beginning to pink a little around the edges, and the early April air was a balmy seventy degrees.

The sea breeze freshens in the early morning on Siesta Key, tickling the undersides of palm leaves and sending orgasmic tremors through trailing bougainvillea. Snowy egrets open their topaz eyes and stretch their blue-toed feet, and great blue herons stilt-leg it to the edge of the shore to pick up breakfast coming in on the tide. The air tastes of brine and fish and sand, and throaty chants of mourning doves underscore the squawk of seagulls rising and circling on air currents. It's my favorite time of day, a time when I have the streets almost to myself and can zoom along on my bike like a gull looking for early-waking grubs and unwary snails.

I always see to the dogs first and leave the cats and occasional birds and rabbits and hamsters for later. It isn't that I play favorites, it's just that dogs are needier than other pets. Leave a dog alone for very long and it'll start going a little nuts. Cats, on the other hand, try to give you the impression they didn't even know you were gone. "Oh, were you out?" they'll say, "I didn't notice." Then they'll raise their tails to show you their little puckered anuses and walk away.

My first stop was at Sam and Libby Grayson's, a retired couple who had gone north to visit their daughter. A wooded area separated the Graysons' street from Marilee's, and with tall trees lining the street and woods behind, it was like being in the middle of a dark forest. The Graysons' house was a two-story ultramodern built of cypress and glass, with a high vaulted cage around the lanai that gave it a look of dignified exuberance. One of the bulbs in the twin coach lights flanking their garage had burned out, and I made a mental note to replace it when I came back in the afternoon.

Until a few years ago, nobody on Siesta Key ever thought about burning security lights. But since everybody north of Georgia seems to have looked up one day and said, "By gawd, I'm moving to Florida!" we've started having break-ins here and there, even a murder now and then. So now people on Siesta Key leave night lights burning so potential burglars and rapists can see better.

I propped my bike in front of the garage and sorted through my keys. Rufus, the Graysons' schnauzer, started barking to show me he was on the job as guard dog, but he knew it was me and his heart wasn't in it. As soon as I pushed open the door, he was all over me, not the least bit ashamed to let me see how glad he was that I had come. I like that about dogs. They don't worry that you might not like them as much as they like you and hold off until they're sure, they just go ahead and declare themselves and take the chance of being rejected.

I knelt down to hug him and let him kiss my chin. "Hey, old sweet Rufus," I said, "How's my old sweet Rufus?" Dogs like you even when you say the same dumb things over and over. Cats expect you to have more self-restraint.

I got his leash out of the wicker basket in the foyer, and as soon as I opened the door, he was out like a shot. I had to hold him steady while I locked the door behind me, and then we both loped off. Rufus plunged off the pavement to pee on a palm tree, then raced on ahead of me. My Keds made smacking sounds on the asphalt, so I moved to the edge of the street where pine needles muffled the noise. I didn't want to cause some retiree to think a criminal was running down the street and haul out his handgun. Something about not having to shovel snow anymore and being surrounded by sunshine and tropical foliage 365 days of the year causes a lot of people to feel so guilty that they compensate by scaring themselves with thoughts of imminent crime. They go out and buy themselves a gun and sort of hope they'll get to shoot somebody with it, so you have to be careful.

Rufus did his business next to a hibiscus bush and I picked it up in a poop bag and kicked a cover of pine needles over the spot before I moved on. I like to be tidy. I let the leash play out so Rufus could feel independent, and he bounced into the middle of the street to check out a fluffy egret feather. He whoofed at it and nosed it around, showing off to let me see he was alert to anything new. Something caught his attention from the woods, and he raised his head and began barking loud enough to wake everybody on the block.

I jerked the leash taut and said, "Shhhh! Quiet!"

He barked again and I turned to look over my right shoulder. I could have sworn I saw a figure slip behind a tree trunk in the murky shadows.

Any number of things could have been moving around back there in the predawn shadows. A snowy egret or a great blue heron could have dived for a baby black snake from one of the oak trees. A squirrel could have awakened early and leaped from a branch with a flash of white underbelly. Or somebody returning from a middle-of-the-night tryst might have seen me and ducked into that dark thicket. God knows, there are plenty of men and women who drift in and out of one another's beds here on the key, and some of them are married to other people. But still, the skin on my shoulders puckered and I felt uneasy, with that tingly feeling that tells you unfriendly eyes are watching.

I yanked Rufus out of the street and set off for the Graysons' house so fast he had to do a scrambling dance to catch up. As we trotted up the driveway, the *Herald-Tribune* delivery man turned into the street and sailed a paper into the flower bed by the front walk. I retrieved it and put it in a wooden chest outside the front door where people leave drop-offs when the Graysons aren't home. Somebody had left a stack of paperbacks rubber-banded together, and in the pale glow cast by the lone security light I could see a yellow Post-it stuck on top with a heavily scrawled "Thanx!"

I fed and brushed Rufus and put out fresh water for him. With him following me like an aide carrying a clipboard, I did a fast check of the house to make sure he hadn't gotten bored overnight and chewed up something. The Graysons' latest acquisition was a full-sized carousel horse that had once been part of John Ringling's collection — Ringling practically built Sarasota, and you can't turn around here without seeing something circus-related. The horse was mounted on a floor-to-ceiling brass pole in the dining room, and it gave the room a happy, carefree look. I took a moment to admire it before I turned on the TV in the den for Rufus. I set it on Nickelodeon so he could watch *Mister Ed*. Then I hugged him good-bye.

"I'll be back tonight," I promised. "You be a good boy, okay?" I don't know why I ask animals questions like that. If one of them ever answers me, I'll probably freak out.

Rufus was sitting in the front hall with his head cocked to one side when I shut the door behind me. I felt guilty leaving him alone, but everybody has to come to the realization sooner or later that we're all alone in this world.

2

It was almost 6:00 a.m. by the time I worked my way to Marilee Doerring's house. On that twisty street, the house next door was the only one visible, but I could see a couple of lights there. The normal world was beginning to wake up. I let myself in with my new door key and flipped on the foyer light. Abyssinians are people cats, and when I'd taken care of Ghost before, he had always come bounding to the door to greet me.

I called, "Ghost?"

Dogs come when you call, and cats answer. But there were no little *nik-nik* sounds of friendly greeting. A stack of outgoing mail was on the foyer table, with the top envelope addressed to the IRS. I figured Marilee must have planned to mail it on her way out of town and forgot. While I gave Ghost time to decide to come out of hiding, I flipped through the other envelopes, most addressed to department stores or utilities, and then slid the lot in a deep-flapped pocket on my cargo shorts. I would put it in her mailbox for pickup as I left.

The living room was to the left, and I ducked in to give it a quick once-over while I called to Ghost again. Sometimes bored animals do something naughty just to announce their annoyance at being left behind when their person leaves, but there were no overturned plants or shredded magazines in the living room. The air seemed oddly humid, with a warm breath coming from the glass doors opening to the lanai. Linen sheers hung over the sliders, and when I stepped closer, I could see that the glass slider was partially open.

I said, "Uh-oh," and hurried to the door. There were a ton of potted plants on the lanai, and a water hose had been left lying on the floor. Marilee had probably been interrupted watering the plants just before she left and forgot to close the slider. Peasant that I am, my first thought was that all that warm air would make the AC run harder and that Marilee's electric bill was going to be enormous. The second thought was that Ghost might have gone outside. The lanai was typical — a tiled pool at the far side and wicker furniture and potted plants grouped under the roof on the inner side. It was screened, of course, sides and top, to keep out insects and falling leaves. In Florida, screened lanais are called "cages," and anybody who is anybody has a caged lanai.

A screened door was at one side, opening to the yard. Most lanai doors have simple latch mechanisms that can be locked, but since a dedicated burglar can simply slit the screen, most people leave them unlocked so pool cleaners can get in. The furniture on the lanai made dark shapes in the murky light as I sprinted to the outside door. It wasn't firmly latched, and I pulled it shut, making sure the latch caught. I could see a light in a back window of the house next door, but no sign of Ghost.

I trotted back inside, pulling the slider shut and locking it behind me, and hurried toward Marilee's bedroom. Unless Ghost had gotten outside through the lanai door, he was probably hiding. His favorite hideaway was atop an immense antique armoire in Marilee's bedroom. Abys have powerful back legs that give them unusual jumping ability, and Ghost vaulted up there when he was nervous or when he was sulking, tucking himself into an invisible small mound.

Calling "Gho-oo-ost," I went down the hall to Marilee's bedroom. As I went through the door, I flipped the bedroom light switch, and the room's vibrant colors sprang alive. I stopped with the hairs on the back of my neck rising. Marilee's bedroom was like something out of *Architectural Digest*, with deep pumpkin walls and a tall dark bed that Pancho Villa might have slept in. Ordinarily, the room was fastidiously neat, but not today. The drawers on the bedside tables stood open, and all their contents had been raked to the floor.

Cautiously, I edged toward the dressing room between the bedroom and bathroom. Somebody had pulled everything crooked, as if they had jerked robes and dresses and skirts and jackets out to dig in their pockets. Handbags that were usually filed on shelves gaped open on the floor. A tall jewelry cabinet stood like a gap-toothed vagrant, with blank spaces where its drawers had been. The drawers were piled on the floor with jewelry spilling from them.

Whoever had done this hadn't been after valuables to pawn or sell, but for something that could be secreted in a small space. Drugs were the obvious first thought, but Marilee had never struck me as a user, and if she was a dealer it didn't seem likely that she would keep her supply in her jewelry cabinet.

In the bathroom, drawers had been similarly ransacked. A hair dryer lay on the counter with its cord plugged into an outlet by the door. It was a brush-type dryer that doubled as a curling iron, with a few black hairs caught in its bristles. Marilee usually left her bathroom so spotless that the errant hairs seemed almost obscenely disordered.

I must admit that while I was appropriately concerned that somebody had broken into Marilee's house, I was more concerned about Ghost. I went back into the bedroom and looked up at the carved cornice at the top of the armoire.

"Ghost, are you up there?"

A faint little *nik-nik* came from the top of the armoire, and Ghost came sailing down and landed at my feet. Cats hate for you to gush at them, so to protect his dignity, I let him wind himself around my ankles before I knelt to stroke the top of his head.

Ghost's hair was ticked, meaning it had several colors on one hair shaft. The overall effect was an iridescent sheen graduating from silver to pale lavender. He wore a black velvet color studded with miniature hearts and keys. The collar gave him a decadent look, like a charming French roué whom you know you shouldn't allow yourself to trust, but you can't resist.

"I was afraid somebody had taken you," I said.

He rubbed his face and neck against my leg to reassure me, gently scratching my skin with the charms on his collar. Now that we had properly greeted each other and I knew he was okay, I headed toward the kitchen. I would give Ghost his breakfast first, and while he ate I would call 911 and report the break-in. Ghost trotted behind me making happy little squeaks of anticipation. I've trained all my cat owners not to leave food out all the time, but to put it out twice a day and remove it as soon as the cat has stopped eating. That way they don't get finicky or fat, and mealtime is a big deal to them.

To a dog, food is simply a necessity of life, and they're not too picky about how it tastes or what it's served in. A weighted plastic feeding bowl suits a dog just fine, and you can give them the exact same food twice a day and they'll think you're the greatest chef in the world. Cats, on the other hand, are snooty gourmands. Oh sure, they may supplement their finicky diet with an occasional mouse head or lizard tail, but that's more to satisfy their hunting instinct than for the taste. Cats like their food fresh and flavorful, and they'll turn up their noses today at what they loved yesterday. If their dishes aren't spotlessly clean, they'll even turn up their noses at food they love.

Cats don't shove their bowls around on the floor, either. They sit in front of them daintily, giving the impression of having patted a linen napkin in place. Cat owners therefore feed their cats in dishes ordinarily reserved for royalty, and the cats accept them as their due. Ghost ate from a hand-painted porcelain bowl, and he lapped his drinking water from an ornately carved silver serving bowl. It held enough water for a trio of cats, but it served the purpose well enough, and both Marilee and Ghost thought its elegance was totally appropriate.

When I stepped through the kitchen door and flipped the light switch, I instinctively turned toward the water bowl, and then did a quick backward dance. I'm not sure, but I think my legs may have pedaled the air for a moment. A man was lying on the floor with his face in Ghost's silver bowl. A strip of putty-colored masking tape ran across the top of his head to the sides of the bowl, holding his nose underwater. The back of his head was caked with dried blood, and he was entirely too motionless to be alive.

For a second, my eyes darted around the kitchen, refusing to look at the body. Everything in the kitchen was normal. A stainless-steel teakettle of Italian design, with a carved yellow bird for a pouring spout, sat shining on the immaculate stove. A yellow dish towel was on the countertop beside the sink, neatly folded so both edges were turned in the way you do with guest towels. Trust Marilee to fold her dish towel that way.

I looked back at the dead man. He wore a navy blue suit, and both sleeves showed white shirt cuffs. His shoes were expensive black wingtips, well polished, the kind pimps and undertakers wear. As well as I could tell with the dried blood on his head, his hair was dark. I couldn't see his face. I tiptoed over and knelt beside him. I don't know why I tiptoed, it just seemed the right thing to do. His body had been carefully arranged so that his arms were out to the side with the elbows bent in a kind of "I surrender" pose. I took his wrist in my fingers and felt for a pulse. The wrist was cold. The man was definitely dead.

Ghost wailed a long insistent falsetto that forced me to do what I should have done already. I got up on rubbery legs and went to the wall phone and dialed 911.

The dispatcher who answered didn't sound like anybody I knew. Old training kicked in, and after I gave her Marilee's address, I said, "I've got a Signal Five, adult male."

Signal 5 means homicide victim. With his head bloody and taped to a cat's bowl, I didn't think it could be anything else.

The dispatcher verified the address and asked my name.

"Dixie Hemingway."

"Are you sure he's dead?"

Ghost had gone into a crouching position with his body stretched long and his nose twitching toward the dead man.

"Oh yes, he's dead."

"What appears to be the cause of death?"

I cleared my throat. "He appears to have drowned in a cat's water bowl."

The dispatcher was silent for a moment, and then rallied. "Inside the house or outside?"

Ghost was slinking toward the man, and I swung my foot to distract him.

"Inside. In the kitchen. I came to feed the cat and found him."

Ghost crept closer to the man's head. I skittered toward him on my Keds and tried to block his progress with my foot. He ignored me and twitched his whiskers.

"Do you know who he is?"

"No, I've never seen him before, and the woman who lives here is out of town."

"Somebody's on the way, ma'am."

Just as I hung up, it occurred to me that

the killer could still be in the house. I grabbed Ghost and ran.

I was pacing the driveway with a seething Ghost in my arms when the green-and-white squad car pulled in. The deputy who got out wasn't anybody I knew, but I knew the type well enough. Hair cut so short it was near-shaven, hard lean body under a crisp dark green uniform, black leather belt bristling with all the accoutrements of authority, and a small diamond stud in one well-shaped earlobe. I could tell from the stiff way he walked that he thought there was something fishy about a woman finding a dead body in somebody else's house before 6:00 a.m.

"You called about a dead man?"

Ghost twisted hard in my arms and glared at the deputy. Either he didn't like the tone of his voice or he was so pissed at being held against his wishes that he hated everybody on general principle. I took a moment to read the name on the deputy's ID tag: Jesse Morgan.

"I'm Dixie Hemingway," I said. "I'm a pet-sitter. The owner of the house is Marilee Doerring. She left town last night and won't be back until next week. I don't know who the dead man is."

"How do you know he's dead?"

"I tried his pulse. He's dead, trust me."

"Where'd you find him?"

"In the kitchen. I went in to feed the cat and there he was."

"And you think he . . . you think he drowned?"

I shot him a look. "Yeah, that would be my guess, since his nose is stuck in a bowl of water."

"Anybody else in there?"

"If anybody was there, they could have gone out the back door after I left. I didn't look around. I grabbed Ghost and ran."

He inclined his head a quarter of an inch toward the cat and said, "That's Ghost?"

"Yeah."

"He doesn't look happy."

"He hates being held."

"So why did you grab him? Why did you bring him outside with you?"

I blinked at him for a good five seconds before I realized he had a point. Ghost had been there when the murder was committed, and he had been there with the dead body, but I had instinctively scooped him up as if I were rescuing him. I knew the reason, but I doubted Deputy Morgan would understand how maternal impulses can kick in even when they don't make any sense.

As if he had asked a really stupid question,

I said, "He could have contaminated the area for forensics."

"Wait here," he said, and walked down the driveway and through the open front door. He had a good walk, which surprised me. I would have expected a rookie's power stomp, but it was a seasoned stride — confident but not cocky.

I crooned under my breath to Ghost, and he gradually sheathed his extended claws. A frightened or angry cat can do serious harm with its claws, but I knew he wasn't that angry. His pride was hurt at being restrained and he just needed to remind me that he could hurt me bad if he wanted to.

In a few minutes the deputy came back with his phone stuck to his ear, calling for a crime-scene unit. When he tucked the phone in its holder on his belt, he said, "I'll need to get some information from you."

"Sure, but I have to do something about Ghost first. I think I'll ask the next-door neighbor to keep him until I can take him to a day sitter."

He looked at his watch. "It's pretty early. Do you think they'll be up?"

"I saw a light there earlier. They have a teenager, and he's probably getting ready for school. I'll just be a minute."

I was off before he could tell me what he

thought of the idea. The house was about forty feet away, with a yard full of ground cover instead of grass, so I sprinted down the street. The house was built on the same lines as Marilee's, but the stucco was more pink than cream, and the front door was bright turquoise.

I rang the doorbell, and while I waited I met Ghost's outraged eyes. I blinked at him slowly, which in cat language means "I love you." That usually calms an agitated cat, but it didn't do much this time. Ghost definitely didn't blink back.

3

The woman who answered the door gave *stiff-necked* a whole new meaning. Her neck rose from her narrow shoulders like a soaring redwood, broader at the base and held stiffly upright by thick cords that showed bruised blue under her sallow skin. In comparison to her neck, her head seemed too small, made even smaller by the way her pale hair was pulled into a tight knot high at the back of her skull. She held her chin tilted upward, with her eyes squinted and the corners of her rubbery mouth turned down. From the deep grooves running from her thin nose to her jawbone, I surmised that her inverted mouth was a habitual expression.

I said, "Sorry to bother you. I'm Dixie Hemingway. I take care of Ms. Doerring's cat. There's been an incident at her house, so the Sheriff's Department will be working there for a while. I can't leave the cat in the house with all the people going in and out, and I don't have my car with me. I was hoping I could leave him with you for an hour or two."

She started to close the door and said, "I don't want to be involved."

Her carefully enunciated syllables oozed with barely suppressed contempt. She definitely felt she was speaking to an inferior, and she wanted me to know it.

I slid my foot in the door before she could close it. "The deputy over there wants me to leave him someplace, and there's really no place else to take him."

She frowned and allowed her eyes to open all the way.

I said, "He can stay on the lanai, and it will just be for a little while."

She spun around and walked away, managing to do that without moving her head. Since she hadn't slammed the door in my face, I assumed I was to follow. I stepped into a large square living room with a glass wall across the back. It was dark inside, not just because no lamps were burning but because the glass was covered by thick draperies. They were more appropriate for a cold clime where you need insulation against frigid winds, not for a sun-filled place like Florida.

Instead of pulling the cord to open the drapes, she pushed the edge aside, unlocked the slider, and held them back while I slipped through the opening. She watched me while I took Ghost to the far corner under the roof. I knelt down and let his hind legs touch the floor between my knees while I kept my hand under his chest to hold his front paws up.

I said, "You're just going to stay here for a little while, and then I'll come get you and take you to Kitty Haven. You'll like it there."

I lowered his front feet to the floor but kept one hand under his chest, ready to lift them if he tried to run. His whiskers were anxiously pointed up, and I talked low to him while I eased my backpack off. I got out one of my emergency Tender Vittles packets, along with a disposable bowl. Semimoist cat food is like Froot Loops for a child — both are poor excuses for nutrition, but they'll do in a pinch. Ghost eyed the pouch and made his skin quiver, either to show revulsion or enthusiasm, I wasn't sure. I emptied the pouch into the bowl and put it on the floor. Slowly, I pulled my hand away from his chest and stroked his head and neck. He dropped his eyelids to half-mast to show me he was not pleased with me, but he didn't run when I stood up.

Instead, he crouched in a martyred sulk, tail wrapped tightly to his side, paws folded under his chest, head looking straight forward. Do whatever you want, his posture said. I have to eat breakfast in a strange place and there's a dead man in my house, but don't give me a second thought. I'll be fine.

I went back inside, and as the woman let the drapes fall shut, I saw Ghost hunker over the Tender Vittles and dig in.

"I don't know your name," I said. "I should have asked."

She switched on a lamp that managed to look both priceless and ugly at the same time, and in its weak glow I noticed that a gleaming grand piano dominated the room.

"I am Olga Winnick," she said stiffly.

A tall skinny boy with white-blond hair and an innocent mouth stepped into the room with his knobby neck angled to the side trying to see what was going on. He was dressed for school in jeans and a white polo shirt with a collar. His eyes were red and puffy, as if he needed several hours more sleep. He stopped like a spooked horse when he saw me.

"Oh, hi," I said. "I'm Dixie Hemingway. Your mother is letting me leave my cat on your lanai for a couple of hours while the Sheriff's Department is in the house next door."

He gave me a tight, self-conscious grin, the way adolescents do when they can't figure out what they're supposed to do next.

Mrs. Winnick said, "My son is a pianist. He isn't interested in what happens next door."

I said, "Is that you? I've heard you. I always thought it was the classical radio station."

He didn't answer, either from embarrassment or because his mother jumped in before he could.

"He's going to Juilliard soon." From the way she said it, she might as well have added "you stupid clod."

I made appropriate noises to show how impressed I was that the kid was a musician, while he looked like he would have been extremely grateful if the floor had opened and let him fall through to oblivion. Neither of them volunteered his name, but I was afraid he would have a nervous breakdown if I asked, so I let it slide.

"I'll pick the cat up as soon as I can," I said. "Would you mind giving him a bowl of water? If he has water, he'll be okay."

Mrs. Winnick turned to look at me full on. "I am allowing you to leave that woman's cat on my lanai. That should be enough."

Her son's face flamed, and he turned and left us.

I got out as fast as I could, with the slamming front door making it clear that Mrs. Winnick felt sorely imposed upon.

Another green-and-white patrol car was pulling into the drive as I got back to Deputy Jesse Morgan, and an ambulance was slowly gliding to the curb. Morgan's eyes flicked to my braless bosom and up again. "Got the cat squared away?"

"For a little while. I have some other pets on my schedule, and I have to go home and get my car. Would it be okay if I do that before I talk to anybody?"

Morgan looked toward the street, where a third deputy was parking in front of the ambulance. Both deputies got out of their patrol cars and spoke to the EMTs standing at the back of the ambulance. An unmarked sergeant's car and a crime-scene truck with forensics people drove up and parked behind the ambulance. People swarmed into the street and up the driveway. I knew most of them. I did not look forward to the moment when they recognized me.

Sergeant Owens spoke to me first. Owens is a skinny fifty-something African-American a foot taller than me, which makes him about six three. He has a long face and droopy eyes like a basset hound. His slow and easy facade masks a lightning-quick mind. More than one person who thought it would be easy to put one over on Sergeant Owens has found themselves in deep doo-doo. I served in his unit, and I speak from experience.

Maybe he already knew I was the one who had called in the report, because he didn't seem surprised to see me. He put out his hand, cordial as if we were in a receiving line, and said, "How are you, Dixie?"

"Except for this little blip on my horizon," I said, "I'm just fine."

The last time I'd seen Sergeant Owens, he hadn't asked me how I was, he'd told me. What he'd actually said was, "You're totally fucked up, Dixie. No way are you ready to go back to work." You have to respect a man who can look you in the eye and tell you that.

Deputy Morgan said, "Miz Hemingway was just asking me if it would be okay for her to take care of some other pets and then go home and get her car before she talks to anybody. There was a cat in the house, and she took it next door. She has to come back and get it and take it someplace else."

Sergeant Owens narrowed his eyes in the exact same look that Ghost had given me from Mrs. Winnick's lanai. Both of them seemed to have expected better of me.

"How long do you think you'll be?"

"Two and a half hours, tops."

"Okay, see you then."

Another crime-scene unit was oozing down the street looking for a place to park when I pedaled away. I was an hour behind schedule, and I felt guilty about it, as if the cats waiting for me were looking at their clocks and tapping their paws. I also felt a bit of envy for the quickened adrenaline all the people at the crime scene were having. I don't care how gruesome and disgusting it is, crime is a lot more fascinating than cleaning litter boxes.

4

It was almost nine o'clock when I finished seeing to the other pets, and I had a no-caffeine-yet headache and slippery armpits. I pedaled home, tossed my dirty clothes in the washer to run later, and jumped in the shower. My hair is the drip-dry kind that I can pull back in a ponytail and forget, so all I had to do to make myself presentable was slather on sunscreen and roll transparent color on my mouth. I love the sun, but I tend to fry when I'm in it, so I pretty much keep the Beaver 43 people in business. I put on clean khaki shorts and a sleeveless knit top, this time with a bra, and in less than fifteen minutes, I was in my Bronco and headed back up Midnight Pass Road. The leather seats were already hot on the backs of my thighs, but a blast from the AC cooled my face and left my nipples pleasantly puckered.

I drove north on Midnight Pass Road to Marilee's street and parked at the curb. A second crime-scene unit had arrived, along with trucks from all the local media. A few neighbors and curious onlookers had gathered outside to stare and talk, and reporters from NBC, ABC, CBS, BLAB, and Fox were interviewing anybody who would talk to them. Crime-scene tape was stretched across the front entrance, and a contamination sheet had been posted by the front door for everybody to sign as they entered and left.

When I walked up the drive, Deputy Jesse Morgan was outside keeping the curious at bay, and Sergeant Owens was just coming out of the house. He saw me and did a U-turn, flapping his hand at me in a gesture that I took to mean "Wait here."

In a moment, he came out with a man in dark pleated trousers and an unlined teal linen jacket with the sleeves casually pushed up. Open-collared white knit shirt. Leather sandals. Smooth bronze tan, like somebody who spent a lot of time on the tennis courts or polo grounds. At first I thought they had found a rich Italian relative of Marilee's, but Owens said, "Dixie, this is Detective Guidry of CIB. He'll be handling the case."

Guidry stepped close and held out his hand. He had a nice handshake, firm and dry. His face was sober edging onto stern, but laugh lines fanned from the corners of his eyes, and his mouth had twin parentheses at the sides. A beaky nose and dark hair cut short, with beginnings of silver showing at the temples and above the ears.

Before he could speak, I said, "I hate to ask you to wait some more, but I'm really worried about the cat. I left it next door and I told the woman I'd come get it in a couple of hours. It'll take me about ten minutes to run it over to the day-care place. Is that okay?"

He said, "You found the body a little before six this morning, right?"

"Around then."

"Have you had breakfast?"

"No, and I'm about ready to start gnawing on my arm."

He grinned. "Why don't you take the cat wherever it has to go and we'll eat while we talk."

I could have kissed him. We agreed to meet in fifteen minutes at the Village Diner and then he and Sergeant Owens went back inside the house. I went to the back of my Bronco and unfolded a cardboard cat-carrying case. I put a folded towel on its floor and loped to the Winnicks', where a black Mercedes now sat in the driveway. The front door flew open before I got to it, and a dark-haired man in a powder blue suit came storming out with an infuriated scowl on his face.

He stopped when he saw me, and I could almost see the deliberate muscle-by-muscle transition as he got himself under control. His shoulders and chest were broad as a linebacker's, but his short legs made him eye-to-eye with me. His face was familiar, the kind you see on billboards and flyers during campaigns for local elections, but I couldn't place it.

"Good morning," he said. He reached to shake my hand, revealing a raw scratch running diagonally across the back of his right wrist. His eyes were a little too close together for my taste, and if he'd ever had a sweet mouth like his son, it had gotten narrowed into one that seemed to have forgotten how to make a sincere smile.

I gave him the tips of my fingers to shake, and he enfolded them in a hot meaty hand. "I'm Dr. Win. I understand there's some kind of problem next door."

I flinched. I knew that voice, and I knew that name. Carl Winnick was a radio psychologist beloved by people who felt they'd been cheated out of their deserved special place by single mothers, minorities, homosexuals, and feminists. He daily filled the airwaves with ranting diatribes about how

45

public schools were teaching sex perversion to eight-year-olds, how white men were losing their jobs to illegal immigrants, and how working women were causing children to become drug addicts. He was best known for fighting to keep alive an idiotic Florida law that required unmarried mothers giving up their babies for adoption to run newspaper ads giving their names and the dates and places where they'd had sexual intercourse. Three years before, he had added me to the list of people he considered a threat to his definition of a family.

He had left the door open, and Olga Winnick stepped forward to grip its edge, as if she had to hold on to something to keep from falling. Her face was wet with tears, and her mouth was open in a rictus of despair.

I said, "I just came to pick up the cat."

He gave a false hearty laugh. "Oh, yes! The cat! Mustn't forget the cat!"

He rushed past me and got in the Mercedes and started the engine. For some reason, I imagined his fingers shaking when he turned the key. As he backed out of the driveway, he gave me a side-to-side wave like a beauty queen in a parade.

Mrs. Winnick was still hanging on to the edge of the door, mournfully watching her husband's departure the way a loyal dog watches her master drive away.

There was no use pretending I hadn't caught her crying her eyes out. "I'm sorry," I said. "This is obviously a bad time to come."

"It's nothing," she said. "We had an argument. Just a heated debate, really."

From the raw wound I'd seen on his hand, I thought it might have been more than a heated debate. I had been on enough domestic-disturbance calls as a deputy to know that husbands and wives who seem the epitome of decorum may go at each other like barroom brawlers.

As I got closer to her, I got a whiff of an odor on her breath that I remembered from living with my mother, the scent of alcohol overlaid with mouthwash. Even this early in the morning, Olga Winnick had been fortifying her courage with booze.

Inanely, I said, "These things happen."

I made a beeline to the back sliders where the heavy drapes were still drawn. As soon as I opened the slider, Ghost came running toward me making little chirping noises of relief. I squatted on my heels to stroke him, then lifted him into the cardboard case and closed it. He whined and poked a paw through one of the air holes, but it couldn't be helped. I retrieved the food bowl and checked the lanai floor for errant Tender Vittles crumbs. There were none. There was also no water bowl.

With the carrying case in both hands, I went through the living room while Mrs. Winnick tracked along behind me.

"It's this place," she said. "Nothing but cheap, predatory women living here, and half of them are Jews."

For a moment there, I had been feeling sorry for her, but the woman was as pompous and bigoted as her husband. It was a good thing they had found each other, instead of contaminating two marriages.

With my back teeth touching, I said, "Thank you so much for keeping Ghost," and bolted.

She stood in the doorway and glared at me all the way back to my Bronco. I guess she thought I was one of the predatory women after her husband.

I put the cat-carrying case in the front seat and talked to Ghost as we drove north on Midnight Pass Road. He had got an arm through an air hole all the way up to his armpit and was waving it frantically while he made piteous mewing noises to alert people that he was being catnapped.

From the traffic light where Midnight

Pass intersects with Stickney Point from the mainland, beachside condos and private clubs stand shoulder-to-shoulder behind hibiscus hedges and palm trees. They all have salty names like Midnight Cove, Crystal Sands, Siesta Dunes, Island House, Sea Club. My personal favorite is Our House at the Beach. If you spend your vacation there, you can truthfully tell your friends, "We're going down to Our House at the Beach."

At Beach Road, I turned left and slowed down so I wouldn't hit any of the half-naked vacationers crossing the street to get to Crescent Beach. It's amazing how many normally sensible women come to the key, deck themselves out in skimpy bikinis, tie a beach towel around their hips, and step out into oncoming traffic with bemused smiles on their lips. I think it's the seaside's negative ions that get to them.

Kitty Haven is on Avenida del Mare about a block off Beach Road in an old Florida-style house — yellow frame with crisp white hurricane shutters and a deep front porch. Except for areas planted with liriope and palmettos and century plants, the yard is completely covered in cedar chips. Walking to the front door through the smell of all that cedar always makes me feel like I'm inside a gerbil cage.

Kitty Haven is like a cross between a brothel and a grandmother's house, with lush velvet, soft music, and a TV screen that plays continuous films of twittering birds and darting fish. A bell tinkled to announce my arrival, and a couple of calico tabbies lolling on windowsills raised their heads to look me over. Marge Preston bustled from the back, leaving a floating wake of wispy cat hairs like the precursors of angel wings. If I were a cat, Marge is the person I'd want for my human. She's plump and white-haired like Mrs. Santa Claus, with a soft voice and a light touch that soothe the most agitated cat. She took the case and held it up to look inside the vents, and I swear Ghost began to purr.

"You'll have to keep his collar," she said.

"Oh, of course."

Marge set the case on the floor and she and I knelt to open it. I stroked Ghost's head, letting my fingers slip down the back of his neck and under his velvet collar. The collar had an elastic insert to allow it to slide over his head, and I brought it out on my fingertips and pushed it up on my wrist.

"I don't know how long he'll be here," I said. "Something happened at his house and he can't go home just yet. His name is Ghost. He hasn't had water or a litter box for over two hours. He's had a lot of stress today, so when you feed him, you might stir in some vitamin C."

Marge made tuttutting sounds as she bustled off to the back room to set things right, while Ghost told her in self-pitying yips and growls how he'd been sorely mistreated.

I got back in the Bronco and whipped around the corner, and nosed into a parking place in front of the Village Diner. Detective Guidry was already seated in the last booth in the corner with two steaming mugs of coffee on the table. I tossed my backpack onto the seat and slid in, grabbing one of the mugs and taking a big hit almost before I was settled.

"God, that's good."

The charms on Ghost's collar winked on my wrist, and I realized I still wore it. I wanted to explain that I wasn't the kind of woman who wore black velvet wristbands decorated with little hearts and keys, but explaining would make me look like the kind of woman who cared what anybody thought, so I didn't.

Judy, who's been a waitress at the diner for as long as I can remember, appeared as if by magic with a full pot and a lifted eyebrow at seeing me with a man. Judy is smart-mouthed and efficient, with an angular frame, a dusting of orange freckles over her nose, and pecan-colored eyes that have the faintly astonished look of somebody whose dreams have been worn to a nub by disappointment. We have a close friendship that exists solely in the diner. We've shared our most hurtful stories, even though we never see each other anyplace else. I know about the men who've treated her like shit, and she knows about Todd and Christy.

I put the mug back on the table so she could top it off. "I'll have the special," I said.

"Uh-huh." She didn't even write it down. I always have the special. Two eggs over easy, extra-crispy home fries, and a biscuit.

"I'll have the same, with a side of bacon," said Guidry.

Judy splashed another bit of coffee in my mug to replace what I'd drunk while Guidry ordered, and swished away with curiosity radiating out of her like lines of light.

I took another sip of coffee and said, "Okay, I'm ready now. Ask me."

He pulled a narrow notebook from his jacket pocket and clicked a pen into readiness. "First, the particulars. Name?"

We went down the list. Name, address, phone, all those details that you give so many times it seems like they would be engraved on the air.

"Age?"

"Thirty-two."

"Occupation?"

"Pet-sitter."

He hesitated with his pen poised above the notebook. "Is that a real occupation?"

"Damn right it's a real occupation. I'm licensed and insured and bonded."

"Insured against what?"

"If I'm walking a dog and it bites you, my insurance will pay your doctor bills."

He got the kind of surprised face that people always give when they find out that pet-sitting is a legitimate profession with its own rules and ethics and legal responsibilities.

"How long have you been a pet-sitter?"

"About two years."

"Sergeant Owens said you used to be with the Sheriff's Department."

"I was."

"Why'd you leave?"

"Is that really important to your case?"

"I don't know. Is it?"

I felt rising anger and took a quick swallow of coffee.

"My husband was a sergeant with the Sheriff's Department. He was killed three years ago, along with our little girl. Sergeant Owens was my superior officer. He and I decided it would be better for me to do something else." I gave him a level look over the coffee mug. "I wasn't real good with people then, and I'm not much better now."

He nodded. His eyes were dark gray, edging toward blue. They didn't give anything away. "Tell me about this morning."

5

There wasn't much to tell, but I told him what I knew. Mostly, that consisted of the fact that I'd found the slider to the lanai unlocked and Marilee's bedroom and bathroom ransacked before I found the dead man.

"Did you notice anything missing?"

"No, but I wouldn't notice anything except the obvious. There was just one thing that struck me as odd. She had left her hair dryer behind. Most women getting ready for a trip stick their hair dryer in their overnight bag last thing after they've finished their makeup and hair. They don't leave it behind, especially when they'll be gone for a week."

"Maybe she had a spare already packed."

"Maybe, but it sort of bothers me. Marilee's an unusually neat woman. She doesn't leave her hair dryer lying out like that."

"Okay, what else can you tell me besides the hair dryer?"

I caught an edge to his voice and let the hair dryer go. I told him what Marilee had told me the day before — that she was leaving town that night and would be gone a week.

"She travels a lot on business, and the only thing different about this time was that I had to go by and pick up a new house key because she'd had her locks changed."

"Did she say why she'd had them changed?"

"No, and I didn't ask."

"Her car's in the garage. Does she usually drive to the airport?"

I stopped to think. "I can't remember ever looking in her garage when she was gone. If she was leaving from the Sarasota airport, I guess she might have driven."

"But you doubt it."

"I really don't know. It's just that Marilee is more the type to take a limo."

"Did she leave a number where she could be reached?"

I felt my face redden. "I told her to leave it for me, but I didn't look for it while I was there."

Judy slid a plate of eggs and potatoes in front of me, and put another in front of Guidry. "I'll be right back with your bacon and more coffee," she said.

To cover my embarrassment at having to admit that I'd let a client leave town without making sure she had left a number where she could be reached, I dug into my backpack and took out my client notebook.

"I have every client's information in here," I said. "When I first interview them, I get names of their vets and numbers to call in an emergency." To emphasize that I hadn't been irresponsible, I added, "Sometimes people go mountain climbing or something where I can't call them directly."

Judy plunked down a rasher of crisp bacon in front of Guidry and refilled both our coffee mugs. I eyed his bacon wistfully. It was exactly the way I like it, stiff, with no icky white bubbles on it.

Guidry moved a pair of slices to his plate and buttered his biscuit while I flipped to Marilee's page in my notebook. "She gave the number of a woman named Shuga Reasnor as her emergency number," I said.

"Shuga?"

I spelled it out for him, and forked up some egg. He had left four slices of bacon on its special plate.

"What's her number?"

I jerked my eyes away from his bacon and peered in the book. I read it off to him, and while he wrote it down, I looked at his bacon

57

again. He sighed and picked up the bacon plate. He raked two slices onto his own plate and then tipped the remaining two onto mine.

"You know you want them," he said.

"Well, just this once," I said. "I never eat bacon. I love it, but I never eat it. All that fat . . ."

"What do you know about Marilee Doerring?"

"Not much. She has some sort of decorating business, I think."

"Husband? Boyfriend?"

"I've never seen a man at her house, and there's never any sign of one."

"You look?"

"I don't look for man signs, but I do give the house a quick once-over every time to make sure the cat hasn't done something that needs cleaning up. Sometimes pets get bored and knock over a plant or poop in the middle of the bed. It's part of my job to check for things like that."

"How many times have you been in the house?"

"Lots. I can get the exact dates for you if you want. I keep a file at home of every visit."

"Isn't a week a long time to leave a pet alone?"

"Yeah, but cats can handle it. I go twice a

day and play with them and comb them and talk to them. During the day they watch TV, and I always leave the blinds up so they can sit on the windowsill and watch the birds and squirrels outside. At night I put the lights and the radio on a timer. They get a little bored and lonely, but most pets would rather be at home alone than with strangers in a strange place."

He was watching me closely. "You really like doing this, don't you?"

"Does that surprise you?"

"It just seems like a big jump, from deputy to pet-sitter."

I shrugged. "It's really not so different. You always have to be alert, you always have to expect the unexpected, and every now and then somebody tries to hump your leg."

He laughed and then sobered. "Do you have any idea who the dead man is?"

"Not a clue. Do you?"

"We're checking it out."

That meant he wasn't going to tell me.

He said, "We'd like to keep the details of how he was killed quiet as long as we can. Have you told anybody about him being taped to the water bowl?"

I shook my head. "I haven't told anybody anything."

"Good. I'd appreciate it if you wouldn't.

Some reporter will get your nine-one-one call and report it, but until somebody does, we're not going to make that public."

"Is Marilee a suspect?"

He shrugged. "Everybody's a suspect."

I had scarfed down a whole slice of bacon before I realized that included me.

Guidry tossed bills on the table and stood up. "You'll be around?"

I nodded. "I'll be on the street behind Marilee's this afternoon walking the Graysons' dog. I'll stop by while I'm there."

"Okay."

He left without any "See yous" or "It's been nice" or "Glad to meet yous."

As soon as he was out of sight, Judy plunked herself down opposite me with coffeepot in hand.

"Okay, who is he?"

"He's a detective. There's been a murder at one of my pet houses and he's the investigator. I found the body, so we ate while he questioned me."

"Well shit, I thought he might be a man. You know, a man for you. Who got murdered?"

I ignored the part about a man for me. In spite of the fact that Judy has had terrible luck with men, she persists in thinking it's time for me to get one.

"I don't know who he was."

"Shot?"

"I'm not sure. I turned on the kitchen light, and there he was, stretched out on the floor."

"No!"

"Yep, DRT — dead right there."

"Good God. Did you freak out?"

"Come on, I used to be a deputy, I don't freak out at things like that. Well, I freaked out a little, but just for a minute."

"Whose house was he in?"

"Marilee Doerring's."

"I know who Marilee Doerring is. She's a piece of work. You know her?"

"Just from taking care of her cat. She's always been fine with me. Pays on time, takes good care of her cat. I don't have any complaints about her."

Judy looked around to make sure nobody was listening, and leaned closer. "See that man at the counter reading the paper? That's Dr. Coffey. He's a heart surgeon. He and Marilee Doerring were engaged a couple of years ago."

A bell dinged from the back to get Judy's attention, and she got up with her coffeepot to go pick up an order.

I studied the man at the counter. He was lean to the point of boniness, with sharp shoulder blades jutting from his back like mountain ridges. His dark hair was shorn high, with a longer shock flopping down to meet the shaved part. It was a cut for a much younger man, a cut meant to be cool and mellow. It made him look like the nerdy kid in high school who never quite fits in, the one who's always on the sidelines watching the popular kids. He was wearing the Siesta Key male uniform — khaki shorts, short-sleeved knit shirt, and Docksiders, which exposed a lot of straight black hair on his arms and legs. For a quick second, I imagined running my hands down his bare back and felt my fingers tangle in a thicket of hair. Ugh.

Somehow I couldn't imagine him with Marilee, but if they'd been engaged, he must have known where she went on her business trips. Before I could talk myself out of it, I got up and went to the counter and took the stool next to Coffey. He turned his head just enough to give me a quick glance to reassure himself I wasn't anybody he knew, and turned back to his paper. He had a smooth rectangular face like a department store mannequin, with a high forehead and long cheeks. His sallow skin was perfect as plaster, and his dark eyes were velvety and dull, like ripe olives that have set out too long and lost their sheen.

I said, "Dr. Coffey, I'm sorry to interrupt you, but I'd like to ask you something."

He looked at me again, this time with a furrow of distaste forming on his unlined forehead.

"I'll be quick," I promised him. "My name is Dixie Hemingway, and —"

Looking flustered and anxious, Judy came trouncing to us bearing his order and her coffeepot. He moved his paper out of the way so she could set his plate down. Scrambled egg whites, dry rye toast, sliced tomatoes. I guess if you're a heart surgeon, you eat like that.

Judy topped off his coffee and looked warningly at me. "Something for you?"

"No thanks, I'm not staying," I said.

She gave an emphatic nod of her head and stomped off with her coffeepot held in front of her like a lancet.

Ignoring me, Dr. Coffey picked up his fork and cut into his egg whites. His fingers were hairy, too, with black hair sprouting between his knuckles. I watched his fork with a kind of repelled fascination. There's something unnatural about eating just the white of an egg.

I pushed Ghost's velvet collar higher on my arm and said, "The thing is, I'm a pet-sitter, and one of my clients left town and didn't leave a number where she could be reached. There's been something of an emergency at her house, and I was thinking you might have some idea where she might have gone. Like where her business takes her, or where her family lives."

He looked toward me again and then stood up so fast it seemed like his knees had suddenly gone stiff and he couldn't sit anymore. "I know nothing about this! Do you understand me? Nothing! If you bother me again, I'll have you arrested. Do you understand?" His voice was venomous, and he was shaking.

I said, "Well, actually, you can't have me arrested just for asking you a question. I'm sorry if I bothered you, but don't you think you're overreacting?"

He extended his arm with his skeletal finger pointing at me like Abraham cursing the Philistines. "Stay away from me!"

Stomping to the front door, he charged out of the diner so fast that several people in the front booths looked around.

Judy came over and leaned on the counter. "Thanks a lot," she said. "You just chased off one of my best customers. Not to mention the fact that he stiffed me for his breakfast."

"All I did was ask him if he knew where

Marilee might have gone. He was going to marry her, he must know something about where her job takes her."

She groaned. "He hates her. She dumped him practically while the organ was playing the wedding march. I mean, people were in the church and everything. She just up and left him standing there."

"Well, that's sort of brave, don't you think? It must have been embarrassing, but if she realized she didn't love him —"

"No, you don't understand! She had got him to put a million dollars in her name just before the wedding. Gave him some big song and dance about how she didn't want to be dependent on him after they were married, and how she didn't want to live in fear that he would dump her one day and she'd be out on the street without a dime. How she wanted to be able to look him in the eye as an equal so they would both know she was with him because she *wanted* to be and not because she *had* to be. You know, like she was a poor little match girl out on the street getting taken in by a prince or something. The poor schmuck fell for it and transferred a million bucks to her account. In her name. Hers to have no matter what happened, like love insurance."

"And then she dumped him?"

"Like a rock. He sued her, I think, but the doofus had given her the money, so she got to keep it. He hates her guts now. It was just two years ago. I can't believe you didn't hear about it."

I didn't remind her that two years ago I'd been doing well to get out of bed and find my way to the bathroom. I wouldn't have known if they'd declared World War III.

She said, "He's got a live-in bimbo now. I saw her early one Sunday morning coming out of cocaine alley."

I knew the place she meant. Everybody on the key, including the Sheriff's Department, knows the areas where drugs are sold. There's a drug bust every now and then, but mostly it's small-time stuff not worth the time and expense to fight, especially when you know the dealers will be back on the street before the ink is dry on the arrest warrant.

"Do you think she was getting it for him?"

"Maybe, but he's never seemed coked up. She does, though. You look at her and expect her feet to be a few inches off the floor."

I looked at my watch and said, "Listen, I've got to run, okay? I'll see you later."

"Let the police handle this, Dixie."

"It's not the police, it's the Sheriff's Department."

"Whatever."

I knew she was right, but it bothered me that I didn't know how to get in touch with Marilee. I had a responsibility, and I wasn't at all pleased with how I was handling it.

6

Before I left, I ducked into the ladies' room, where two very large black women were at the sinks. One of them I recognized as Tanisha, a cook in the diner, but I didn't know the other one. I whipped into a stall, and they went dead silent, the way women in a rest room do when they've been interrupted midconversation. When I flushed, the sound seemed to release them.

"So I says to him, I says, 'You can kiss my big fat black ass.' "

"Uh-huh, that's good."

"I told him, 'You can start in the middle and kiss your way thirty-six inches to the right, and then you can go back to the middle and kiss your way thirty-six inches to the left. You can just kiss my big fat ass.' "

I went out to wash my hands, and they went silent again. I kept my gaze directed toward my hands, but I could feel them watching me. I pulled a paper towel from the holder and turned around and leaned my butt on the counter.

I said, "I absolutely cannot leave here without knowing what happened next. What'd he say?"

They both laughed. Tanisha said, "Girl, he didn't say nothing. He just stood there with his mouth hanging open, and I walked. I don't take that shit from nobody."

I grinned and tossed my wadded-up paper towel in the bin. "I wish I could have seen that."

I left them giggling and punched the door open with my knuckles — I'm squeamish about putting the flat of my hand on a bathroom door because half the women who go in there don't wash their hands — and headed for the parking lot.

The temperature had climbed and the Bronco was like a pizza oven. I started the car and let the AC run while I pulled out my cell phone and client book and flipped to Marilee's page. I read Shuga Reasnor's number while I dialed it.

The voice that answered had the husky, half-choked sound of somebody blowing out cigarette smoke and talking at the same time. "Hello, this is Shuga," she said.

I had been pronouncing the name "Shooga," but when she said it I realized the name was "Sugar," with an exaggerated southern accent. Probably a lot of people would think that was cute.

"This is Dixie Hemingway, Miss Reasnor. I take care of Marilee Doerring's cat, and she gave me your number to call in case of an emergency. Has Detective Guidry been in touch with you yet?"

"Noooo." She drew out the word while she registered all the implications of what I'd said.

Damn. I should have checked with Guidry before I phoned. Now I'd given her a heads-up that a detective would be calling her.

"The reason I'm calling is that Marilee's out of town, and I've taken Ghost to a day-care center. I expect he'll be there for a day or two, and I just wanted to make sure that was okay with you."

"You've left who?"

"Ghost. Her cat."

"Hell, I don't care. I don't know why she left my number."

"You don't happen to know where she went, do you?"

She laughed uneasily. "I didn't even know she was gone. What did you say your name was?"

"Dixie Hemingway. If you should hear from Marilee, I'd appreciate it if you would have her call me." Before she could ask any more questions, I gave her my number and thanked her, then punched the disconnect button.

"That was really dumb," I muttered to myself. "Really, really dumb."

Before I backed the Bronco out, I slid Ghost's velvet collar off my wrist and put it in my backpack. It was 11:55. I should have been at Kristin Lord's house an hour ago. A murder really screws up a work schedule.

When I got to the traffic light at Beach Road, I automatically turned my head to look at the fire station. I've done that all my life. Once when I was about seven years old, my father was in the driveway with some other firefighters polishing the fire truck when my mother and Michael and I drove by. My mother honked at him, and he gave us a big grin and waved. It's one of my favorite memories.

Kristin and Jim Lord were the kind of people who prove the theory of karma and reincarnation — they had less sense than a pair of sand fleas but were filthy rich, so they must have been really, really good in a former life. I'd known them since high school, but we'd never been friends. They ran with the kids who knew the difference between Polo and Izod — and cared — and I ran with the kids whose idea of making a fashion statement was not wearing yesterday's T. Kristin had a huge crush on my brother for a while, and I don't think she ever forgave him for rejecting her.

Kristin met me at the door of their multimillion-dollar mansion with a smile frosty at the corners. "You're a little late, aren't you?"

Kristin was slim, with glossy brown hair cut to curve around her square jaw, and heavy dark eyebrows that made straight slashes above beautiful hazel eyes. Her nose was out of a plastic surgeon's catalog, but her lips were naturally full and wide. Her upper lip was thicker in the middle, giving her a slightly rabbity look. If she were so inclined, she probably gave her husband great blow jobs — further proof of a previous life of good deeds, at least for him. She was wearing a pair of wrinkled white cotton capris and a free-hanging pink-and-white-striped shirt that covered her newly bulging tummy.

"I got tied up," I said. "Sorry."

She made a little snuffing sound with her perfect nose to show her displeasure, and spun around to walk ahead of me, her raffia flip-flops making sucking noises on the cool Italian tile.

Kristin was four months pregnant and she

had developed an acute case of Fear-Of-Cat-Poop. Specifically, she was afraid of catching toxoplasmosis from her cat's litter box. Cats can only get toxoplasmosis from eating a diseased rodent, and a pregnant woman can only get it if she touches the diseased cat's feces and then eats something without first washing her hands. Kristin's cat had probably never even seen a rodent, much less eaten one, and what woman doesn't wash her hands after changing a litter box? But it was Kristin's fear and her cat and her money, so I allowed her to pay me twenty dollars a day to groom her cat and change its litter box.

The cat was an American Shorthair named Fred. Shorthairs are low-maintenance cats, so it was almost a crime to take money for what little I did. Fred's litter box was in a guest bathroom, and I kept the door closed because Kristin was so spooked about it. A litter box shouldn't have more than a quarter inch of sand in it, and flushing it away took a nanosecond. I spritzed it inside and out with my all-purpose water and Clorox mix, rinsed the hell out of it with hot water, dried it with paper towels, and spread another quarter inch of sand on the bottom. I replaced the bag of litter under the counter, and washed my hands and dried them. The whole procedure had taken two minutes, tops.

When I went out to the lanai for Fred's grooming, he and Kristin were both pretending not to be excited that I was there. Fred was doing a jug imitation, sitting tall with his long tail curled around his toes the way some executives curl a long line back under their signatures. Kristin was sitting in a cushioned redwood chair, eager to gossip. Dishing dirt was Kristin's favorite pastime. She had done it when we were in high school, and she was still doing it. She had never been fastidious about facts, and if somebody's reputation was hurt because she'd passed on malicious gossip, it never seemed to bother her.

Kristin said, "It was on the news this morning about that dead man in Marilee Doerring's house. They said you found him, but they weren't giving his name until his next of kin is notified. Who was he?"

My heart did a somersault at hearing that anything about me was on the news, but I kept my face still and lifted Fred to the table.

"They gave my name?"

"They just said a pet-sitter, but I knew it was you."

As if he sensed that a dark cloud had lowered around me, Fred looked over his shoulder with sad eyes.

Fred was large and muscular, brown, with a white muzzle and throat and white paws. Like all American Shorthairs, he was sweet and affectionate. When I ran my hands lightly over his body, telling him by touch where I was getting ready to brush, he arched his back and began to purr. I dipped a hand into my grooming kit for my small slicker brush and pulled it through the hair on the back of Fred's neck, careful to keep the brush flat so the bristles wouldn't dig into his skin.

"I don't know who the man is," I said. "Like they said, they have to notify his family before they announce his name."

Fred tilted his head back so I could get under his chin, and I made short strokes on his snowy throat and chest. He stretched his head up higher. If he could have spoken, he would have said, "Yes! Yes! Now a little to the right! Oooh, that's good!" Since he couldn't talk, he purred louder.

Kristin said, "The Sheriff's Department won't say how he was killed until they do an autopsy. Isn't that odd?"

I shrugged. "They always do an autopsy whenever a person dies in mysterious circumstances."

Kristin did a disappointed pout with her bunny mouth. "I know Marilee Doerring from the yacht club. People don't like her much. Well, men like her, but women don't."

I put a protective finger over Fred's sensitive spine and combed in short parallel strokes on each side. Fred gave a warning flick of his tail, and I went back to his neck and throat, making sure I was keeping the teeth of the brush comfortably pointed straight at his skin and not tilted to the side.

"I think it's because Marilee's so flashy," said Kristin. "Lately she's been wearing an *enormous* square-cut diamond that's *soooo* ostentatious. The thing just screams zircon!"

My experience with diamonds being limited to the small kind that nobody would mistake for a zircon, I continued combing Fred and stayed quiet.

Kristin gave a little self-deprecating laugh. "God, I sound catty, don't I?"

I don't know why people say they're being "catty" when they make unkind remarks about other people. Cats are never like that.

Kristin shifted in her chair and said, "It's not because she's pretty that I don't like her. I'm not afraid of pretty women. And it's certainly not because she has money! It's that you always get the feeling Marilee's trolling for men. If a man's anywhere in her vicinity, you can almost hear the music from *Jaws* playing."

I thought of Olga Winnick and said, "Predatory music?"

"Exactly! Marilee is a predatory woman."

I was imagining Kristin and Olga Winnick together talking about how predatory Marilee was, when Kristin's eyes settled on my wedding band.

"You're a widow. Why do you still wear a wedding ring?"

The question caught me off guard, causing my hand to jerk so the bristles of my slicker brush bit into Fred's skin. He growled a warning and waved his tail, and I quickly went back to his throat to placate him. I've never thought of myself as a widow. Widows are old women with blue hair and a lifetime of memories. I don't belong in that group, I'm just a formerly loved.

Kristin looked up at me as if she'd suddenly had an attack of sensitivity. "I hope you don't mind my asking."

I didn't answer, but just to scare her, I turned Fred so that his anus faced her while I brushed the hair around it. She watched with pale dread, so hyperalert for bits of cat poop that she forgot her question. Fred whipped his tail back and forth to let me know his patience was wearing thin. To reward him for not jumping down, I combed his neck and throat again.

He pushed his head up against my hand and purred his thanks. I picked him up and set him on the floor, packed my slicker brush away, spritzed the table with my handy-dandy water-Clorox mix, and wiped it dry with paper towels.

"I'll let myself out," I said. I had been there only about five minutes.

Kristin looked disappointed. She would have paid me another twenty dollars just to stick around and dish dirt about Marilee. Fred stuck his left back leg into the air and curved around to enthusiastically lick the inside of it. He didn't even say good-bye.

7

It was one o'clock when I put my grooming equipment in the back of the Bronco and started home. The sky was a clear Crayola blue, with a relentless white sun that lasered the top of my head. Something was nagging at me, but I couldn't put my finger on it. I'd been up since 4:00 a.m. and my brain wasn't working on all cylinders.

The lane leading to my apartment is covered with oyster shells that have leeched lime and become hardened by rain into a concrete-hard surface. Australian pines, mossy oaks, sea grape, and palms line one side of the drive, and the other side edges the sandy beach. It's a private drive with a sign at its entrance proclaiming it not for public access, but people turn into it anyway and nose down to see what lies at its end.

On most of Siesta Key, a private road like ours will take the curious to a multimillion-dollar house whose owners are readily recognizable from movies or book jackets or TV talk shows. Our road leads to a weathered two-bedroom house where my brother and his partner live, and to a detached four-slot carport with an upstairs apartment where I live. My grandfather bought the house from Sears, Roebuck in the fifties for a thousand dollars, now the house and garage apartment together are worth about fifty cents. The beachfront property they sit on is worth about five million. Or at least that's what we've been offered for it. We wouldn't sell at any price, so it doesn't matter.

Michael and Paco were in the carport putting away fishing gear, both with the bleezy, sun-blasted look that men get when they've happily spent arduous hours sweating and squinting at a blazing sea. Michael is thirty-four, blond and blue-eyed like me, but a lot taller and wider. He's a fireman, and when he's suited up in his fire-fighting gear he's roughly the size of Sasquatch. Women fling themselves at Michael the way mating lovebugs splat themselves on car windshields in the spring. I wouldn't be surprised if some of them bear razor scars on their wrists at the futility of it, because he and Paco have been together for over twelve years and counting.

As slim and dark as Michael is blond and broad, Paco is with the Sheriff Department's SIB — Special Investigative Bureau — which means he gets involved in cases that require him to take on disguises his own mother wouldn't recognize. Cases that we don't question him about. Michael is my best friend in the whole world, and Paco is my second-best friend. When I lost Todd and Christy, Michael and Paco sort of sandwiched me between them and kept the world out until I was ready for it.

Michael works twenty-four/forty-eight at the firehouse, which means a twenty-four-hour shift on, followed by forty-eight hours off. He usually spends his off-time fishing. Paco works mysterious hours that nobody can predict, many of them after midnight. When he isn't working or sleeping, he goes out in the boat with Michael. I never do. I love to look at the Gulf and I love the sound and smell of it, but I don't like being on it. It's too big and willful for me. I don't much like things I can't control, at least a little bit.

I got out of the Bronco and shaded my eyes against the glare. Out in the Gulf, sunlight sparked diamonds off glittering waves undulating toward the beach where they gently exploded into lacy white froth. A few gulls halfheartedly squawked and spiraled overhead, but most of them had retreated to shady nooks for a siesta.

I said, "What'd you get?"

"Some nice pompano. A couple of snapper."

"There was a dead man in one of my houses this morning."

They both stopped what they were doing and stared at me with identical expressions of shocked concern. I felt like a kid with a great Show and Tell.

"Marilee Doerring's house," I said. "I found him in the kitchen with blood on the back of his head and his nose taped in the cat's water bowl. I'm not supposed to tell the part about the water bowl yet."

Michael said, "Well hell, Dixie. What'd you do?"

"Called nine one one. Sergeant Owens came out, and a detective I never heard of before. Paco, do you know a guy named Guidry?"

"Nope, must be somebody new."

Having delivered my impressive news, I said, "Well, I'm going to go take a nap," and left them staring after me as I dragged my weary butt upstairs to my little private world.

I have a wide covered porch, a living room with a one-stool breakfast bar and galley kitchen at the side, and a bedroom barely big enough for a single bed, a nightstand,

and a double dresser. Photographs of Todd and Christy sit on the dresser. They're the last things I see before I turn off the lamp, and the first things I see when I get up in the morning.

Off the bedroom, I have a tiny bathroom, a laundry room, and a big walk-in closet that doubles as an office. It's where I handle my pet-sitting business — at a desk in a windowless cubicle in front of a wall of shelves holding folded Ts and shorts and jeans, Keds and sandals and a couple pairs of heels. A lone rod across the short end holds a few dresses and skirts.

I went inside just long enough to go to the bathroom and check my answering machine. I had three calls from women asking for my pet-sitting rates. I didn't return any of the calls. I'd already had way more than my daily quota of people, and the day was only half over.

I went back to the porch, switched on both ceiling fans, and lowered myself into the hammock strung in the corner. The surf was tumbling in its endless rhythm and gulls squawked overhead. My thoughts tumbled and squawked along with them as I let the terrible truth of the morning settle in. A man's life had been taken, and whoever did it had made sure his dignity was stripped away, too. I felt personally violated. I didn't know him, but he was a fellow human being.

I drifted to sleep and dreamed that Christy was running on the beach throwing chunks of bread to the seagulls, laughing into the sky as they swooped down to catch them in their beaks. Her hair was almost white in the sunshine, and it bounced on her shoulders from a ponytail high on the back of her head. I was thinking I'd let her play until all the bread was gone and then call her into the shade so she wouldn't burn.

I woke up without knowing I was awake, with the edges of the dream blending with the sounds of the gulls and the surf. I lay there for a moment with my eyes shut before I realized it had just been a dream.

Those of us who've lost loved ones to terrorists or religious fanatics or doped-up drivers or some other senseless violence ask, "Why? Why? Why?" But after awhile, the question becomes "Why not?" Why should we get to have our loved ones around us when people all over the world are keening the loss of mothers, fathers, sons, daughters, brothers, sisters, lovers? So many people dying for so little reason.

Todd and Christy were killed when a ninety-year-old man slammed his Cadillac into them in a Publix parking lot. If I say it fast like that, I can keep my voice even, but just.

Todd and I had talked on the phone before he left to pick Christy up at day care. "We need some milk and Cheerios," I said. "I think we're out of orange juice, too."

"Christy and I will get it on our way home," he said. "See you a little after six."

For the rest of my life, I'll play that conversation over and over in my head, wishing I could rewind it and do it over, wishing I had said, I love you, my darling, and I always will, wishing I had told him how safe he made me feel, how protected and cherished.

He and Christy were both killed instantly. Todd was thirty. Christy was three.

The man who hit them said he had accidentally hit the gas instead of the brake. He felt terrible about it. His son came to see me after the funeral and told me his father was a good man who had resisted giving up his independence even after macular degeneration had robbed him of most of his sight. Florida allows people to renew their driver's license over the phone, so he had just kept driving in spite of his family's objections. The son said he had taken the car away from his father after the accident, and that his father had wept every day since it happened.

From grief and guilt, he said, not just because he couldn't drive. As if that made us even.

For a long time I was so consumed by anger that it almost destroyed me. Anger at the state for allowing people to renew their driver's license without an eye exam. Anger at a man for continuing to drive after his vision and reflexes were shot. Anger at his family for not taking his car away sooner. In the end, forgiveness came not because I stopped feeling the gash of bitterness, but because I was exhausted by it. My anger has settled down from a flaming roar to a dull simmer now, like a volcano that seems calm but may erupt when you least expect it. It's the volcanic part that's the problem, the part I can't control — especially if I see somebody abusing a child or a pet. Then I go totally apeshit, and there's no telling what I'll do.

I got up feeling flushed and swollen and went inside and stood in front of the open refrigerator and glugged an entire bottle of cold water. I carried another bottle to my closet office, and put in a call to Lieutenant Guidry. He wasn't in, so I left my number. Then I called Shuga Reasnor.

She answered the phone on the first ring, and her voice had that mix of desperation and annoyance that people get when they've been hovering around a phone for a long time hoping it would ring.

I said, "It's Dixie Hemingway, Ms. Reasnor. I just wanted to ask you something. Do you know Dr. Coffey?"

She waited so long to answer that I thought for a moment she might have laid the phone down and walked away. Then she said, "Why do you ask?"

"I saw him in the Village Diner, and I asked him if he knew where Marilee might have gone. I thought since they were engaged, he might have some idea. He got very angry. Wouldn't even talk to me. It seemed odd."

"He's odd. He's mean and he's odd. Stay away from him. Don't talk to him about Marilee."

"Do you think he's dangerous? Do you think he might have been the one who killed the man in Marilee's house? Jealous, maybe?"

"Gerald Coffey's too big a coward to kill anybody. He might hire somebody to do it, but he wouldn't do it himself."

"But you think he might do that? Hire somebody?"

"I didn't say that. I just said he didn't have the balls to kill anybody himself."

"If you think of anything that the Sheriff's Department ought to know about Dr. Coffey, I hope you'll tell them."

"Yeah, I'll do that."

We said our good-byes and hung up. I knew she wasn't going to tell Guidry about Coffey. Shuga Reasnor didn't sound like a woman anxious to help in the investigation. In fact, she sounded like a woman with something to hide.

I spent the next hour attending to business. I called the people who wanted to know my rates, which is twenty dollars a day to make a morning and afternoon visit. If they want a sitter in the house overnight, it's forty dollars. For twenty-four-hour care, the fee is sixty dollars. Most pets are accustomed to being home by themselves during the day, but I have a crew of retirees who do sleepovers and round-the-clock care.

All my fees are spelled out in a contract I have my clients sign, along with our respective responsibilities. If a pet becomes ill and needs medical care when the owners are gone, I pay for it. If some disaster happens that causes water to be shut off or the pet to have to be evacuated, I supply whatever is needed, including new quarters. When the owners return, they reimburse me for my expenses. Taking on the care of a beloved pet while its owners are away is like taking on the care of a child. I have to trust the owners, and they have to trust me.

The first woman said she had found somebody else, and the next one slammed down the phone when I told her my rates, as if I'd said something obscene. The other woman said she thought they were extremely reasonable. Everything is relative. I made an appointment to stop by the approving woman's house to meet her cat and get the pertinent information, then spent the rest of the hour entering the morning's visits into my client records.

I keep meticulous records, recording the date and time I arrived, the time I left, and what I did while I was there, along with notes about anything a pet needed or did that was out of the ordinary. If a pet has a medical condition that requires medications or vitamins or treatments, that's recorded. I have the history of illnesses, injuries, and pregnancies, along with the dates of all immunizations, the number on the animal's ID tag, and whether it's been declawed, spayed, or neutered. I know each pet's preferences in food, toys, TV programs, and music. I'm probably too compulsive about keeping all that information, but I'd rather have it and not need it than need it and not have it. Someday it might be important to know precisely when I gave a bath or a vitamin or a prescription medication.

At four o'clock, I got a banana from its special little hanger in the kitchen and ate it as I went down to the carport. A great blue heron standing on the hood of the Bronco watched me as I got a sixty-watt lightbulb out of the storage closet. I tossed the last bite of banana toward the shore, and the heron fluttered to the sand to get it. I threw the peel in the garbage can, got in the Bronco, and drove back to the Graysons' house, where Rufus was ecstatic to see me. We played a short game of roll the ball on the living room floor before his supper. While Rufus ate, I hauled out a ladder from the garage and changed the burned-out bulb in the coach light. I put the ladder away, closed the garage door, and brought in the Graysons' mail. I checked the house for any doggy accidents, giving the carousel horse a pat on the rump as I walked by. Everything was in order, and I washed Rufus's food and water bowls and gave him fresh water before we went for a walk. We walked the quarter block to Midnight Pass Road and jogged past the wooded area, where

Rufus insisted on stopping to bark at unseen squirrels or rabbits. I finally persuaded him to walk with me to Marilee Doerring's street.

8

A deputy's car was in Marilee's driveway and the crime-scene tape was still on the door, but there were no CSU cars. That meant the ME had come and put the body in a bag and taken it away, but the forensics people weren't finished getting photos, latent prints, hair, fiber, and all the other evidence they gather. Next door at the Winnick house, a yard vacuum lay in the driveway with an orange extension cord snaking under the partially opened garage door.

I parked behind the deputy's car and went to his open window. He was making notes, and he looked up at me with the flat, impersonal look that law-enforcement people learn.

I said, "Hi, I'm Dixie Hemingway. I found the dead man this morning, and I told Detective Guidry I'd stop by this afternoon when I was in the neighborhood."

"He's not here."

"Okay, I'll call him later. Thanks."

Rufus was contemplating a bird of paradise plant as if he thought it needed to be peed on, so I pulled his leash and started back down the driveway. Passionate piano music started coming from the Winnicks' house, and I turned my head that way. Now that I knew it was the kid practicing and not the radio or a CD, I was truly impressed. Not that I know diddly about classical music. My taste runs more to jazz and blues and country, but I know talent when I hear it, and the kid could play. Even Rufus cocked his head and listened with doggy respect.

Mrs. Winnick suddenly rose from behind a row of low shrubs between the two lots and walked rapidly around to the driveway. She wasn't wearing gardening gloves or carrying a trowel or any other gardening tools, and I had the distinct impression that she had been hiding behind the shrubs. She seemed to deliberately avoid looking my way. Maybe she was pissed that I hadn't told her about the murder.

She leaned down to get the handle of her yard vac and switched it on, intently looking at the driveway and moving the wand back and forth over the pavement. She wore black stretch Lycra tights with a boxy white T that stopped at her hipbones. Except for her skinny butt, her body was surprisingly muscular. Her butt wasn't muscular. It was the kind that hangs in two saggy loops, like basset ears.

Rufus and I retraced our walk toward his street. At the wooded area, where an abandoned drive disappeared into the trees, he stopped and barked again, tugging eagerly at the leash. The wooded swath between Marilee's street and Rufus's street is about fifty feet wide, and runs all the way from Midnight Pass Road to the bay. A wooden fence runs along both sides to separate it from people's backyards. Originally, it spanned a private driveway to a house on a peninsular extension into the bay. The owners had died years ago and the property was frozen in some kind of litigation for so long that the house fell apart and the land leading to it reverted to its original wild state. A useless metal gate stretched across the old shelled drive as mute testimony of how quickly nature reclaims its own.

I explained to Rufus that the woods were too brambly for dogs and women in shorts, and he reluctantly abandoned the idea of exploring it. When we got to his house, I turned on some lights and the kitchen radio and he and I kissed each other good-bye.

My next stop was across Midnight Pass Road at the Sea Breeze, a pink stucco honeycomb of condos tucked into a slim slice of land at the edge of the Gulf. Every condo has a curved stucco roof over its balcony, so the balconies look like dark caves cut into the side of a mountain. The whole thing resembles an excavated Indian ruin. Inside, it's anything but a ruin, with a marbled lobby dotted with great urns of green things and tasteful paintings by local artists. Sarasota probably has more artists per capita than anyplace in the world, so it's not hard to find good art here.

I took the stainless-steel and mirrored elevator up to Tom Hale's condo. Tom is a round man — rosy round face, warm round black eyes behind round steel-rimmed glasses, round head of curly black hair, round little belly that rests lightly on his lap. Until a wall of shelves at a home-improvement store fell on him and crushed his lower spine, Tom headed a large CPA firm. He had gone to pick up some piano wire to hang a large painting in the house he shared with his wife and two children, but you know how it is, you can't go to one of those places without wandering around looking at all the neat stuff. As he remembers it, he had no reason to walk down the aisle between towering stacks of lumber and ready-to-hang doors. Nobody ever knew what caused the shelves to topple over, but they did, spilling all their contents onto the floor and anybody who happened to be there. Luckily, only one other person was in the aisle at the time, and he escaped with a concussion and broken arms. Tom wasn't so lucky.

He sued, of course, but it took several years before the case finally settled, and by that time his CPA firm was kaput because he'd spent so much time having surgery and learning how to function in a wheelchair. The lawyers for the store claimed that he was partly responsible for his own pain and paralysis because he was an intelligent man and should have known better than to walk down that aisle. The jury didn't buy that argument, and they awarded Tom half a million dollars. His lawyers got half, plus reimbursement for all their expenses. Then his wife divorced him because she couldn't bear living with a man in a wheelchair, and she and the children moved to Boston where her parents lived. In the divorce settlement, she got most of the money that was left, and Tom got a studio apartment in the Sea Breeze. The only thing standing between him and utter loneliness was a greyhound named Billy Elliot, a former racing dog that Tom had rescued. I suppose Tom identified with the dog.

Tom and I trade services. He does my taxes and I go by twice a day and walk Billy Elliot for him. I could hear Billy Elliot's nervous toenails skittering on the marble floor before I opened the door. He started to jump on me when I came in, then crouched in fear when I held my palm flat and said, "Down!" It always breaks my heart to see a dog cower like that, because it's a clear signal the dog has been beaten in the past.

I knelt beside him and stroked his smooth neck. "You'd feel terrible if you jumped on somebody and knocked them down," I said. "That's why jumping's not allowed."

He thumped his tail on the floor and grinned hopefully at me. From the kitchen, Tom yelled, "Hey, Dixie! Come tell me about that dead man!"

Billy Elliot followed me in and stood whipping my legs with his tail while I gave Tom the condensed version of finding a dead man in Marilee's kitchen.

Tom said, "Have they contacted Marilee?"

"We don't know where she is. She didn't leave me a number."

"Maybe her grandmother would know."

"Marilee has a grandmother?"

"Everybody has a grandmother, Dixie.

Marilee has one who lives at Bayfront Village. Name is Cora Mathers."

It was news to me that Tom and Marilee knew each other, but Tom did taxes for a lot of people on the key.

I said, "Wasn't Cora Mathers the *Leave It to Beaver* mother?"

"No, that was June Cleaver. Ward and June Cleaver. The kid who played the Beaver was Jerry Mathers. Maybe his mother's name was Cora."

"I wonder whatever happened to him."

"He probably bought his own island or something. Unless somebody screwed up and he didn't get the money from all those shows."

"You think it would be okay if I called Cora?"

"Oh, sure. From what Marilee's told me about her, she's a pistol."

Billy Elliot whuffed sharply, letting us know that he had enjoyed as much of our chitchat as he could stand. He and I took the elevator downstairs, and as soon as I thought we were far enough away from the front door, I let him pee on a bush. Then he stretched his body out and took off like he was back on the track chasing a fake rabbit. Even fattened up since his racing days, he was still faster than most dogs, and I ran behind him like a maniac. When we finally stopped, I had to bend over and take deep breaths while he pranced around and gave me annoyed little huffs because I had slowed him down. We trotted back to the Sea Breeze and took the elevator back upstairs, where I unsnapped his leash and stored it away. Tom was busy with somebody's return and merely grunted and waved as I left.

It was close to eight o'clock when I fed the last cat and went home. Michael and Paco were on the terrace between the house and the carport, firing up the grill.

Michael said, "Hurry up, Dixie, we're waiting for you."

I ran upstairs, peeled off my clothes, and tossed them and my Keds on top of the things already in the washer. I took a quick shower, toweled my body and hair dry, and pulled on a short strapless cotton dress and some flip-flops. My answering machine was blinking, so before I went downstairs, I punched the play button and got Shuga Reasnor's voice.

"I've been thinking about it," she said. "And I'd like to talk to you some more about the cat. Could you come to my place? Please call me as soon as you can. Or just come on by. I'll be here all day." She left her address and hung up, and the machine's robotic voice announced that the call had come in at 4:37. I glared at the machine. I didn't want to go see the woman, and I didn't want to call her back.

I took a deep breath and dialed her number. I got her machine, which thrilled me so much that I punched my fist into the air in a "Yes!" sign.

Shuga's recorded voice said, "You have reached. . . ." and gave her phone number. Why do people give you their phone number when you've just called it?

Talking fast in case she was monitoring her calls and might pick up, I said, "Miss Reasnor, this is Dixie Hemingway. I got your message, and I'll try to stop by your place tomorrow morning around nine o'clock."

I was so relieved that I didn't have to talk to Shuga Reasnor three times in one day that I almost skipped down the stairs to the terrace, where the outdoor table was set, the grill was ready, and the wine was chilling in a bucket.

Michael said, "Well, the queen has arrived, so we can eat."

I stuck out my tongue at him, and Paco shook his head. "You two are so mature," he said.

Michael is the cook of the family. Even when we were kids, he was the family cook. He's the cook at the firehouse, too. Michael believes that George Foreman's grill has done more for the civilized world than Einstein's theory of relativity, and he loves to do things that take a long time, like ribs and briskets and turkeys.

Michael was four and I was two when our mother left us the first time. Our father was pulling a twenty-four-hour shift at the firehouse and didn't know she had gone, so Michael took care of us until he got home. He fed us cold cereal with milk until we ran out of milk, and then we ate cold dry cereal. He climbed on a chair and got the peanut butter jar from the cupboard, and he found a jar of grape jelly in the refrigerator. We didn't have any bread, so we ate it with a spoon.

When our father came home, he found us curled up together like puppies, jelly-smeared and confused, but none the worse for wear. Our mother came back in a few days, and our life took up as if she'd never been gone. She left us for good when I was nine and Michael was eleven. Our father had died putting out a fire by then, so we went to live with our grandparents in their house on the Gulf. Now we've come full circle. Michael moved back into the house when our grandparents died, and I moved into the garage apartment after Todd and Christy died. And Michael's still feeding me.

We were so practiced at getting dinner together that we all went into action like a circus act. Michael brushed olive oil on three pompano, dusted them with salt and pepper, and stretched them on the grill. Paco brought out a big wooden bowl of salad and a tray of sliced eggplant and zucchini from the kitchen, and I slathered the veggie slices with oil. Michael laid them on the grill with the pompano, and Paco tossed the salad with olive oil and lemon juice. Michael turned the fish, and I poured the wine. Michael turned the veggies, and Paco pulled out my chair. Michael flipped pompano and veggies onto a platter, and Paco and I grabbed our forks.

If there's any better way to end a day than sitting on a terrace with your favorite people while you eat fresh-caught fish and watch a spectacular sunset, I've never found it. The men had shaved and changed out of their scrungy shorts and sweatshirts with the sleeves cut out. Michael wore white linen pants and a crisp cotton shirt with thin blue and white stripes, and Paco had on black pants and a white linen shirt.

Easy with themselves and the world, they exuded that special masculine energy that goes along with vibrant health and well-honed muscles. There were women all over Sarasota who would have given one of their ovaries to be with either of them, and I had them both. I also had their undivided attention.

Over dinner, I told them everything I knew about the murder. I told them about finding the lanai door open and the bedroom and closet ransacked, and about finding the dead body. About leaving Ghost with Mrs. Winnick and how weird she was, and about meeting Dr. Win and how it had looked like the Winnicks had just had a fight. I gave them a word-by-word account of my conversation with Guidry and told about speaking to Dr. Coffey and Shuga Reasnor. I told them what Judy had said about Marilee and how she'd dumped Dr. Coffey, and about his bimbo girlfriend coming out of cocaine alley.

At appropriate intervals, one or both of them said, "Huh," and when I mentioned Dr. Win, they both twisted their mouths to simulate throwing up. They were especially interested in the gross details about the dead man, and shook their heads with prim disapproval when I told them how Marilee had conned Dr. Coffey. I guess men don't get much pleasure out of hearing how a woman has tricked a man into giving her a million dollars.

9

When I was done telling it all, Michael set his wineglass down with a firm thud. "Stay out of it, Dixie. Let the homicide guys handle it."

Paco nodded soberly. "Dixie, you can get in the middle of something you don't want to be in. Stay out of it."

"I'm staying out of it! Did I say I wasn't staying out of it? I'm just concerned about the cat. What if Marilee Doerring never comes home? Some people don't, you know."

I saw the look on their faces and stopped. Okay, so I was getting a little overheated about the cat.

"I'll stay out of it," I said. "Don't worry."

Michael smiled and said, "Okay, folks, let's get off this subject. I make a motion that we all go over to the Crab House for a while."

Paco got up and started gathering plates. "Good idea. Come on, Dixie, let's hustle."

I knew what they were doing. Neither of

them wanted me to go to bed thinking about death and loss. To tell the truth, I didn't want me to do that, either. It was almost my bedtime, but the day's excitement and my long nap had left me wide-awake.

The Crab House is a bayside waterfront bar that has entertainment ranging from female impersonators to stand-up comics to rhythm and blues. It's the kind of place where you don't have to arrive on a Ducati and look fetching in black leather, but it helps. There's a wooden porch across the back where people can eat dinner beside the dock. Inside, tables line the perimeter of an oblong room separated from the porch by a glass wall. Half the patrons come from the key and half from boats that tie up at the dock. They're mostly gay, mostly good-natured, and mostly free of prejudice toward straights. My kind of place.

The bandstand and a small dance floor is to the right of the entrance, and even before we opened the door, we could hear rollicking honky-tonk piano music. Several people were dancing, and as we went toward the tables, we automatically began bobbing our heads and dipping our knees to the music. We took a table in the corner and ordered margaritas from a finger-snapping, hip-twitching waiter.

Over the music and laughter, Michael shouted, "Who's that playing?"

"That's Phil," the waiter yelled back. "A real cutie pie, and people just love him."

He sort of jitterbugged away to get our drinks, dodging around two men taking turns whirling and dipping each other in a parody of a fast waltz. The place was really jumping, mostly because of the music. All over the room, people were wagging their heads and grinning at one another like idiots.

The waiter boogied back with the drinks and did a little shimmy before he boogied off. We laughed and clicked our margarita glasses. Michael's idea had been a good one. Being in a fun place was a good way to get life back in perspective.

From where I sat, I had a good view of the pianist's back and his blond head. He had broad shoulders and wore a black jacket flocked with some sparkly designs. He was built with long bones. When he stretched an arm out to reach the end of the keyboard, his long fingers seemed to dance across the keys, lifting with playful little flips. He was obviously having fun playing, and the fun was infectious. I couldn't have said what it was that gave the music such a joyous sound. Whatever it was, it had a bouncing enthusiasm that drove deep into the psyche and flushed out every iota of cynicism.

A man in creased jeans and Doc Martens boots stopped beside my chair, and we all looked up. "Uh, I hope I'm not out of line here, but would you care to dance?"

Michael gave him a lazy grin. "Which one of us are you asking?"

The man gave him a startled blink. "Well, her, of course."

Obviously, he wasn't a native. I was guessing New York. Michael and Paco swung their heads toward me with eyebrows hopefully raised. The man met all their criteria. He was about our age and clean. His boots were polished and neither his fly nor his jaw gaped open.

I shook my head. "No thanks."

He reddened and turned away. I looked at Michael and Paco and shrugged. I knew they would both like me to meet a man and fall in love again. As much as they had liked Todd, they were ready for me to replace him, and it bothered them that I wasn't willing to entertain the idea, that I wasn't even willing to dance with a new man.

It isn't that I think love can't happen twice in a lifetime. I'm not that naïve. And I don't feel any constraint from Todd, no sense that his spirit hovers between me and a second love. If anything, Todd would want me to find somebody new and start a new family. It's the new family idea that stops me. When Todd and I had Christy, we were so caught up in the pink cloud of starting a family that we never once considered the idea that everything has its polar opposite. If a family can be started, it can also be ended. The ending is an amputation of your soul, and I can't risk that again. I also can't place that restriction on love. You either love completely and absolutely, with faith in the future, or you don't love at all. Since I can no longer have faith in the future, I choose not to love.

A little after midnight, the pianist switched moods. So softly that people stopped talking to hear, he began playing "He Ain't Heavy, He's My Brother." All around the room, people grew somber and reflective. For men who had literally carried their lovers in their arms as they died of AIDS, it was more than a sentimental ballad. Gradually, the playing grew more intense and passionate, filled with almost palpable anguish. The room had gone completely quiet and still, and as the song ended, I looked toward Michael and Paco and caught a look between them that made my heart catch. They never make a display of their feelings for each other, but their love is definitely not for weaklings.

Suddenly shy in the face of it, I drank the last of my margarita and began to scoot my chair back. I had to get up at 4:00 a.m., and Michael had to be at the fire station at 8:00. As usual, nobody knew what Paco had to do.

"We'd better go," I said.

They nodded and began to dig in their pockets for money while I headed toward the exit. The pianist got up to take a break and turned toward me. By this time, I felt as if I knew him. Through his music, he had laid himself out in a way that was almost too transparent — whether it was joy or pain he felt, there was absolutely nothing between him and his listeners. Our eyes met across the room and I opened my mouth to shout "Great music!" or "Bravo!" or something to show my appreciation. He suddenly looked stricken and turned away. At the same moment, I realized who he was. He was the Winnick teenager, the shy classical musician destined for Juilliard.

The kid took off toward the rest rooms at the back and left me rooted to the floor. The Crab House was a far cry from Juilliard, and I couldn't believe the sanctimonious Winnicks had given their blessing to their son's night job.

Michael and Paco caught up with me, and Michael took my arm as if I needed steering.

Paco held the door for us, and we moved out into air that was damp and warm, with a strong briny scent from the bay. Our footsteps made crushing noises on the shelled parking lot. Somewhere in the starlit distance, an outboard motor made muffled chugging sounds and night peepers called from the dark treetops.

I contained myself until we were in the car, Michael and Paco in the front and me in the back. Then I leaned forward and said, "You know who the piano player is? He's the kid who lives next door to Marilee Doerring. The house where the murdered man was!"

Now here's one of the differences between men and women. If they had been women, both of them would have turned around with their jaws dropped and their eyes stretched wide. They would have said, "No! You've got to be kidding!"

Being men, Michael said, "Huh," and Paco didn't say anything at all.

I said, "He can't be more than sixteen years old!"

That made Paco turn. "Nah, he's older than that. He's eighteen or nineteen."

Michael said, "God, it's nearly one o'clock. We're all gonna hate getting up in the morning."

Sometimes men are just no fun.

Michael was right about hating to get up next morning. When the alarm went off at four o'clock, I crawled out of bed with a dull margarita headache and a queasy stomach. There was a time when I could stay out till after 1:00 a.m. and get up at 4:00 with at least a modicum of alertness, but no more. If I hadn't known that half a dozen animals were depending on me, I would have hit the snooze button and slept another hour. Bleary-eyed, I switched on the bedside lamp and padded barefoot to the bathroom where I automatically got myself splashed and brushed for the day. I grabbed clean shorts and a T from the closet shelf and started pulling them on as I went down the hall. Then I remembered I was going to be seeing people, so I went back to the closet and got a bra. I shook my Keds to make sure no critters had crawled in during the night, then slid my feet into them and laced them up.

Out on the porch, I stopped a minute to inhale the fresh briny odor of morning sea air. A soft breeze was cool on my skin, and I could see the dark curved backs of dolphins jumping the waves in the milky light. So long as I concentrated on my work and had moments like this, I was okay. Not great, but okay. At least I was a lot better than I had been three years ago.

I clattered down the stairs, shooed a congregation of gulls off the Bronco, and got in. I would have preferred the bike, but I didn't know what the morning would bring. I went down the drive and turned onto Midnight Pass Road, where I didn't meet a single car. I didn't even see an early-morning jogger. I could have been the only person in the whole world.

Both coach lights were burning at the Graysons', and I mentally patted myself on the back for remembering to change their lightbulb. Rufus and I had our usual morning love-in, and as soon as we went out the front door, he started barking and straining at the leash. I had to shush him sharply to get him to shut up, and I took him toward the bay instead of toward Midnight Pass Road for his morning poop. Something was definitely calling to him from the woods.

After his walk and brushing, I put my bill on the kitchen counter, along with a note asking the Graysons to call me as soon as they got back that afternoon. Otherwise, I would make an evening call to take care of Rufus, and they'd get billed whether they were home or not. You have to be strict about these things. Sometimes people don't notify their pet-sitter that their flight has been delayed or that they've decided to extend their trip for a few days. I don't intend to neglect any of my charges, and I don't intend to pace around wondering if their owners might not have returned when they said they would. Ergo, they have to verify they've returned or pay for an unnecessary trip. I gave Rufus an extra-big hug when I left. I was going to miss him.

When I let myself into Tom Hale's condo, Tom and Billy Elliot looked up at me and Tom waved, but then their attention went back to the TV. A woman with spiky black hair and ruby red lips was holding a blue-balled microphone close to her lips and speaking low, the way sportscasters do at a golf match. Behind her was a wide wrought-iron gate, through which one could see a massive house.

"Mrs. Frazier hasn't made a statement yet, and so we're just waiting here to see what the next development will be. From what the Sarasota County Sheriff's Department has reported to us, the medical examiner's office has not yet released the body to the family."

A man's off-camera voice said, "Any new information about the connection between Harrison Frazier and the woman whose house he was found in?"

"Well, that's the interesting thing, Joel. According to the Frazier family spokesperson, there is no connection between the two at all. The family believes he must have been killed somewhere else and moved to the house."

Tom hit the mute button on his remote and said, "Well, there's a classic case of denial."

"That dead man in Marilee's house was Harrison Frazier?"

"Yep, and if he wasn't dead already, getting caught in Marilee's house would kill him."

Harrison Frazier was one of Florida's wealthiest men, with a family that practically went back to Ponce de León. The epitome of good breeding and good taste, the name Frazier graced an opera house or botanical garden or library in almost every city in Florida.

"You think Harrison Frazier and Marilee knew each other?"

"Come on, Dixie, why would somebody dump a dead body in Marilee's house? Of course they knew each other."

"You think she killed him?"

"Marilee never seemed the type."

"Anybody's the type, Tom. Any one of us could commit murder."

His face tightened. "I've sure had moments when I could."

"We all have. Most of us are just lucky enough that the moments pass."

"Still, Marilee's a gentle soul. I just can't see her shooting somebody."

"Is that what they said? That he'd been shot?"

"I just assumed. Wasn't he?"

I shrugged. "I don't know. He might have been."

It seemed like the time to get out, before he could quiz me about what I had seen. I snapped Billy Elliot's leash on his collar and started toward the front door. Tom said, "Dixie, did you call Cora Mathers?"

I shook my head. "I haven't had a chance yet. I'll do it later."

10

Billy Elliot and I took the elevator down-stairs, and when we came out the front door he leaped forward in a headlong dash. I welcomed the hard run. It helped get the cobwebs out of my head from my night of dissipation. We tore around the paved parking lot enough times to equal at least a mile before he slowed to a satisfied trot. For once, he had been able to run as long as he wanted to. I was half-dead and my thigh muscles were burning like a hot poker had been stuck to them, but at least I had sweated out the vestiges of alcohol.

Back upstairs, I let Billy Elliot inside and yelled good-bye to Tom, then drove to Marilee's house and sat in the driveway looking at the blank house. There was no deputy in sight, but the crime-scene tape was still up. I looked toward the Winnick house, but it looked as closed down as Marilee's. I decided to stop by again after I'd finished for the morning. If Guidry wasn't there, I would call him and find out when I could bring Ghost home.

I backed out of the driveway and headed toward Midnight Pass Road. In the rearview mirror, I saw the Winnicks' garage door rise and a white Jeep Cherokee back out. At the intersection, I stopped, and the Jeep drew up close behind me. The Winnick kid was driving, and his face in the rearview mirror looked desperate. He braked and jumped out of the car and ran to my side. I put down my window and looked into scared red eyes.

"On your way to school?"

"No ma'am, today's Saturday."

God, I had reached the age when I didn't know what day it was! Not only that, but people taller than me called me "ma'am."

The kid looked apprehensively toward his house. "Would it be all right if we went someplace and talked?"

I had cats to take care of, but I didn't have the heart to refuse him. Besides, cats don't have to be fed at exactly the same time every day. If they were living in the wild, they'd be on a random bird and rodent schedule. Okay, the truth is that I wanted to hear what he had to say.

I said, "I'll meet you at the Village Diner."

He followed close behind me and we both nosed into parking spaces in front of the diner. He opened the diner door for me without any uncertain diffidence, and I wondered which of his parents had taught him proper manners. Probably his father. The man had the soul of a sea slug, but he probably held out women's chairs. The kid was wearing jeans and a neon yellow waffle-knit knit shirt with a blue-and-white-striped collar and trimmed pocket. I would have bet good money that his mother had chosen it and that he didn't know how nerdy it was.

Judy gave me a questioning look when she saw me with another person of the male persuasion. I waggled my fingers in a wave and we took the same booth that Detective Guidry and I had sat in. Judy was right behind us with coffee and mugs.

Deadpan, she said to the kid, "You want coffee, sir?"

He blushed and shook his head. "Apple juice, please."

Apple juice had been Christy's favorite, too. For a minute, I saw him as his mother probably saw him, two or three years old and just learning to speak up to strangers. It's probably those cute overlaid memories that allow parents to look at their gangly adolescents without stabbing themselves.

Judy said, "You ready to order?"

"I'm not hungry," he said.

I understood how he felt. I never can eat when I'm worried, either.

Judy knew what I wanted, so she gave me another look and left us alone.

A woman came in dragging a whining little boy who looked about three years old. Cute kid. Skin the color of a Starbucks frappaccino and a mass of dark curls flopping over round black eyes. The woman had the same coloring and silky black hair, but she was carrying close to two hundred pounds of puffy fat on a five-foot frame, and she had sour, angry lines etched into her face. She had a death grip on the child's hand, alternately jerking and dragging him the way you have to pull a twisted garden hose. She stopped at a booth across the aisle and snarled, "Shut up and get in there!"

The Winnick kid and I watched the little boy try to scrabble onto the plastic-covered seat. His legs were too short and the plastic didn't give him anything to grab, so his feet flailed the air. The woman smacked his bottom with the flat of her hand, which caused him to jerk his head up and bang it on the underside of the table. Most kids would have cried, but he didn't, and the fact that he didn't was telling. This kid was accustomed to pain, and he knew that crying would only bring more of it.

She shoved him the rest of the way in and took the opposite seat. "Now you behave yourself," she said. "You sit there and be quiet."

Judy came to take the woman's order, and the kid and I turned our eyes away from them. I sipped coffee and watched his hands fiddle with the bundle of flatware rolled into a paper napkin. His hands were broad, with long skinny fingers and knobby knuckles.

To the tabletop, he said, "I know you saw me last night."

"I heard you, too. You were terrific."

He shrugged and blushed. It was hard to believe he was the same person as the confident pianist of the night before.

"The waiter said your name was Phil."

He blinked a couple of times and said, "It's Phillip, really." The poor kid couldn't even come up with a decent alias.

I said, "Do you play regularly at the Crab House?"

"Yeah. From eleven to one." He raised bloodshot eyes to me. "I climb out my window and walk over there."

"Ahhhh. So I guess that means your folks don't know about it."

He gave a choked laugh. "Among other things."

"You must not get much sleep."

"School will be out in a couple of months, and I'll be leaving in August."

"For Juilliard."

"Yeah."

"Are you excited about that, going to Juilliard?"

"Sure."

"Your mom's really proud of you."

"Yeah, it's all she talks about. She has lots of scrapbooks and pictures."

I had a quick image of Olga Winnick alone in that darkened house, working on her photo albums and scrapbooks, creating records of a happy family that didn't exist. Phillip was her way of vindicating herself to the world, but the woman didn't know her real son, she only knew the one she had created.

"How'd you get the job at the bar?"

He flashed me a quick look that was almost sly. "Somebody I knew told the owner about me. He had me audition and hired me."

I would have bet good money that the somebody he knew was also an older lover. He raised his head and looked at me head-on. "Are you going to tell my folks?"

I rotated my coffee mug and realized I hadn't even considered telling them. I'm not sure what that says about me, but that's how it was.

"If you were my son, I'd want to know that you were climbing out a window and playing at a bar. But you're not my son, and you're what, eighteen? Anyway, it's none of my business. I think you're probably not getting enough sleep, but other than that, I don't see anything wrong with it. It's an honest job, the place is safe, and it gives you a chance to do what you like to do."

He kept looking at me, waiting for something else.

I smiled. "That's all, Phillip."

Judy came with a coffeepot in one hand and my breakfast in the other.

Phillip said, "If it's not too much trouble, I think I'd like some pancakes."

"No trouble at all. You want bacon or sausage with them?"

"Yes ma'am."

"Which?"

"I guess both."

Nothing stimulates your appetite like finding out you're not hopelessly doomed after all.

I tucked into my eggs for a while, and he rhythmically tapped his fingers on the table. His hand span was probably twice as wide as my two hands laid side by side.

Across the aisle, the little boy said, "Look, Mama! A moon!"

He was holding up a triangle of toast with a bite mark in its center. The shape did look a little moonlike. He was a smart kid, noticing something like that so young.

With her cheeks swelled with hunks of sausage, his mother said, "Schtop playing wif your food."

His face fell and he bent his head back to his cereal.

Phillip said, "The police came and talked to my mom and dad and me about that murder."

"They're not police," I said. "They're from the Sheriff's Department."

"Oh. Well, they asked if we'd seen anything over there, or if we'd heard anything."

"Did you?"

He blushed, shifted in his seat, and looked out the window. "Not really."

Judy swished to the table with a plate of pancakes and another plate piled high with bacon and sausages. "More apple juice?"

"Yes ma'am, if it's not too much trouble."

She sped off to get his juice while I eyed his bacon and thought about what "Not really" meant.

Judy came back with another glass of juice and poured more coffee in my cup. "Anything else?"

"We're fine," I said.

Across the aisle, the woman said, "You eat every bite of that. You wanted it, you eat it. I'm not paying for shit you don't eat."

"Poor kid," said Judy, and moved on with her coffeepot.

"Phillip, do you know Ms. Doerring very well?"

"Nnnn-nnnn." He shook his head with his mouth full of pancake. I sipped coffee and watched him chew. He had put all the sausage on his plate but none of the bacon.

He swallowed and said, "My dad's helped her with some things, but I've never even talked to her."

I said, "Do you mind if I take one of your pieces of bacon? I don't usually eat bacon, but that looks so good. . . ."

"Oh, sure! Sure! That's fine!" It was like taking candy from a baby.

Perfume companies ought to bottle the smell of crisp bacon. Forget pheromones. I'll bet a woman with a little spot of bacon grease behind her ears would attract every male within a five-mile radius. Taking little bitty bites to make it last longer, I said, "What kind of things?"

It took him a minute to pick up where we'd left off. "Plumbing and stuff."

"She calls him to do things like that?"

He chewed awhile and considered how to answer. "She doesn't exactly call him. A few times her garage door has been open when he came home and she was out there, you know. I guess he saw her and went over to see if she needed any help."

No matter how hard I tried, I could not imagine Marilee Doerring out in her garage getting down a plunger to unstop her toilet or searching for a washer to fix a dripping faucet.

"That's nice of him."

"Yeah."

We both ate silently for a while, him taking huge forkfuls of food and me fighting down the rage I felt at the memory of Carl Winnick devoting an hour of radio time to say that Christy would not have been killed if I had been home where I was supposed to be instead of out acting like a man in a deputy's uniform. He had even objected to the department giving me widow's benefits, saying taxpayers shouldn't have to reward me for being a bad wife and mother.

I studied Phillip's face and reminded myself that the kid wasn't his father. The kid wasn't anything like his father. There was no reason to blame the kid because his father was an arrogant idiot.

I said, "I got the impression from your

mom that she doesn't like Ms. Doerring much."

"My mom thinks she's a slut," he said. "She probably is."

The easy way he said it took me by such surprise that I choked on a swig of coffee. While I coughed and sputtered and fanned my face with my napkin, Phillip grinned. "Bet you didn't think I knew that."

I was beginning to like this kid a lot. After four years of college away from his parents, he would probably be as smooth as his dad, but he wouldn't be a phony. This kid was the real deal.

The woman across the aisle stood up and yanked her dress down over her folds of fat. "Come on," she said, "we don't have all day."

I watched the little boy slide off the seat and follow his mother to the cashier's stand.

I pulled bills from my backpack and laid them on the table. "My cats await," I said. "I'll probably see you around."

Phillip's mouth was full, and he smiled up at me with a tiny slick of syrup on his chin. I resisted the urge to spit on a napkin and wipe it off, and headed for the front door. The woman was at the cashier stand counting out change and snarling at the little boy. Outside, I stopped and put my foot up on a railing separating the parking spaces from the walk. I untied and retied my shoe while I waited for the little boy and his mother to come out.

The door opened and the woman put her hand between his little shoulder blades and shoved him forward. "Goddamn it! Go on!"

In about two nanoseconds, I spun away from the railing and pinned her to the diner's stucco wall with my forearm across her throat. "You have a beautiful child, lady, and he deserves a lot better than you. You either start being nicer to him or I swear to God I'll see that he's taken away from you and given to somebody who'll love him."

All the rage had left her face. She was afraid, and she had every right to be. Something hit my ankle, hard, and I looked down. The little boy was glaring up at me, ready to kick me again.

"Leave my mama alone!"

I stepped away from her and she grabbed her throat with both hands as if she was afraid it had a hole in it. The diner door opened and a family came out — mother, father, three preadolescent kids. They flowed around us without paying us much attention, the father teasing one of the kids and the others laughing the way close families do at their private jokes. They moved down the sidewalk to their minivan and got in, still laughing and talking.

The woman was watching me with frightened eyes. The little boy had moved to hug her leg and she had a hand on top of his head.

"Okay," I said, "that's all."

I walked briskly down the sidewalk and around the corner to my car. My hands were shaking so much I barely managed to get the door unlocked. I put my head on the steering wheel and waited for the adrenaline tremors to leave. I felt sick. I felt ashamed. Sergeant Owens had been right about me. I wasn't ready to deal with people yet.

Maybe I never will be.

11

After I got myself together and saw to the other cats, I drove to one of the ritzy streets coiling around the edge of Roberts Bay to see Shuga Reasnor. Half-hidden behind a cluster of royal palms, her house was a behemoth of glistening white stucco shaped in a wide V, its upjutting wings giving it the look of an albino frigate bird in flight.

In the circular driveway, I got out of the Bronco and pulled my shorts out of my crotch before I climbed three wide stone steps to the entrance. The front door was a thick slab of glass that allowed a view all the way through the house to the lanai. I couldn't see it, but I knew the pool would be damn near Olympic in size and either equipped with every accessory known to man or built with a cascading waterfall. Or both. I rang the bell, a brass plate the size of a turkey platter, and stood looking up at the glass door while I waited. If that sucker broke as you walked through it, a shard could slice your head right off.

Through the glass wall at the back of the house, a woman moved into view out on the lanai. She came through the slider and walked toward me, giving me a thorough examination as she came.

"Are you Dixie? Sorry it took me so long, I was watering plants on the lanai. Come on in."

Shuga was tanning-booth brown, with the kind of long blond hair that you get only by being fifteen years old or paying a bundle for extensions. Her skin was smooth and taut like a fifteen-year-old's, too, and her body was trim and youthful. She was wearing a short black tank top and low-rider white jeans that showed her flat belly and smooth swirl of navel. Only her knowing eyes and corded hands gave away her age, which I estimated as somewhere between thirty-five and forty-five. Barefoot, she led the way into her living room, her feet leaving faint damp prints on the black tile. Outside the sliding glass doors, a water hose lay coiled like a green anaconda in the midst of a jungle of potted plants.

Swooping over a coffee table the size of my bed, she plucked a cigarette out of a nicotine bouquet stuck in a crystal holder, and waved her hand at me in a gesture that managed to invite me to smoke and to sit at the same time. Her fingernails were like Porsche fenders, sleek and curved and bright red. I shook my head at the cigarette offer and lowered my butt to a curved sofa covered in a rose-colored linen. Like Shuga, the room was beautifully done, but it had a hint of street toughness that no amount of cosmetics or money could overcome.

She got right to the point. "I wasn't entirely truthful over the phone. I don't want to talk about the damn cat, it's Marilee I'm worried about. The detective talked to me, so I know about that man in her house. That what's his name person. But that's all he would tell me. You know how the police are, they won't tell you a thing, even if you're a person's best friend. You work there, you're bound to know more than the police do."

She said the last with a pasted-on smile, as if she had suddenly remembered that she needed something from me and ought to be sucking up.

"I don't exactly work there," I said. "I just stop in twice a day to take care of the cat."

"And you don't know where she went?"

"No, that's why I called you. She didn't leave a number where she could be reached."

"The detective said she was going to be gone a week."

She gave me a pointed look with one raised eyebrow, as if it was my turn. I stayed silent. If she wanted me to play coy guessing games, I wasn't playing.

She sighed and blew out a stream of smoke. "What I want to know is how they can be sure she left town? Has anybody checked to make sure?"

I thought of the hair dryer left on her bathroom countertop. "Do you have any reason to think she didn't?"

She took another hit from the cigarette and looked out at the plants on the lanai, as if hoping to find inspiration out there. Abruptly, she dropped into a chair and gave me a hard stare. "I might, but Marilee would kill me if I told anybody."

"Miss Reasnor, if you know something that bears on a crime, you should tell the detective."

"Call me Shuga," she said throatily. The seductive way she said it was well practiced.

I gave her a level stare and her mouth twisted impatiently. "People have secrets," she said. "Everybody has secrets. You probably have secrets." She slitted her eyes and peered at me as if assessing what kind of secrets I had.

"And you're afraid Marilee will be mad at you if you tell one of her secrets."

"Hell yes. Wouldn't you be mad if your best friend told one of your secrets?"

I shrugged and stood up. I didn't have time for this. "Don't tell it, then."

She crossed her legs and swung her foot like an agitated cat swinging its tail. "I made a phone call last night to the place where she might have been going. She wasn't there."

I sat back down. "I thought you said you didn't know where she was going."

"I didn't know there had been a murder when you asked me."

"And you lied to the detective after you knew."

"I'm not *sure* that's where she was going. It wasn't like she had *told* me she was going there."

Her leg swung faster, and she sucked so hard on the cigarette, it almost disappeared into ash. Then she slapped her free foot on the floor and leaned forward and looked hard at me.

"It's damn funny. It's just damn funny. The murder's all over the news, why hasn't she called?"

To tell the truth, I'd been wondering that myself.

I said, "If you're really concerned about her, you should give the investigators all the information you have."

She leaned over and stubbed out her cigarette in a crystal ashtray that already had several lipstick-tipped butts in it. She lit another cigarette, and this time her hands were shaking. "I'll think about it," she said. "I really will think about it. You won't tell them what I said, will you? I mean, I don't know that's where she was going."

I stood up to go. "Not unless I think I have to. I can't promise I won't."

She nodded, and for a moment her face looked as old as her hands.

I pushed through the great glass door and went down the steps to the Bronco, conscious all the way of Shuga Reasnor's eyes watching me. I was sure of two things — she had been hoping to use me, and she had been lying through her teeth. I just didn't know what she had lied about.

I am blessed and cursed with an excellent memory for the things people say and how they say them. It began when I was a kid and had to pay close attention to what my mother said so I could figure out which things were lies and which were the truth. It was the only way I could predict what was going to happen from one minute to the next, and even then it didn't always work. I got better at it over time, and now it's second nature to me, like having a built-in lie detector.

I threaded my way through the serpentine streets, running through the entire conversation with Shuga, hearing her voice and its inflections. I passed the village and the fire station, driving on automatic, while my mind kept going over the meeting. Then I played it again, like rewinding a tape and starting all over. She had been nervous, but honest people can be nervous when they're talking about things they don't want to talk about, and her reluctance to betray a friend's secret could account for her uneasiness.

As I turned onto the shell-topped lane leading home, a black Harley-Davidson came roaring toward me. The driver had a bandanna tied over bushy black hair. A thick beard covered the bottom of his face and dark glasses hid his eyes. He wore a black leather vest and faded jeans. Black boots. I stopped at the side of the drive and let him go by, watching his right hand. As he passed, his first two fingers extended and then folded back around the handlebar.

He sped out to Midnight Pass Road, and I drove on down the lane. The two fingers were the signal Paco and I had agreed on he'd use whenever he was working a case in disguise. Otherwise, I might have thought a serial killer was on the property.

I started replaying the meeting again, but this time seeing it instead of hearing it. Seeing Shuga's face, her swinging leg, her fingers stabbing out her cigarettes. Liars always give themselves away one way or another. Some liars sweat profusely, some raise their voices to a telltale falsetto, and some cut their eyes up and to the right, as if they're seeing a vision of the story they're inventing. I was dead sure Shuga Reasnor had been lying about something, but I hadn't caught her giveaway sign.

I pulled into the carport and sat with the motor running, staring straight ahead at the Gulf but blind to everything but the mental images in my head. Like watching a movie, I slowed it down to an almost frame-by-frame run, and then I had it. When Shuga spoke of the dead man, she had called him "that what's his name person." As she said it, she had cut her eyes for an instant toward the right edge of the ceiling, the way people do when they're inventing a lie. Now that I had the sign, I realized even her words had been a giveaway. She had tried too hard to feign ignorance of the man's name, when it was known to every Floridian who was halfway sentient. Shuga Reasnor knew Harrison Frazier. She either had a personal relationship with Harrison Frazier or she knew that Marilee did.

A little voice in my head said, "No shit, Sherlock! You just figured that out?"

I should have realized it from the beginning, the way Tom Hale had. I had been so focused on putting one foot in front of the other that I hadn't given the details of the murder much thought. Now I felt the way Snow White must have felt after the Prince kissed her and brought her out of her coma. In a way, I had been in a coma for three years, and now I was beginning to wake up.

I climbed the stairs to my porch and opened the French doors to let the sea breeze blow out all the morning's stale air while I went to the bathroom and brushed my teeth. I checked my answering machine, which had no messages, then went out to the porch and sank into the hammock.

I thought about the aura of hard knowing that surrounded Shuga Reasnor, and about her opulent lifestyle. My guess was that she had gotten her money the hard way, either on her back sequentially or in a marriage bed to somebody who had conveniently died with no other heirs. For all I knew, Marilee might have gotten her money the same way.

Had Marilee been present when somebody conked Harrison Frazier on the back of the head? Had she been there when somebody taped his face nose-down in Ghost's water bowl? Maybe Marilee had been having an affair with him and his wife followed him and killed him. If so, what had she done with Marilee? It could have been Marilee who killed him. He was big, but a woman can swing a baseball bat or golf club hard enough to knock a man out. But surely Marilee wouldn't have been stupid enough to kill a man in her kitchen and leave him with his face taped inside her cat's water bowl. Unless she'd counted on people thinking she wouldn't be stupid enough to do that and therefore they'd think she had to be innocent. And where the hell was Marilee anyway? If she had killed him, she could be halfway around the world by this time. With all the money she had, she could buy a new identity, dye her hair, lay low, and she might never be found.

No matter who killed Harrison Frazier, Shuga Reasnor was right, it was damn strange that Marilee hadn't called.

The hammock swayed ever so gently in the sea breeze and seagulls squawked and circled in the cloudless blue sky. The surf surged onto the beach in an unbroken rhythm, and I stayed wide-awake. Finally, I gave up trying to sleep and grabbed my car keys. Olga Winnick thought Marilee was a slut. Kristin Lord thought she was predatory. Tom Hale thought she was a gentle soul. Shuga Reasnor knew a secret about her that she was afraid to tell. All I knew about her was that she was neat and clean and took excellent care of her cat. I wanted to see what her grandmother had to say about her.

12

Sarasota has a slew of retirement communities and assisted-living facilities, and Bayfront Village is one of the most exclusive. Its main building is a pink brick monstrosity constructed in a vague mix of Gothic spires, Mediterranean arches, red tile roof, and Art Deco turquoise trim. I drove up a fake cobblestone drive and pulled under a portico, where a uniformed valet courteously opened the door for me. As he drove off to park my Bronco in some secret spot, wide glass doors automatically sighed open when they felt my presence. Inside, the cavernous lobby appeared to have been decorated by a committee of feverish designers who saw an opportunity to unload all the mistakes former clients had refused. Overstuffed sofas upholstered in foxhunting scenes kept company with Hindu statues and gilded rococo. Plaster cherubs with fat cheeks mingled with sleek Danish modern and ruffled chintz.

Silver-haired men and women were

moving around, some going outside to cars drawing up under the portico. A lot of them pushed little three-wheeled canvas walking aids that looked like empty doll carriages. I wasn't surprised. The decor alone was enough to give them vertigo. Most of them wore sweaters, in spite of the fact that it was sizzling outside.

Feeling obscenely young and fit, I passed an easel supporting a large cardboard sign giving the week's activities. The sign was outlined in flashing lights, a tacky way of attracting attention, in my opinion, but I read it as I went by. One of the events being announced was a talk by Dr. Gerald Coffey, entitled "Help for the Heart."

I went up to the front desk and told a calm young woman in a tailored black suit that I was there to see Cora Mathers.

"Is she expecting you?"

"No, I should have called, but I just took a chance and came over."

"I'll call her. What's your name?"

"Dixie Hemingway, but she doesn't know me. Tell her I'm her granddaughter's cat-sitter."

"Her granddaughter's cat-sitter?"

"I take care of her granddaughter's cat when she's out of town. She left without giving me a number where she could be reached, and I'm hoping Mrs. Mathers knows how to contact her."

She nodded and punched numbers into a phone pad. I could hear buzzes on the other end of the line, and after nine or ten of them, I was ready to turn away. The young woman didn't seem fazed, however, so I waited. After what must have been thirty rings, a voice answered. The young woman explained my reason for coming and then listened intently while the person gave a lengthy response. She said, "Okay, Mrs. Mathers, I'll tell her," and put the phone down.

"She says to go on up," she said. "She's on the sixth floor. Turn right when you get off the elevator, her apartment is number six thirteen."

The elevator was mirrored, so on the ride up I smoothed my hair and tried to brush some wrinkles out of my shorts. At the sixth floor, I stepped out and turned right, and saw a tiny woman with wispy white hair planted in the middle of the hall waving a heavily freckled arm side to side like a highway construction worker. She wore a pair of wide-legged shorts in an exotic parrot print, with a bright red blouse that fell loosely over her thin hips. Her pale legs were as scrawny as a child's, and she would have had to get on tiptoe to be five feet tall.

"Here I am," she called. "Come on." She was beaming at me with such a sweet face that I felt a stab of yearning for my own grandmother.

When I got close, I said, "Thank you for seeing me, Mrs. Mathers. My name is Dixie Hemingway."

She turned into her doorway and crooked her finger at me to follow. "I know," she said. "Debby told me when she called. Are you related to Ernest Hemingway?"

"No, afraid not."

Taking tiny steps that moved her along in minuscule increments, she said, "I wouldn't regret it if I were you, he wasn't a man with a strong character. Oh, he was strong enough when he was young, all that swagger and boasting, but when the going got tough, he couldn't take it. Shot himself, you know. Got old and shot himself. Being young is easy, you know, anybody can do that, but it takes guts to be old."

We had now made it through a small foyer lined with framed botanical prints. Her apartment smelled like chocolate chip cookies.

I said, "Oh, this is lovely."

I wasn't just being polite, it really was. To

my left was a bar in front of a small galley kitchen, and I could see a spacious bedroom to the right. Directly in front was an airy living room with a glassed wall across the back. The floor was pale pink tile and the walls were a deeper shade of pink. A pale green linen Tuxedo sofa sat in front of a glass-topped coffee table, and a couple of armchairs in a muted green and pink chintz faced the sofa. Between the kitchen and the sofa was a skirted round table with two pale green ice-cream chairs. The effect was graceful and serene, enhanced by white wicker and greenery on a narrow sunporch that ran across the back of the living room and bedroom.

"It is nice, isn't it? I'm so blessed to have it. Marilee bought it for me, you know. Sit down and I'll make us some tea. You're in luck, I just finished making chocolate bread."

I took a seat at the round table and said, "I never ate chocolate bread."

"Well, it's my own invention. Marilee gave me a bread-making machine, oh, it must have been fifteen years ago now, and I use it every week. I start it and then at just the right time I throw in some chocolate chips. I won't tell anybody when I throw them in, that's my secret."

She ministepped around the bar to the kitchen, where she clattered down two mugs from a rack and poured boiling water into a fat brown teapot. "I keep water simmering all the time," she said. "You never can tell when somebody may drop by for a cup of tea."

"You must have a lot of friends here."

"Well, not a lot, but a sufficient amount. You don't want too many people coming and going, but enough so you don't feel alone. Of course, Marilee stops by pretty often, too, and that's nice."

She put the tea things on a tray and added a plate of fist-size hunks of brown bread studded with dark bits of oozing chocolate. Next to freshly fried bacon, the scent of hot melted chocolate may be the most tantalizing smell in the world. I got up and carried the tray to the table.

"It's Marilee I wanted to talk to you about, Mrs. Mathers," I said.

"Call me Cora."

"Do you happen to know where she's gone? She forgot to leave me a number when she left."

She pulled out a chair and sat down across from me. "This is about that Frazier fellow, isn't it?"

"Sort of. I'd like to let her know about it before she comes home."

Pouring tea into our cups, she said, "Well, dear, I expect she knows by now, don't you? I'm sure it's been on all the news. Here, butter some bread while it's hot. I don't slice it, I just rip off chunks of it. I don't know why, but it seems better that way."

While Cora watched intently, I smeared butter on a hunk and took a bite. I closed my eyes and moaned. "Oh God, that's good."

"Better than sex, isn't it? Of course it's been a long time since I had sex, so I may not remember it clearly. I'll bet you have plenty of sex, pretty young woman like you."

I sipped some tea and avoided her eyes. "Cora, have you heard from Marilee?"

She swallowed a bite of bread and took a sip of tea before she answered. "I don't imagine she'll be wanting to talk to me right now. Not with that Frazier fellow dead in her house."

"You knew him?"

"I never met the man."

My head felt like it had been twisted like a doorknob and allowed to spin back into place. I buttered another bite of bread and chewed it slowly while I studied Cora's face. Her eyes were overhung by crepey eyelids, but they were bright and alert. I said, "Why don't you think Marilee will want to talk to you?"

Her lips tightened and she slapped a pat of butter on a bit of bread. "Well, Frazier's the man who ruined my granddaughter's life, isn't he? Don't think I'm saying Marilee hasn't made the best of it, because she has. But that's all water over the dam now, isn't it?"

The words lay on the table along with the bread and butter and tea. I could pick them up and learn something very personal about Marilee that she probably didn't want known, or I could mind my own business and stay ignorant.

I said, "I don't know about that, Cora. To tell the truth, I never understood what that meant, water over the dam, under the bridge, whatever."

"Well, it's just too late, isn't it? What's done is done, and you can't go back and undo it, can you?"

"I guess not. Uh, Cora, would you mind telling me how Marilee knew Harrison Frazier?"

"Well, yes, I would mind, dear. That's personal and private business of Marilee's, and I don't go around telling my granddaughter's personal and private business, now do I? Have some more tea."

"No thanks. Can you tell me where she is? I really think I should contact her."

"No, can't tell you that, either. But here's what I'll do: If she calls me — and she usually does call when she's off on one of these trips — I'll tell her you want to talk to her. How's that?"

"Cora, the Sheriff's Department would like to know where she is. It isn't just me."

"Well, I'll tell them the same thing I told you. I don't know, and even if I did, I wouldn't say, because that's Marilee's private business."

"But you're not worried about her?"

"Oh my, no. Marilee can take care of herself. I'll say that for her, she can take care of herself." She waved her arm toward the glass wall as she said that, presumably to indicate the vastness of the visible blue sky as a symbol of how well Marilee could take care of herself.

I said, "Marilee left the number of Shuga Reasnor to call in case of an emergency. Do you know Ms. Reasnor?"

"Oh my, yes, I've known her since she was a little bitty thing, only her name wasn't Shuga then, it was Peggy Lee. Her mother was a fool for Peggy Lee, so that's what she named her little girl. Poor little thing, that's about the only thing her mother ever gave her. Her daddy wasn't much better. Drunks, both of them. If I hadn't fed Peggy, I think she might have flat starved to death. She's done all right for herself, though. Last time I saw her, she looked like Miss Gotrocks herself."

"You saw her lately?"

"No, it was several months ago. Marilee had picked up my heart pills at the drugstore and forgot to bring them to me before she left town, so Peggy Lee brought them to me. I told her she looked like a movie star. Between you and me, though, I don't think that's her own hair."

"So she had a key to Marilee's house?"

"Oh my, yes. Those two have always been in and out of each other's house like it was their own."

"Cora, did you know Marilee had her locks changed? I had to stop by and pick up a new key before she left."

"Is that a fact? Well, no, I didn't know that. But then I wouldn't, because I don't have a key myself. The only time I go over there is when Marilee comes and gets me, so why would I?"

I was stumped. So far as I knew, Marilee hadn't broken any laws or done anything wrong. If her grandmother didn't want to say where she'd gone, she wasn't obligated to do so. Furthermore, I was a pet-sitter, not a criminal investigator. I had already stepped over a line by coming here, and if I went any further, I would be getting into serious unethical territory.

I stood up. "I'd better go," I said. "If Marilee calls, I'd appreciate it if you'd ask her to contact me. I've put her cat in a day-care center until the house is released, and I'd like to discuss that with her."

"I'm sure whatever you've done is just fine."

"Would you like me to put the tea things away before I go?"

"Well, if you don't mind, dear, yes, I would. Things get heavier when you're old."

I set the teapot and mugs and plates on the tray and carried them around to the kitchen counter. The refrigerator door had notes attached by magnets, and there were several snapshots of a pretty dark-haired young woman.

I called, "Are these photos of Marilee when she was young?"

Through the open space above the bar, I saw Cora's face close like a flower pulling its petals inward. She looked much older, and infinitely sadder.

"No, dear, those are not of Marilee."

Her voice held such finality that I knew I had violated some unspoken rule by asking.

"I'm sorry," I said. "I didn't mean to pry."

"Oh, of course you did, but it's all right. I'm not angry. I just can't discuss what it isn't my business to discuss, now can I?"

I reminded myself that I had no right to ask questions, and said my good-byes, leaving her hunched over the little round table.

Downstairs in the lobby, I veered behind a couple of elegantly dressed women standing in front of the blinking activities display.

"Excuse me," I said, "my grandmother is thinking about buying an apartment here. Could you tell me how you like living here?"

They turned and started talking at once, the gist of which was that the chef in the dining room put out a fabulous Sunday brunch, that there were always classes and workshops and outings planned, and that everybody who lived there was interesting. They could have done commercials for the place.

I nodded toward the blinking display. "I noticed that Dr. Coffey is going to do a talk about bypass surgery. Does he do that often?"

They sobered and nodded. "Yes, he does," said one. "I suppose he's operated on so many of the people living here that he needs to let us know that it's available for us."

I looked toward a tanned silver-haired couple striding out the door carrying tennis rackets. "Everybody looks awfully healthy. He can't do *that* many bypasses."

One woman fingered a string of cultured pearls at her throat and said, "Looks can be deceiving. Several people have been active one day and in the hospital the next. It's really alarming."

The other woman said, "Like Mary Kane. She had a big party for Sunday brunch, and that night she went into a diabetic coma. She just insisted on eating those cherry blintzes, and why not? She was eighty-five years old and she'd lived with diabetes for years and years. She knew what she could do and what she couldn't do, but I guess that time she overdid it. Two days later Dr. Coffey did a triple bypass on her."

I waited for the end of the story, and when neither of them volunteered it, I said, "And was it a success?"

"She never woke up. They had to transfer her to a hospital in St. Pete, and she was there for three months before she finally died. Dr. Coffey said she was just too frail to survive. Poor thing, and she never even knew she had anything wrong with her heart. All she knew about was her diabetes."

"Almost the same thing happened to Mr.

153

Folsom, remember? He seemed fine too, just complained of emphysema from smoking before he knew better. And then, boom, Dr. Coffey found four of his arteries blocked and had to do bypass surgery on him. He didn't wake up, either, but he didn't suffer as long as Mary did. He passed away just a few days after the surgery."

They both fixed me with eyes frightened and resigned, while little warning bells went off in my head.

13

I said, "Dr. Coffey must be awfully busy."

"Oh, he is! At least one person a week from here has a bypass, and that's just the people living here."

"It must be awfully hard for their families, having them die so suddenly like that."

They nodded, but with a look of some disturbed confusion. "Actually, none of them has had a family. They've all been alone."

Somehow that didn't surprise me.

While the valet retrieved my car, I calculated Dr. Coffey's income from bypass surgeries. The going rate was around $150,000 per artery, so a triple bypass could bring him a cool half million. If he did just two of those a week, the million dollars Marilee had conned Coffey out of would be only a week's income. In light of the fact that she had bought her grandmother an apartment that probably cost at least a half million, and in light of the fact that it sounded like some of his patients hadn't needed the surgery anyway, it didn't seem so bad for Marilee to have taken advantage of him.

I drove south on Tamiami Trail, passing Marina Jack, where a few cotton-ball clouds were reflected in the glassy blue water and naked masts of sailboats stood sentinel around yachts sleeping in the sun. A million questions were running through my mind. Why did Cora say Harrison Frazier had ruined Marilee's life? If Marilee knew Frazier, had she had her keys changed to keep him out? And where the hell was Marilee, anyway?

When I got back home, I put a Patsy Cline CD in the player, and Patsy and I sang together while I took the sheets off my bed and gathered up more laundry to put on top of the stuff in the washing machine. I added detergent to the wash and turned it on, and while the washer filled, Patsy and I sang another song. I got out the Swiffer and punched a clean cloth into its head, and Patsy and I sang some more while the machine started chugging. The thing about Patsy is that she kept it clean and simple. Nothing oily or mysterious. The world would be a better place if everybody thought like Patsy.

One minute I was running the Swiffer and singing with Patsy, and the next minute I was yelling *"Oh shit!"* and running to open the washer. The laundry was twisted and bloated under murky water, looking like the slimy fetuses of some horrible monster. I jammed my arm in and yanked up Ts and towels, Keds and shorts until I hauled up my khaki cargo shorts with the flapped pockets. I spread them over the washer's agitator head to hang in sodden folds while I fumbled the Velcro flap open and fished out Marilee's letters that I'd taken from her hall table.

Making moaning noises, I laid each wet, ink-smeared envelope on top of the dryer. I imagined myself explaining to Marilee that I'd had good intentions about mailing the stuff, but just, you know, forgot. I imagined myself telling Marilee that I would pay her IRS fine for being late. Then I started getting mad and imagined myself saying, "You didn't actually tell me to mail it, you know. You went off and left it, and a lot of people wouldn't even have noticed it. It's really not fair to expect *me* to pay the penalty!"

I went to the kitchen for paper towels and blotted as much water from each envelope as I could, but they were all a sorry sight. Some of them had more or less disintegrated over the checks and invoices they held. I recognized the familiar Florida Light and Power envelope, and also Verizon and Teco, but not the others. One bedraggled check was made out to a pool-cleaning service, but the ink was too blurred to make out the name, and another check was stapled to an invoice from a home-security company. The check was a loss, but the print on the soggy invoice was clear enough to see that it was for $785, for the installation of a Centurian wall safe.

"Huh," I said brilliantly. Marilee must have had something she deemed important enough to hide in a wall safe. Something she wanted to keep close at hand instead of in a safe-deposit box at the bank. Perhaps the person who had trashed Marilee's bedroom had been looking for whatever it was.

All the envelopes were business size except one pale blue square of heavy linen-woven stock. The dark blue ink of the address had run badly and the flap had come unstuck, but the thickness of the envelope seemed to have kept the paper inside relatively dry. I raised the flap all the way, just to see how wet the letter inside was, just to see if it might be salvageable. Well, okay, I raised it to see if I could see anything written on it. I know I shouldn't have, but I did.

Marilee's handwriting was round and girlish, with little hearts dotting the *i*'s. The sentence at the top of the opening in the envelope said, "I can't wait to see you!"

Carefully, I extracted the damp letter from the envelope and gingerly carried it to the kitchen and laid it out on paper towels. It was two pages long, and I laid each page out as precisely and clinically as a pharmacist laying out prescription pills. So long as I focused on drying these moist sheets, I could ignore the fact that I was tampering with the U.S. mail, violating Marilee's privacy, interfering with a homicide investigation, and generally sticking my nose into things that were none of my business.

I left the pages drying and went back to the washer and restarted it, then finished Swiffering and dusting and plumping up the cushions on the living room furniture. I have one chair in my living room. It matches a rattan love seat with dark green linen cushions patterned with bright red and yellow flowers of a purely artistic species. Originally, both love seat and chair sat in my grandmother's little private parlor off the bedroom she shared with my grandfather. The idea had been that she could retreat there when she wanted privacy or just to get away from the noise of a man and two children — the two children being me and Michael. But she never found time for privacy, so the furniture stayed like new. When I moved into the apartment over the carport, I appropriated it for myself. Like my grandmother, however, I'm not very good at just sitting, so when I die, my living room furniture may still be as good as new. But of course I won't have a granddaughter to inherit it. Unless Michael and Paco adopt a child, there won't be any relative to inherit anything. We'll all just die without leaving a trace, like sculptured sand people obliterated by the tide.

By the time I put clean sheets on my bed and cleaned the bathroom, the wash was ready to go in the dryer. I tossed it all in and turned it on, then went to the kitchen to check on the letter. Most of the ink was too blurred to read, but I took it to the porch and sat down at the table.

Dearest Lily,
It still seems strange to call you Lily! It's a pretty name and I like it, but I had intended to name you Bonnie, and that's what I've always called you in my mind. My Bonnie. I guess when you're only fifteen, you aren't real good at naming babies. Ha! I guess I know why they named you Lily, but that's something else I'll tell you when we're together.

The next paragraph was blurred, then some clear lines: "You have a right to know all the truth, not just part of it. Honey, please don't feel bad about keeping it a secret that —"

That was the only legible but except for "I can't wait to see you!"

I read those few lines over and over, and each time I had to blink hard to keep from crying. Obviously, Marilee had given birth to a daughter when she was only fifteen, and evidently she had found her. Finding a daughter you gave up at birth would be like having a dead child returned to you, a fulfillment of the heart's deepest yearning.

I leaned back in my chair and looked out at the sea. Sunshine sparked diamonds off the glittering waves. In the distance, triangular sails moved slowly along the horizon. A few shorebirds were leaving tracks down on the sand. A snowy egret, perched on one leg on a mooring post, was blissfully turned the wrong way to the breeze so his feathers could ruffle. From the rooftop, a pelican sailed to the edge of the shore and gulped something from the lapping water. No matter what happens in the world, the ocean keeps rolling. It's the one thing you can depend on.

I went inside and got an apple from the

fridge and went back to the porch and watched the waves rolling in while I ate it. I thought about calling Guidry and telling him about the letter, but I didn't. I didn't want to explain about reading it, and it might not have anything to do with Harrison Frazier's murder. I thought about what Shuga Reasnor had said about Marilee having a secret, and this was probably it.

I was beginning to feel very protective toward Marilee Doerring. I didn't want to give her secret away unless it became absolutely necessary. I'm a real pushover for people who are good to their pets and their grandmothers and the babies they gave up when they were fifteen.

I threw the apple core down to a congregation of black gulls and went inside to get my things for the afternoon pet visits. I locked the French doors when I left, even though any dedicated intruder could easily burst through them. I drove down the tree-lined lane to the street, where a vacationing couple on the sidewalk paused to let me pass. The woman was short and round and sun-pinked, with a mass of curly brown hair sticking out in all directions from a tennis cap. She wore flower-printed shorts and a yellow spandex bandeau stretched over breasts as big as honeydews. Her arms were held out chest-high like chicken wings, with wrist weights attached like cuffs. As I drove by, she marched in place with her arms swinging and her cheeks puffed out while she energetically whooshed air in and out. Her husband was almost two heads taller, and he was ambling along behind her with his hands in his shorts pockets. They were so cute that I waved at them as I turned onto Midnight Pass Road. The husband waved back, but the wife gave me a startled look and resumed her power walking.

The Graysons hadn't called, so I went first to their house. One of their three garage doors was up and Sam Grayson was standing beside the driver's side of his BMW. Sam was a sexy, seventyish Cary Grant look-alike with a high forehead and silver hair cut in an almost military burr. Tall and lean, he moved with a loose-limbed grace that always made me wish I could dance with him just once.

I parked behind one of the closed doors so he could back out, but he walked out to meet me. "We forgot to call you, didn't we?"

I said, "Welcome home. How was your trip?"

"Oh, it was great. Just great. We got to spend time with our daughter and the grandkids, and we've got enough snapshots to bore our friends for months."

"That's true friendship."

"Yeah. Come on in and say hello to Libby."

We went up the front walk and he opened the door and stood aside. Rufus came galloping to kiss my knees, and Libby Grayson came from the kitchen, drying her hands on a dish towel. As beautiful as Sam was handsome, Libby had shoulder-length silver hair and brilliant blue eyes that sparkled with intelligence and good humor. Together, they looked like the couples in retirement community ads — the ones who are so fit and sexy, they make you wish you were that old so you could look so good.

"Oh, Dixie, I'm sorry I didn't call! Oh well, it gives us a chance to thank you for taking such good care of Rufus. Look how he loves you! I'll bet he didn't even miss us."

I leaned down to stroke Rufus, wishing he wouldn't act so happy to see me.

Libby said, "Sam, pay Dixie."

He took the bill from her and read it, then got out his wallet.

While he counted out twenties, Rufus trotted over and sat next to Libby and smiled at me, as if he understood it wasn't polite to two-time her to her face.

I said, "I love the new carousel horse."

Sam handed me a neat stack of twenties and said, "He's a rare one. Made of cast iron instead of the lighter stuff. You wouldn't believe what a project it was to get him mounted on that brass pole!"

Libby said, "He's so heavy, the brass pole had to be lined with galvanized steel. First we had to find a brass pole that was exactly one and a quarter inches in diameter, because the holes in the horse are one and a half inches. Then we had to find galvanized-steel pipe the right diameter to fit inside the brass pipe. It took *weeks* of phone calls!"

Rufus yawned and trotted away toward the kitchen. I knew just how he felt. This was way more information than I needed about pipes, but they were getting such a kick out of telling it that I tried to look interested.

Sam said, "We hired a guy to cut the pipes and fit them together. He had to drill a hole through them and attach the horse. When he fitted them into the brass plates on the floor and ceiling, it was like watching brain surgery. If he'd cut either pipe a quarter inch too short or too long, we'd have been back to square one."

I started edging toward the door. "Well, I'd better run. Oh, by the way, somebody left some books for you in the chest."

We all said our good-byes, and as I backed out of the driveway, Sam was leaning over the chest digging out all the accumulated newspapers. I wondered if he and Libby would actually read them or toss them in the trash. My bet was that they would trash them. Who needs so much news?

At Tom Hale's condo, I found Tom reading in his wheelchair and Billy Elliot lying on the floor with his head propped on Tom's feet. Both man and dog looked up at me when I walked in. As if we were in the middle of a conversation, Tom said, "Dixie, do you know what a fewterer is?"

"It sounds like something dirty."

"In medieval days, a fewterer was the keeper and handler of the greyhounds."

"So you're a fewterer?"

"I guess you're one, too, Dixie. We're two fewterers."

"Well, that was always my ambition, Tom, to be a fucking fewterer."

I got Billy Elliot's leash and he and I went downstairs to run. As I ran down the edge of the parking lot behind him, a dark Blazer pulled to my side and eased along with me. I looked over and saw Lieutenant Guidry eyeing me with that calm level look that only cops have. I could have been jogging along stark naked and he probably wouldn't have changed expression. I pointed to the building's front door, and he nodded and pulled away, making a U-turn and parking by the entrance.

14

Billy Elliot barreled along like he was back on the track with his greyhound buddies, and my muscles burned with the effort of keeping pace. We rounded the end of the parking lot and thundered around the central esplanade of palmettos and hibiscus. At the entrance, where Guidry waited, I pulled Billy Elliot to a halt but left him enough leash to explore a bit. I dragged my aching legs to Guidry's window, panting like Billy Elliot but managing to keep my tongue from lolling out the sides of my mouth.

Guidry grinned at me. "Now I see how you can get away with eating all that bacon."

I made a wheezing sound.

"I got a message you'd called," he said.

"Yeah, I wanted to know when I can bring the cat home."

He gave me a blank look for a moment and then remembered. "Oh, the cat. Well, the forensics people are finished at the house, but the crime-scene tape will have to stay up until I get the ME's report."

"When do you think that'll be?"

He looked at his watch. "I'm on my way to the morgue now. It'll just take a few minutes. Wanta come with me?"

I stared at him. Was he nuts?

"The time comes when you have to get back on the horse," he said. "Maybe this is your time."

"Maybe you're way out of line, Lieutenant."

"Could be. Or I could be right."

"This conversation is over."

I spun away from him and jerked Billy Elliot out of the esplanade. I pulled him short and opened the front door.

"You can't hide out indefinitely," yelled Guidry.

I pulled Billy Elliot into the elevator and leaned against the wall while it climbed to Tom Hale's floor. My heart was pounding hard and a surge of adrenaline had made me start trembling. Guidry had no right to tell me what to do with my life. He had no right to tell me anything.

By the time I got Billy Elliot settled in his apartment, I was trembling not only with anger but also with embarrassment for letting Guidry get to me like that. I was the tough one, the one who kept her cool in an emergency. At least that's who I used to be.

Now I was quivering like a wuss because a detective had suggested that it was time for me to stop hiding from the world. My shaking continued all the way down in the elevator, so hard that my teeth were clamped hard together. The worst thing in the world is knowing that somebody else is right and you're wrong. It was time for me to stop hiding. I just wasn't sure I was strong enough.

When I went out the front door, I made a little involuntary groan. Guidry was still sitting there with the car idling.

He said, "You ready to go?"

I clomped down the steps and went around the back of the car to the passenger side and got in. Guidry looked straight ahead as I opened the door.

"We have to make this fast," I said. "I have other pets to take care of."

"Half an hour, tops," he said, and put the car in gear.

Sarasota County doesn't have its own morgue, they use Sarasota Memorial Hospital's facilities. We were ten minutes away, and neither of us spoke a word the entire trip. I sat with my arms crossed across my chest and hoped Guidry believed I was trembling from the air-conditioning vents blowing on me. He kept his attention on the traffic, and if he noticed my shaking, he didn't mention it. We parked in the back parking lot at the hospital and took the rear entrance into the maze of hallways that make big hospitals seem like cities. If I ever commit a major crime, I'm going to head straight for the nearest big hospital. You could spend an entire day in a waiting area pretending to be a relative keeping vigil on a loved one, every day moving to a different area. You'd have plenty of bathrooms, you could sleep on the couches, and if you had money to put in food-vending machines, you could hide out indefinitely.

Guidry and I still hadn't spoken. It was as if we had a tacit agreement that we would do this thing without conversation. He led the way to the autopsy room and opened the door for me to go in first. There was a small square waiting room with a scuffed beige linoleum floor and a few plastic molded chairs. A battered wooden coffee table heaped with dog-eared magazines with torn-off rectangles where addresses used to be, and a TV monitor mounted on the wall like in a hospital room. A half wall separated an attendant in green surgical scrubs from the waiting room. He stood on his side with his fists pushed against the counter and stared suspiciously at us. On the wall behind him, a filing cabinet held a coffeepot and some mugs and a jar of Cremora, but he didn't seem inclined to offer refreshments.

Guidry gave his name, and the young man picked up a phone and spoke briefly. In a few seconds, the inner door opened and a tall Cuban-American woman came out carrying a manila envelope. She had warm almond eyes and white hair cropped tight against her skull.

She and Guidry shook hands, and Guidry said, "Dr. Corazon, this is Dixie Hemingway."

We shook hands, and if she thought it strange that Guidry had brought along somebody in rumpled shorts and a T, she didn't show it.

15

Dr. Corazon pushed a pair of reading glasses to the top of her head. "Your man had a subdural hematoma that would have resulted in his death, but he probably died of a laryngeal spasm. Officially, he drowned."

Guidry frowned. "I don't understand."

"If a person dies within forty-eight hours of being immersed in water, it's officially called drowning. Fifteen percent of drowning victims don't have water in their lungs, but die of hypoxia caused by a laryngeal spasm. In other words, they choke to death. Mr. Frazier had enough water in his lungs to kill him, but he also had a laryngeal spasm. It's impossible to say which killed him, but the hematoma would have caused his death if he hadn't had a laryngeal spasm or taken water into his lungs."

Guidry said, "I guess it doesn't matter. Whether it was the blow to the head or drowning or choking to death, it was still homicide."

"Well, that's the problem, Lieutenant. It does matter. The blow to his head was inflicted by a blunt object moving in a right-to-left trajectory. The tape applied to his head to keep his nose and mouth underwater was done left to right."

Guidry and I both stared openmouthed at her. I found my voice first. "You mean he was killed by two people?"

"I mean he was first struck in the back of the head by a right-handed person, and then taped to the cat's water bowl with his nose and mouth underwater by a left-handed person."

Guidry said, "Maybe it was one ambidextrous person."

"That's possible too."

"Any idea what hit him?"

"Blunt instrument, Lieutenant. You know what that means."

We all knew. A blunt instrument can be just about anything.

"Here's another thing," said Dr. Corazon. "He was nude when he was struck, and there was a time lag before somebody dressed him and tried to drown him. I know that because there was dried blood on his body, under his clothes."

I said, "If they let him lie around long enough for blood to dry on his body, maybe he was already dead when they stuck his nose in the cat bowl."

She shook her head. "No, he had some water in his lungs. He was still breathing when somebody taped him down in the water, but he wasn't fully conscious. I know that because there are no petechiae, little broken blood vessels from struggling to breathe."

Guidry said, "Can you give me a time of death?"

"This isn't TV, Lieutenant. He died between the time he was last seen alive and the time he was found dead."

He grinned. "Can't you narrow it down a bit more?"

"From the lividity, best estimate is around two a.m."

"Any idea how much time elapsed between the time he was hit and when he died?"

"Several hours, probably."

Guidry thanked the ME and took the manila envelope from her. She said, "Good luck, Lieutenant. Nice meeting you, Ms. Hemingway."

We smiled at each other and she bustled off to her grisly inner sanctum. Guidry held the door open for me, and I went through like an obedient puppy. We retraced our way through that peculiar combined odor of chemicals and putrefaction and body wastes that permeates every hospital, both of us with our heads down to keep from breathing deeply, both of us thinking hard. I suppose Guidry was thinking about his case, but I was thinking how strange it was that I had stopped trembling the minute the medical examiner had come out to talk to us, when it was the ME I had been dreading so much. The last time I'd spoken to an ME, it had been to get the details of the autopsies on Todd and Christy, but somehow that memory hadn't surfaced while Dr. Corazon had spoken. Instead, I had snapped into cool, objective detachment.

We went through the exit and stepped into the heat of the parking lot. I said, "I looked through the house before I found the body. I didn't see any blood spatters."

Guidry said, "He was probably taking a shower when he got hit. Forensics found blood traces in the bathtub drain."

"Somebody had cleaned the tub?"

"Yeah."

We trudged across the hot pavement to Guidry's car, and he beeped it unlocked. We slid into its stifling heat and he started the engine and turned the air conditioning up high. I looked at my watch. We had been inside the hospital only fifteen minutes.

I said, "When I stopped by to pick up her house key, Marilee said she was just about to take a shower."

He turned his head and gave me a look. "You think that's significant?"

"Not unless she was about to take a shower with Harrison Frazier."

"Do you have any reason to think she was?"

"Come on, Lieutenant, they were bound to know each other. Harrison Frazier wasn't the kind of man to go around breaking in a woman's house."

"Not unless he was accustomed to using a key and she'd had the locks changed."

Right then and there, I should have confessed that I had read Marilee's letter to her daughter. I should have told him that Shuga Reasnor knew things she hadn't told. But Marilee was a kind woman who gave her grandmother bread makers and expensive apartments, and she deserved a chance to have a relationship with a daughter she'd given up when she was fifteen without it becoming public knowledge. Besides, Shuga Reasnor was right. If Marilee was okay, she would be pissed sixteen ways from Thursday if she came home and found her most intimate secrets blabbed to the world.

For all those irrational reasons, I kept quiet.

Guidry said, "Do you happen to know whether she's right-handed?"

I shut my eyes and replayed her arm stretching toward me with the door key dangling from her fingers. "She handed me the new key with her left hand."

He nodded and didn't say anything else. I didn't, either.

At the entrance to the parking lot at the Sea Breeze, Guidry stopped to let a woman on a yellow three-wheeler cross in front of us. Red-faced under hair dyed an improbable shade of magenta, she was leaning over the handlebars and pedaling with grim therapeutic exertion. A pole jutted at an angle from the rear of the trike, with a triangular orange alert flag attached to its end like a waving tail. We watched her move down the sidewalk the way jungle animals might watch a lioness chasing prey.

We pulled into the parking lot, and I pointed silently to the spot where my Bronco was parked. When Guidry stopped behind it, I said, "So when can I bring Ghost home?"

He gave me an "Oh for God's sake" look.

I said, "Come on, the cat didn't do anything wrong. Let him come home."

"Maybe late tomorrow."

"You'll let me know?"

"Yeah."

I shut the door and walked to my own car, beeping it unlocked as I went. Guidry drove off without saying good-bye, which suited me just fine. I was glad I'd gone with him, but I didn't want any conversation about it.

By the time I finished with the last cat and drove home, it was after 8:00 p.m. Before I went upstairs, I stood a few minutes looking out at sailboats silhouetted against a sky so clear and blue, it caused my heart to swell with inchoate longing. Sailboats always seem carefree to me, even though I know a lot of them are manned or womaned by people who are anything but carefree. I went upstairs and unlocked the French doors, tossing my shoulder bag on the desk in the closet-office as I walked to the bathroom. In the kitchen, I opened a bottle of cold Tecate and poured it in a wineglass. I added a wedge of lime and took it out to the porch to drink while I watched a brilliant orange sun sink toward the horizon.

When it touched the rim of the earth, pulsating for an instant on the water, a shimmering gold ribbon moved over the sea to the shore beneath me. When I was little, I believed that golden path was stretching out especially to me. I thought that if I were brave enough, I could step out on it and walk to the edge of the sea where I would find an enchanted world. I was never brave enough, so every sunset was an occasion of both wonder and chagrin.

When the sun had slid under the horizon and left only a faint reflection of itself behind, I went inside and took inventory of the refrigerator. With both Michael and Paco away, I would have to fend for myself. Except for mayonnaise and mustard and pickles, about all I had was some sliced cheese and beer and a package of corn tortillas. The freezer section held a box of Boca burgers, some ancient hamburger buns swathed in a thick layer of ice crystals, and some Ziploc bags holding mystery leftovers.

I thought about having a bowl of Cheerios, but except for breakfast twelve hours ago, all I'd had to eat all day was an apple, and I was famished. Also, the shrink I saw after I lost Todd and Christy said it was important to eat a real meal when I was alone — if you don't take good care of yourself when you're alone, you'll end up thinking you're only important when you're with another person.

There was a little Greek place in the village where I could get great lamb shish kebab if I could get there before they stopped serving. I jumped in the shower, and then ran still damp into my office-closet to pull on a short denim skirt and a white stretchy T. I dug my feet into a pair of white canvas mules, grabbed my shoulder bag from my desk, and was on my way out when I noticed the blinking red light on my answering machine. The strap on my bag must have been covering it before. I hesitated a moment, then punched the playback button.

"Um, Miz Hemingway? This is Phillip Winnick? Uh, would it be okay if . . . I'd like to talk to you about . . . you know, the club and all. It's very important. Ah, you can't call me, so I guess I'll try to call you later? And would you mind not mentioning this to anybody? Please? Thank you. Ah, it's Phillip Winnick." Then in an anxious rush, he said, "I'll talk to you later. It's Phillip Winnick." Somebody must have told him it was important to give his name more than once when he left a message.

I threw my bag over my shoulder and went downstairs to the Bronco and headed for the Crab House instead of the Greek place. Phillip wasn't there when I arrived,

181

but the waiter who led me to a table on the back porch said he was due at 11:00.

The waiter said, "Would you like a drink?"

"A margarita, please, but I'm starving, so I'll go ahead and order."

"Stone crab?"

"Absolutely."

"Fries?"

"Extra-crispy."

"Salad?"

"Please, with blue cheese dressing."

"Caesar or house?"

"House."

"What kind of dressing?"

"Blue cheese." There must be a law that says waitpersons must ignore you if you tell them what salad dressing you want before they specifically ask you.

He flashed a wide grin and buzzed off. Without Phillip's music, the Crab House was quiet. Two guys at a table next to me were being so careful and polite that it was clear they were on a first date. On the other side of me, a man and woman were leaning forward with their elbows on the table and their hands interlaced. They had drinks on the table, but from the way they were gazing into each other's eyes, they were already intoxicated by romance. A motorboat chuffed up to the dock and a man in cutoffs jumped out to tie it up while two women and a man stood up and made tugging and fluffing motions to clothes and hair before they climbed over the side and stepped onto the dock. They all trailed onto the porch and took a table at the side, laughing and talking amongst themselves with the kind of easy camaraderie that old friends have.

The waiter brought my margarita and a board holding a miniloaf of hot bread that had a big lethal-looking knife stabbed into it. He said, "A guy at the bar paid for your drink."

I looked through the glass wall and saw a large ruddy man at the bar grinning at me. He had a bullet-shaped bald head and eyes like black ball bearings. He raised his glass to me and began to slide off his bar stool with the clear intent of coming out to the porch.

"Take it back," I said.

"It's paid for. You might as well drink it."

"Take it back, and tell the bartender to make me another one."

He set the glass on his tray and hightailed it away to the bar. My admirer turned to him and asked a question, and then looked out at me with a dark scowl when the waiter answered. The bartender looked out at me, too, and his lips firmed into a tight-mouthed smile as he dumped the margarita and whipped up another one.

I cut a thick slab of bread with the giant knife, and was using the knife to smear butter on the bread when the waiter brought a new drink. He carried it out on a tray held shoulder-high and set it down with a flourish.

"He says you've got an attitude."

"Tell him I've also got a sharp knife."

"Whoa, hon, just take it as a compliment. Men are gonna hit on you. That's just life."

He left and I looked toward the two men on my right. They had forgotten their first-date anxiety and were grinning at me. When they caught my eye, they raised their wine-glasses in a toast. I smiled back and sipped my margarita. Inside, the bullet-headed man put money on the bar and stomped out, his pants creasing around a thick wad in his crotch.

By the time I got the stone crab, I had eaten enough bread and salad to be in a better mood. Stone crab is probably what God eats every night of the year, but in Florida we mortals only have it from mid-October to mid-May. Florida law prohibits fishermen from killing the crabs, but stone crabs can regenerate lost claws, so fishermen break one off and throw the crab back into the sea. That only leaves them one claw to defend themselves with, but they're not boiling to death like they would be if they were lobsters.

The claws are steamed right there on the boat, and then they're chilled and delivered to restaurants like the Crab House, where people like me eat them without giving a thought to the crab's trauma. Mine came with mustard sauce and a wooden mallet for cracking the claw, and I happily cracked and slurped away.

16

While I ate, I watched boats bobbing at the dock and idly listened to bits and pieces of conversation from neighboring tables. I learned that somebody named Tony was a real bitch and a half, and that somebody named Grace had finally gotten the money she had married for when her husband's rich and ancient mother died. Grace, they said, was hell-bent to move back east where people would be impressed with their new wealth, but the husband was refusing to give up his golf and tennis life just to hobnob with some snooty New Englanders. Poor Grace. All that money and no place to flaunt it.

It was almost eleven o'clock when I ate the last morsel. I put some bills on the table before the waiter came back, adding a hefty tip to make up for being churlish earlier, and stood up and started inside. The waiter saw me leaving and scurried over with a questioning look.

I said, "I'm going to sit at the bar and listen to the piano player."

He looked over my shoulder at the money on the table and smiled. "No prob," he said. "The pianist should be here any minute."

"You know him?"

"Just to speak to. Seems like a real nice guy."

"He is."

"Oh, he's a friend of yours?"

I smiled, suddenly feeling proud to know Phillip. "Yeah, he's a friend."

Inside, only a few people were at the bar. All men, and all with the appraising look of people who realized the evening was growing old and if they hoped to hook up with somebody, they'd better do it soon. None of them gave me a glance. I took the stool at the end near the bandstand and ordered another margarita.

The bartender grinned when he set it in front of me. "This will be your third, right?"

"Counting the one I didn't drink."

"That guy, what an asshole! What'd he think, anyway?"

"Maybe that works for him sometime."

"Not with a woman like you. He shoulda known that."

Behind me, Phillip's voice said, "Miz Hemingway?"

I spun around, to see him standing there looking at me in disbelief, as if I were a genie he had conjured up from a bottle. Up this close, I could see the black flocked jacket he wore had been made for a much larger man. He looked like a little boy dressed up in his father's suit coat.

"Gosh, you snuck up on me, Phillip!"

"Oh, I'm sorry! I didn't mean to scare you."

"You didn't, I just didn't see you come in."

"I came in the back."

"Can you talk a few minutes before you start playing?"

He grinned nervously, and I wanted to hug him. He was all wrists and ears and cheekbones, too ill at ease to know how to handle this unexpected moment.

"Come on," I said, "let's go sit at a table for a minute. You want something to drink?"

He shook his head, then licked dry lips and nodded. The bartender, who had been silently watching us, filled a glass with club soda and handed it to him.

"Okay," I said briskly, and walked the length of the bar to a tiny two-top in the back corner. Phillip trailed along behind me carrying his club soda, and we both dropped into chairs like falling rocks.

He still seemed nonplussed that I was there, so I leaned toward him and said, "You left a message on my machine that you wanted to talk to me."

"Oh. Yeah. That. Well, see, I got to thinking and all . . . you know, about what happened next door. You know, how the policeman asked if I'd seen anything?"

"Uh-huh. And did you see something?"

"Well, that's just it. I mean, I should have told him, but my mother was there and I didn't want her to know I'd been outside at that time, you know. But the cops probably should know . . . I thought maybe you could tell that detective guy."

I could tell this would take all night if I didn't prompt him. "Okay, what did you see that you didn't want to talk about in front of your mother?"

A deep port-wine blush rose from his throat and suffused his face. "It was when I was coming home Friday morning. I was crossing behind Miz Doerring's house and I saw a woman come out of her house and get in a car in the driveway. A black Miata. The car swung in the driveway, the woman came out of the house and got in, and it drove off. I thought it was Miz Doerring, but now I'm thinking maybe it was somebody else. You know, like the killer."

I waited, but he seemed unable to continue. I said, "Could you see the driver?"

Phillip's flush deepened. "The top was up, so I couldn't see. I just saw the woman."

I took a sip of my drink and pretended not to notice his discomfort. "And you could see her well enough to think it was Marilee Doerring?"

He looked down at his plate, and for a moment I thought he might cry. "Not really. I guess I didn't really look good. It could have been her or it could have been some other woman."

He averted his eyes and his throat bobbled in a nervous swallow. I tried to put myself in his place, a kid coming home after an evening that had to be kept secret from his parents and seeing a woman he thought was a neighbor get into a car and drive away.

"Did the woman see you?"

He bobbled his head in a staccato motion I took to be an affirmative nod. "I think maybe she did. She looked over her shoulder toward where I was and it seemed like she jerked a little bit — you know, like she was surprised or scared or something."

"And then what?"

He looked directly at me for the first time. "Then she got in the car and left."

Carefully, I said, "What time do you think this was?"

"I don't want to get anybody else mixed up in this."

"I'm not asking you where you'd been or who you'd been with, just what time you saw a woman leaving Marilee Doerring's house."

"It was a little after four."

I remembered the flash of movement in the woods that morning when I was walking Rufus. That had been around 4:30.

"Did you see me that morning?"

He blinked at me. "You? No, ma'am, I didn't see you."

Poor kid, he was obviously terrified, and with good reason. If the woman he saw thought he could identify her, he could be in a lot more trouble than his family finding out how he spent his nights.

"Phillip, if we're going to be friends, you have to do something for me."

"What?"

"You have to stop calling me 'ma'am.' And my name is Dixie, not Ms. Hemingway. Got that?"

He gave me a weak smile. "Okay."

"You were right to tell me about the woman, and it's something Lieutenant Guidry needs to know. I'll tell him what you saw, and he'll probably want to talk to you again. If he does, don't be scared. I'll tell him to be sure and talk to you in private, and he's not going to repeat anything you say to your parents or to anybody else. He's a nice guy, you can trust him."

"Okay."

I was so proud of him for having the guts to confess what he'd seen that I didn't check his story with my built-in lie detector.

We looked at each other for a second, sort of cementing a new friendship, and then he gave me a genuine smile. "I have to go play now. Are you going to stay for a while?"

"I'd love to, but it's way past my bed-time."

We got up and walked together down the aisle toward the piano. Before I left him, I turned and gave him a hug. "I'll come back another night, when I can stay."

He was blushing and smiling when he waved good-bye.

When I stepped outside, all the lights were out in the parking lot, the only illumination coming from a waning moon. Nobody else was around, and the spaces between the cars were black wells where anything could have been hiding. I stood a minute outside the door, wondering if I should go back inside and tell the manager about the lights, then decided to let it go. My footsteps made quick scrunching noises in the loose shell as I stepped across the dark lot toward my car.

Part of me was proud that Phillip had trusted me enough to confide in me. The other part was dismayed. Now I knew something that could get the kid in a lot of trouble. If he had seen the killer leaving Marilee's house, he would most likely be called upon in the future to say so in public, bringing upon himself the full glare of media attention that would inevitably reveal that he was gay. He was a good kid, and I didn't want to be the one who outed him. But I had to let Guidry know about the woman he'd seen.

A pair of egrets fluttered low over my head, making those guttural egret sounds that always remind me of somebody trying to cough up a popcorn husk. I turned my head to look over my shoulder, and realized with a sense of shock that I was afraid. That's the trouble with allowing yourself to start feeling emotions after you've been closed down for a long time. You can't feel selectively. You have to let the whole gamut of feelings in, even fear.

As I started jogging toward my car, a form detached from the shadows and ran after me. I picked up my speed and ran like hell. Thanks to Billy Elliot, I had recent experience in covering ground fast. I beeped the car unlocked, tore the door open, and leaped inside, pulling the door shut and locking it a second before the man slammed a fist against the passenger window and pushed his face against the glass. Even with his nose and mouth mashed flat in a grotesque mask clearly intended to frighten me, I recognized the bullet-headed man from the bar. I threw the Bronco into reverse and whipped out of the parking space, almost hoping the man would be foolish enough to run after me so I could run him down. He didn't. He ran behind the row of cars and ducked out of sight. I sat with the motor churning for a couple of minutes and then pulled out of the lot.

Driving north on Midnight Pass Road, I watched the rearview mirror for headlights in case the man was following. At the drive to my house, I passed it and drove straight ahead to the firehouse, where I backed into a parking place across the street. From where I sat, I could see all the traffic on Midnight Pass Road, and I could also see the firehouse where Michael was sleeping. Just knowing Michael was nearby made me feel calmer. Traffic was sparse, and after awhile I decided I hadn't been followed, so I drove home. Paco's car was in the carport, but his Harley was gone, so I knew he was still on an undercover job. I ran up the stairs to my apartment two at a time.

Everything in the apartment seemed exactly as I had left it, but I still felt jittery. The malevolence of the man's eyes looking at me through the passenger window weren't what scared me. What had me feeling uneasy was that he had seemed so determined, as if he had a particular goal and I was it. I lowered the metal storm shutters, checked the answering machine, brushed my teeth, did a few turns around the apartment to work off my nervous energy, and finally went to bed with a million questions buzzing in my head.

If the woman Phillip saw had been Marilee, she would have been leaving Harrison Frazier dead in her house. Did that mean she had killed him? And if she had, who had been driving the car she got into? If it hadn't been Marilee, who was it? It could have been Shuga Reasnor. She knew Harrison Frazier, and maybe she had some personal reason to kill him. Maybe she had lured Frazier to Marilee's house on some pretext and killed him there. Maybe Marilee had a good alibi of where she was at the time Frazier was killed. Maybe she and Shuga had planned it together, thinking nobody would connect Shuga to the killing. I wondered if Shuga had an alibi for that night. I would ask Guidry when I talked to him.

I turned over and pounded my pillow and tried to go to sleep. It wasn't my job to find Harrison Frazier's killer. My job was to take care of Ghost. But who the hell had killed Frazier? Maybe his wife had followed him to Marilee's house and conked him on the head and had somebody pick her up afterward in a black Miata. That didn't seem very likely, though. And why did Marilee have her locks changed before she left town? It had to have been because somebody had a key to her house and she didn't want that person to go in, but who? And why? Maybe she and Shuga Reasnor had had a falling-out and she was making sure Shuga couldn't get in while she was gone. Maybe Dr. Coffey still had a key to her house from when they were engaged and she'd just gotten around to making sure he couldn't use it. Maybe Coffey had hired a woman to go in and kill Harrison Frazier. No, that was dumb. Why would he do that? If he wanted anybody killed, it would be Marilee, not Frazier.

I turned on my back and took deep breaths. Why had that man in the parking lot been after me? Had he been so pissed off that I'd given him the cold shoulder that he'd waited out there for me all that time? Surely it wasn't the first time he'd been turned down by a woman. Surely he wouldn't have let something like that cause him to become so violent. Maybe he had been on something. Maybe he had snorted or shot up or ingested his drug du jour after he left the bar and got so high that he came back for lust revenge. Maybe it was just coincidence that he had chosen me, maybe he had just been there to go after any woman coming out alone.

My eyelids popped open. Oh shit, I should have called the Crab House and warned them that a psycho was loose in the parking lot. I should have told them to be sure no woman went out by herself. I turned over again and smacked the pillow. It was too late now, it was after two, and the Crab House was closed. But if somebody had been raped in that parking lot, it would be all my fault.

On that cheerful note, I finally drifted to restless sleep.

17

Thunder woke me in the night. Hard rain was pelting the roof and making drumming music on the storm shutters. It was a comforting sound. I love sleeping in a storm, safe and dry while a deluge rages outside. I went back to sleep, and when the alarm sounded at 4:00, I smacked it off and groped my way to the bathroom to splash water on my face. I estimated that I'd had all of two hours sleep, tops.

The rain had stopped, so I left the Bronco at home and took my bike, riding out into a glorious Sunday morning. On the lane to the street, I stirred up a flock of wild parakeets in the damp treetops, and their chattering brought answering cello tones of mourning doves from their hiding places. The temperature was around seventy degrees, the humidity low enough to be tolerable, and the air had a fresh, just-washed smell. Even with a sluggish brain from last night's fear and sleeplessness, I loved the feel of the day.

With the Graysons back home, I only had Billy Elliot to dog walk. The rest were all cats, which was good. Cats are a lot easier than dogs, and I needed an easy day. My plan was to wait until eight o'clock and call Guidry with last night's information, see to all the cats, and go home and sleep. Michael would come home this morning, which meant we'd have a good dinner at home tonight. Maybe Paco would be home, too, and I could catch them up on everything that had happened.

Tom Hale was asleep when I went into his condo, but Billy Elliot met me at the door. We went outside and ran like idiots, and then I kissed Billy Elliot good-bye inside the condo and panted my way back to my bike. It was still dark, but the sky was taking on a vanilla tinge of false dawn, and birds were beginning to wake in the trees and call sleepily to one another.

My next stop was at the home of twin calico tabbies named Stella and Marie. If they had been humans, they would have been lounge singers. Stella spent her time on the windowsill, looking longingly at her reflection in the glass, and Marie lolled on the sofa, waiting for somebody to come do her nails. When I groomed them, they preened and posed with delicious self-absorption, and when I ran the vacuum to pick up hair they had flung on the carpet, they both turned their heads and gave me languid looks of total disinterest.

I cleaned their litter box while they ate, then washed their food bowls and put out fresh water for them. "I'm leaving now," I said. "I hope you won't miss me too much."

From the windowsill, Stella lowered her eyelids to half-mast in grudging acknowledgment of my existence, but Marie merely flicked the tip of her tail and yawned. I was still grinning when I got on my bike and started to the next stop. A pale coral tint was washing over the sky by then, gilding the eastern edges of puffy little clouds with a darker salmon pink. In another hour, the sun would be fully up and traffic would get thicker.

As I pulled onto Midnight Pass Road, a bakery truck coming back from making a delivery of breakfast croissants and bagels sped by, barely swerving enough to avoid hitting me, and sending a fine spray of puddle water onto my legs. Unnerved, I jerked onto the shoulder and planted my soaked Keds on the ground. I was in the entrance to the old abandoned road leading into the woods behind Marilee Doerring's house. Muttering words that would have made my grandmother wash my mouth out with soap if she'd heard, I took some deep breaths to get my heart quieted down.

A faint sound caught my attention and I looked toward the rusty metal gate stretched across the old road. The road had once been paved with crushed seashells, but time and weather had taken its toll, and now weeds and low-growing vegetation covered most of the shell. The sound came again, low and urgent. Thinking an animal had been hit by a car and had crawled into the bushes, I got off my bike and walked down the road.

As I got closer, I glimpsed a flash of blue fabric, and realized it wasn't a hurt animal moaning in the bushes, but a person. I stopped. The odds were against it, but this could be somebody pretending to be hurt and I might be walking into a trap.

I called, "Is someone there?"

The moaning sound came again. I went closer, and then rushed forward. Phillip Winnick, caked with blood and dirt, lay sprawled in the tangled wet underbrush. Somebody had worked him over good.

I knelt at his side. "Phillip? Phillip, it's me, Dixie. I'm going to call for help. It's okay now. Phillip?"

His bruised lips struggled to form a word, but it was so faint, I couldn't hear. I leaned close to his face and said, "Tell me again, Phillip. I didn't hear you."

Weakly, he breathed a prayer into my ear. "Please don't tell my mother." Then he passed out.

I called 911 on my cell and gave them the location. Then I sat cross-legged beside Phillip and talked to him while I waited for the ambulance. I wanted him to have a voice to hold on to for the moments that he floated to awareness.

"This is a shitty thing somebody did to you, Phillip, but it's not the end of the world. You'll get over this, and you'll be good as new."

A surge of alarm went through me and I looked quickly at his hands. They didn't appear to be injured, and I sent up a silent thank-you for that.

"Your hands aren't hurt, Phillip, and you'll be playing the piano again soon. I know this is a terrible experience, but you'll get through it. People get through these things, and you will, too. I'll help you, and so will a lot of other people."

I babbled on, as much for myself as for him, until the ambulance came. Two EMTs jumped out and lifted Phillip onto a stretcher so quickly and so gently that I wanted to hug them both. A deputy's car was just behind the ambulance, and Deputy Jesse Morgan came and stood beside me while the EMTs eased the stretcher into the back.

"Miz Hemingway," he said. I wondered if he had talked to some of the other deputies about me.

I said, "Can I ride to the hospital with Phillip?"

"You know him?"

"He's Phillip Winnick. He lives next door to Marilee Doerring, where the man was murdered Friday." I was trying to be as cool as he was, but my voice cracked a little bit when I said that.

He gave me a slow, level look. Oh yeah, somebody had been talking to him about me.

"How long have you known him?"

I read the look in his eyes and said, "I met him that morning when I took the cat over there."

"So he's not a close friend?"

One of the EMTs got in the back of the ambulance with Phillip and hooked him up to oxygen and some kind of IV, while the other came back to talk to Deputy Morgan. They stepped away and spoke out of my hearing, then Morgan came back to me and the EMT got in the ambulance and drove away.

"I'll notify his parents," he said. "You'll have to get permission from them to visit him in the hospital."

Defeated, I clamped my lips together and forced myself not to yell at him. Morgan was right. Phillip's parents were the only people with the legal right to be with him in the hospital, and they had to be notified. But the thought of how his judgmental parents might react made my heart hurt.

Morgan pulled out his notebook. "How did you happen to know he was here?"

"I didn't. A truck almost ran me down and I pulled into the road and heard him moaning."

"He say anything to you?"

I shook my head. "I don't think he was conscious."

"So you don't know why he was out here at this hour?"

"I have no idea."

He looked down at me with coolly appraising eyes. "You seem to be having a run of really bad luck. First finding a dead man and now finding somebody beat-up."

"Is that a question?"

He flipped his notebook closed. "You'll be available later?"

"Sure."

He got into his car to go to ring the Winnicks' doorbell and tell them their son wasn't in bed asleep like they thought he was, but in an ambulance going to the emergency room at Sarasota Memorial Hospital. I started back down the old road toward my bike. As I did, something caught my eye at the end of the gate where a stunted key lime's branches pressed against the upright supports. I walked to the end of the gate to get a better look.

Key limes have long, lethal thorns, and this one had a wad of black human hair snarled on a thorny limb. The hair was long and curly, and it appeared to have been left there recently. I thought of Marilee's shiny black hair caught in the brush of her hair dryer, and a cold snail trailed down my spine.

When Christy was barely walking, I went to pick her up at the day-care center one day and found another mother raising hell because her little girl had a bald spot on her head. The day-care women were red-faced and almost in tears. They said another toddler had just reached out and grabbed a handful of the child's hair and yanked it right out. They said he had never done any-thing like that before and he had done it so quickly, they hadn't been able to stop him. The mother threatened to sue, and she was weeping when she took her child home. I didn't blame her. Who wants their baby yanked bald-headed, even if the yanker is just a baby, too?

I leaned my elbows on top of the gate and looked into the woods, where the tracks of the old road ran about fifteen feet before they disappeared into a tangled mass of live oaks, palms, hibiscus, lime trees, palmettos, ferns, and twisting potato vines. The foliage was so thick, I couldn't see anything except green. Steam was beginning to rise from the damp ground and the thick foliage absorbed it and breathed it out again.

I put a foot on one of the gate's crossbars and boosted myself up. I told myself to mind my own business and let Guidry investigate. I answered myself back that I only wanted to have a look beyond where the road became obscured. I slung a leg over the gate and scaled it. My Keds made gritty sounds as I walked down the devastated road to the spot where it disappeared into the brush. With both arms stiff, I parted the foliage hanging in front of my face. The road was visible for another few feet and then disappeared again in leafy branches. I let the branches close behind me and walked to the next barrier.

It was like being in the Amazon. Thick branches joined overhead to make a canopy that blotted out the early-morning sky, and I could feel the surrounding foliage exhaling its hot breath. An odor of decay or of something dead rose from the steaming thicket. I've never been claustrophobic, but this was nuts. There was nothing to see here, no reason to be here. I had to get out of this place and go take care of my pets. But first I parted the next tangle of branches and got a stronger whiff of the odor — a sweet, heavy smell that reminded me of something, but I couldn't remember what. I pushed a branch aside and looked ahead at the exposed road. More long black hair fanned out on the shadowed ground. For a second, that's all my brain allowed my eyes to see. But you can only hide from the truth for an instant when it's stretched out in front of you. Marilee lay across the road. She was faceup, with her arms slung out to the sides and her legs bent in an awkwardly lewd way. She wore a white skirt and a navy shirt tied at the waist. Animals had eaten away some of the flesh on her arms and legs and the entire lower part of her face. Her eyes stared upward in horror. I gagged and covered my mouth, then turned and ran, batting at the closed branches hanging over the road and making whimpering sounds deep in my throat.

I scrambled over the gate and ran to my bike. I made a diagonal cut across Midnight Pass and pulled into the parking lot of the Sea Breeze. Then I got my cell phone out of my hip pocket and dialed 911.

The operator who answered was cool. I gave her my name and location, and told her what I'd found. She kept her voice at a level monotone. "Please remain where you are," she said. "Somebody will be there in just a few minutes. Can you describe yourself, please, so they'll recognize you?"

That was smart. She was getting me to talk about how I looked, not how the corpse looked. She was also keeping me on the line while she sent somebody out, just in case I was a psycho who had dumped the corpse in the woods myself and was planning on pretending to be an innocent bystander when the deputies hauled it out.

"I'm on a bike," I said. "It's okay, I'm not leaving. I'm an ex-deputy."

She and I both knew that could be a lie, too, but she stayed cool. "That's good," she said. "I'll tell them to look for a woman on a bike in the Sea Breeze parking lot."

Just as she said it, a green-and-white patrol car pulled in. Deputy Jesse Morgan parked and got out of the car and walked to meet me.

"Miz Hemingway," he said. Carefully, as if I were a bomb that might explode any minute. "You've found another dead body."

18

Morgan tilted his head toward the Sea Breeze. "Is the body in there?"

I pointed across the street. "No, it's in the woods behind that gate. It's Marilee Doerring. That's the woman whose house the other body was in. Animals have been at her, but I recognized her."

I was trying to be as cool as he was, but my voice cracked a little bit when I said that.

Flat-voiced, he said, "What were you doing in the woods?"

I could feel my face getting hot. "After you left, I saw some hair hanging on a key lime branch. I went back there to check it out."

"Uh-huh." He gave me that slow, level look again. "Can you show me the body?"

"I can show you where to find it, but I'm not going back there again."

He looked down at me with the same coolly appraising eyes and then nodded. "Fair enough," he said. "Let's go."

We walked across the street and down the

stretch of road to the gate. I pointed to the hair on the lime tree. "Somebody must have been carrying her body around the end of the gate and her hair got caught in the thorns."

"Don't touch it," he said. "Did you touch it?"

"Of course I didn't touch it!" That felt better. Anger always makes me feel stronger.

I said, "Just climb over the gate and walk straight back. I'll wait for you, but I need to get to my animals, so don't take too long."

He gave me another level look and climbed over the gate. His legs under his dark green shorts were muscular and tan. He walked like a man who was at home in the woods, pushing through the branches without any tensing or awkwardness. He disappeared from view and I waited, imagining him pushing through the next branches and seeing Marilee the same way I'd seen her. When he stepped back through the branches, he was calling for a crime-scene unit. He rang off, put the phone back in its holder on his belt, and fixed me with a penetrating look.

"You'll be available later?"

"Sure. I just have to see to my animals

first, and then I'd like to go home and soak in Clorox for a while."

He grinned. He had a nice grin, he should have done it more often. "Where will you be after you soak in Clorox?"

I sighed. "I'll be wherever Lieutenant Guidry wants me to be."

I gave him my cell phone number again so they could get in touch with me. When I left him, he was climbing over the gate again to guard the body until the CSU people arrived.

For the rest of the morning, images of Phillip's beaten body and Marilee's mutilated body sprawled on the musky ground alternated in my head. I kept remembering how Rufus had barked at the wooded area every time we went walking. I should have known he was trying to tell me something. Dogs can smell dead bodies from a distance, even bodies that have been buried in shallow graves. If I had investigated the first time he barked, if I had told Guidry about Rufus barking, if, if, if . . .

Death has a way of forcing us to look at the ultimate question that hovers just below our consciousness. That pitiful body in the woods was no longer Marilee's home. It was just rapidly decaying flesh, no more human than a fish carcass rotting at the edge of the sea. So where was Marilee? Where was the mind that had informed her body when its heart beat?

When Todd and Christy died, an astonishing number of people said stupid things like "They're with Jesus now," as if Jesus was making Christy's breakfast in the morning and brushing her hair into a ponytail, or that Jesus and Todd were hanging out together and watching old movies on TV. I didn't want them to be with Jesus, I wanted them to be with me. I hoped nobody would say inane things like that to Cora Mathers. Oh God, had anybody told Cora Mathers that Marilee was dead? It would be terrible for her if she learned of it on the news, but I didn't know if Guidry even knew that Cora existed.

I called Guidry and left a message about Cora on his voice mail, giving him her address and phone number. The Sheriff's Department has a Victim Assistance Unit staffed by the kind of people who know how to help you through those first few days when you keep thinking it's all a nightmare that you'll wake from any minute now but you don't.

When I thought about Phillip, I couldn't keep from empathizing with the pain his parents would feel when they saw him. They were bigoted idiots, but they loved their son. Maybe this awful thing would make them realize how much they loved him, and maybe when they learned the truth about why he had been out that morning, they would be so grateful he was alive that they would let all the other crap go.

The big question, of course, was why Phillip had been beaten. Oh, I knew well enough that ignorant young men who are so horrified and ashamed of their own homosexual urges go out gay bashing just for the hell of it. People who are filled with self-loathing need to find a target for their hatred, and now that lynching black men has become socially unacceptable, hurting gay men has taken its place. But the timing of Phillip's attack made me suspicious. It seemed almost too coincidental that he'd been attacked right after he'd told me about seeing a woman leave Marilee's house on Friday morning. I couldn't shake the feeling that his attack had more to do with what he knew about a murder than because he was gay.

At eight o'clock, I called Guidry again and left a message for him to call me. At nine I called the hospital and asked about Phillip. The receptionist said there was no patient by that name at the hospital. They were either shielding him from publicity or he wasn't in the system yet. At ten, I called again and got the same answer. I called Guidry again. He wasn't available, so I left my name and number again.

Feeling cut off from the world, I pedaled home through church traffic. At the Summerhouse, I pulled my bike to a stop to allow a wedding party to spill over the walk. The bride and groom were young and laughing, the bride radiant in miles of lace and tulle, the groom tall and gallant, all the wedding guests gazing after them with the bedazzled smiles that wedding guests always have — hoping this union would live up to the fairy-tale wedding promises of happy ever after but knowing full well that nobody really lives happily ever after, not even beautiful young people who are truly in love.

One of the bridesmaids saw me waiting and gave me a little shrug and smile, meaning "I'm sorry you're inconvenienced." I smiled back and shook my head slightly, meaning, "It's okay."

When the walk cleared, I pedaled on, grinning a little bit at how we two-legged animals aren't so different from the four-legged kind. If that bridesmaid and I had been dogs, we would have wagged our tails and sniffed each other's butts to communicate our friendly feelings. Instead, we wagged our heads and smiled.

Michael's car was parked under the carport with its trunk open, showing about a zillion paper bags from Sam's Club. That meant he had made his weekly run to stock up on food for us and for the firehouse. Michael loves Sam's the way women love shoe stores, and he buys as if he's preparing for marauding invaders who will cut off every supply of sustenance.

I got a couple of bags out of the trunk and started to the house with them and met Michael coming out. When he saw me, the grin on his face faded and he gave me a look that can only come from a big brother who bathed in the same tub and peed in front of you for the first years of your lives together. "What's wrong?"

For a second, I felt like bawling. "You know the kid we saw at the Crab House Friday night? The one who lives next door to where the man got killed? He was beaten up this morning, really bad."

Michael gathered up bags from the trunk and slammed the lid closed. "How'd you hear about it?"

"I found him. He was in the bushes there on Midnight Pass where the old road goes into the woods. I called nine one one and they sent an ambulance."

"Poor kid. Is he going to be all right?"

"I don't know yet. But there's more. After the deputy left, I noticed some hair on a lime tree, and I went into the woods there where that old road is, you know, and Marilee Doerring's body was in there."

Then I did bawl. Just stood there with a bag of groceries in each arm and cried like a baby. "Animals had been at her, Michael."

"Good God. That's awful. Come in the house, I've got coffee on."

I trailed behind him with the bags, and we both deposited our loads on the kitchen counters. The house Michael and I grew up in is pretty much the way it was when we came to live in it, except for the kitchen. Michael and Paco knocked out a wall where a bay-windowed breakfast room used to be, so it's a lot bigger and sunnier now. They also installed commercial ovens and a Sub-Zero refrigerator and freezer. A butcher-block island sits in the middle of the floor, with a salad sink on one side and an eating bar on the other.

Michael heaved a spiral-sliced ham from one of the bags and set it aside, then made short work of stowing the other stuff away, while I splashed water on my face at the sink and mostly got in the way. He slit the wrapper on the ham and motioned me to the bar.

"Pour us some coffee," he said.

While I got out mugs, he deftly peeled off several slices of ham and threw them on the big griddle between the rows of burners on the stove. I carried two mugs of steaming coffee to the bar while Michael got eggs from the refrigerator and cracked a bunch of them one-handed into a mixing bowl. The ham on the griddle was sending up clouds of damp steam and beginning to smell divine.

He said, "Why do you think the kid was beat up?"

I shrugged. "Either the obvious reason or because he saw the murderer leaving Marilee Doerring's house Friday morning."

He stopped whisking eggs and looked hard at me. "How do you know that?"

"He told me last night. I ate dinner at the Crab House and talked to him before he started playing. He said a woman left Marilee's house around four o'clock and got in a black Miata that had just pulled into the driveway. He thinks she saw him watching."

Michael turned the ham slices and got butter and a slab of Parmesan cheese from the refrigerator. "Have you told the detective?"

I watched his serrated knife cutting thick slices of sourdough bread. "I've left several messages for him to call me, but I haven't heard from him."

He threw a wad of butter on the griddle, smeared it into a big puddle, and flopped the slices of bread in it.

I got up and held out two plates, and he flipped ham slices on both of them. I said, "I knew all along that Marilee wouldn't have left her hair dryer behind like that."

Michael grunted and put another glob of butter on the griddle next to the frying bread. As soon as he turned the beaten egg into it, he sliced transparent shards of Parmesan on top and started lifting and turning it with a spatula. All that golden brown fried bread and dark red ham and bright yellow eggs was making my taste buds itch. I got forks and knives and hurried to pour more coffee to replace what I'd drunk.

Michael topped the ham slices with scrambled eggs, flopped the fried bread on the side, and slid the plates onto the bar. We sat side by side and dug in, neither of us speaking until we'd finished eating. Then Michael got up and refilled our coffee mugs and sat down with a sigh.

"I wish you weren't involved in this, Dixie."

"I wish I weren't, too, but maybe I'm supposed to be. Maybe this is how I'm supposed to start getting my life back together."

"How? By finding dead people and a kid beaten up?"

"Guidry said something yesterday that may be true. He said I couldn't hide forever. I can't, you know? I have to come out some time and start living again."

"Hell of a way to come out."

"This morning when I was coming home, there was a wedding party just leaving the Summerhouse. The bride and groom were so happy and young, you know? Just looking at them made me wish I could turn back the clock and be that innocent again."

"Feeling jealous?"

"I guess so, a little."

"Of what, that they were happy and young, or that they were in love?"

"Don't start that, Michael."

He raised his hands, all innocence. "Start what? I just asked a question."

I got up and carried our plates to the sink and rinsed them and put them in the dishwasher. Michael came behind me and squeezed my shoulders.

"Go take a nap," he said. "You look like shit."

I turned and hugged him hard, my love for him a shining sun in my heart.

19

I slept in the porch hammock until almost three o'clock, and woke up feeling dehydrated but less fragmented. I'm always relieved and grateful to find myself sane when I wake up, because for a long time I wasn't. For the first year after Todd and Christy were killed, I was a mess. Too tired to breathe, with every cell in my body bruised and aching. My nose ran for an entire year, and I barely had the energy to wipe it. I slept whole days, and when I was awake, I stared at the TV without changing stations. Just watched whatever was on, because I couldn't absorb words anyway. I didn't dress or bathe. Didn't answer the phone. I would go for days without eating and then have a giant pizza delivered and eat it all at one sitting.

Michael and Paco tried to get me to eat, to get out of my house, to wake up, but I couldn't. I just flat couldn't. Then one day in the spring, when Todd and Christy had been gone a full year, I caught sight of myself in the bedroom mirror and stopped cold. I looked awful. I looked unhealthy. I looked like a wraith. If Todd could have seen me, he would have said, "For God's sake, Dixie, what good is this doing?" If Christy could have seen me, she would have been afraid of me, I looked that scary.

That was a turning point. I got myself and my house cleaned up and went out and got my hair cut. I sold the house where I'd been so happy with Todd and Christy, and got rid of all the furniture. I donated Christy's toys to Goodwill, except for her favorite, a purple Tickle Me Elmo, who now sits on the pillows of my bed, fat and silly. When I look at his goofy face, I hear Christy's laughter spilling out like silver coins. I suppose I will keep Elmo with me forever. More than Christy's photos, and even more than my memories of her, Elmo keeps her close and keeps me sane. Mostly.

For a while, I thought I might like to move away from the key and all its memories, but Michael and Paco talked me into taking the apartment over the carport, and I'm glad they did. This is where my heart is. It's where I belong. Now occasional rips in the fabric of reality come when I least expect them. I can be going along minding my own business, attending to responsibilities, bathing and dressing and feeding myself like a normal person, and then one day I'll see Todd walking down the sidewalk ahead of me. I'll know it's him, the same way I recognize my own reflection in a mirror. It's his hair, his shoulders, his long legs. I know his walk, the way he swings his arms a little off rhythm with his steps. I'll open my mouth to shout to him, my heart flowering with a burst of pure joy, and then he changes into somebody else — a man I don't know at all, a man totally unlike Todd, and I am weak-kneed and dizzy with disappointment and fear.

It has been three years. I am long past the time grief experts allow for normal grieving. Mine is pathological, they say, and it's time I got over it. They don't explain how to do that. They merely look at me with tight lips and annoyed eyes and tell me I *have* to. I would if I could, believe me, because every time it happens, I fear that next time I won't realize it's a delusion and that I'll actually rush up to a stranger and throw my arms around him and take comfort in his foreign smells, his alien substance. If that ever happens, I may never return.

I drank a bunch of water and called the hospital again, and this time they gave me the nurses' station on Phillip's floor. A harried nurse told me he was "resting comfortably" — whatever that meant — and got off the phone before I could ask if I could see him. I called Guidry again and left another message for him to call me on my cell, then I ate a little tub of yogurt from the fridge while I stood on the porch and looked out at the glittering waves in the Gulf and told myself everything would work out all right. Phillip would recover from his injuries, Guidry would find whoever killed Marilee and Frazier, and I would find a good home for Ghost. Life would go on, and so would I.

After I took a shower and put on fresh shorts and T and Keds, I went to my office-closet and took care of business, entering records on my file cards and returning calls. A man had left a message asking me to take care of his python, and I called him up and gave him the name of another pet-sitter, one who isn't squeamish about feeding live mice to reptiles. Somebody else wanted to know if I knew how to hatch eggs laid by a dove on their front lawn, and I gave them the number of the Pelican Man. I figured anybody who has devoted his life to rescuing injured pelicans must know how to hatch dove eggs. When I'd gotten my books in order and all my invoices ready, I got in the Bronco and drove to the Kitty Haven to visit Ghost.

He was in one of Marge's private rooms, which is to say he was in a cubicle about three feet wide, six feet deep, and eight feet tall, with a sleeping basket, a scratching post, padded shelves at several levels, and a kitty door low in the back to his private toilet. A screened door across the front had a hinged insert to allow the attendants to move food and water in and out without letting Ghost escape. It was an ingenious setup, but it was still a cell, and he knew it.

Like all Abyssinians, Ghost had a muscular body and the slender head and almond eyes characteristic of cats that originated in Asia. Abys are a highly intelligent breed, and once an Aby falls in love with you, it's one of the most loyal animals in the world. Ghost had been with Marilee since he was twelve weeks old, and as far as he was concerned, she was his everything. I took him into the visitors' room and brushed him and played chase the peacock feather with him, but both of us were off our game. I finally sat down cross-legged on the floor in a dejected heap, and Ghost climbed into my lap and curled himself between my legs. Without his charm-trimmed velvet collar, he looked even more forlorn and orphaned.

I ran my fingertips over his ticked silver

fur and said, "Things are bad, Ghost. Really bad. Marilee's not coming back, and Phillip has been beaten up. Maybe to scare him so he won't tell all he knows about what happened at your house. You know what it is, don't you? You know who he saw that morning."

He sighed and closed his eyes and laid his chin on my knee, as if he were worn-out from the heaviness of knowledge he couldn't express. He had known all along that Marilee was dead. As an eyewitness to two grisly murders, he could identify the killer or killers of both Marilee and Harrison Frazier. He just couldn't do it in words.

"Don't worry," I whispered. "I'll make sure you have a good home."

He opened his eyes and gave me a look of hurt accusation, and I couldn't blame him. This had happened on my watch, and I had let him down.

I slipped him some kitty treats when I left, and promised him I would come back and get him as soon as Lieutenant Guidry said I could. Even with Marilee dead, there was no reason he couldn't stay in his own home until I could find him another one. He gave me a glum look and whirled his head to the base of his tail and gnawed at it. I wasn't sure what that meant in cat language, but I was pretty sure it wasn't something nice.

Just as I was getting in the Bronco to make the rest of my afternoon visits, my cell rang — Guidry finally returning my calls.

I said, "Phillip Winnick saw a woman leave Marilee Doerring's house about four o'clock Friday morning. He says she got in a black Miata and drove off. He didn't tell you before because he doesn't want his parents to know he was out of the house at that hour."

"When did he tell you this?"

"I saw him at the Crab House last night and he told me then. But there's more. Did you know I found him beaten up this morning?"

"Yeah, I know."

I didn't ask him if he knew about Marilee. Of course he knew.

I said, "I think somebody didn't want him to tell what he saw."

Guidry was silent for a moment, and I could almost hear his brain digesting what I'd told him, along with its implications.

He said, "Can you meet me at Sarasota Memorial in the next ten minutes?"

Before I could stammer out an answer, he said, "In the main lobby," and hung up.

I stared at my phone for a few seconds,

then flipped it closed and started the Bronco. Guidry always seemed to be one step ahead of me, and I wasn't sure whether I liked that or hated it.

At the hospital, I left the Bronco for a valet to park, then hurried past a group of hospital personnel out on the sidewalk for a cigarette break. As I veered round them, they all gave me the defiantly sullen looks that smokers have acquired. Wide automatic glass doors slid open for me, and I went through to the lobby, my eyes searching for a man who looked too rich and well dressed to be a homicide detective. A hand touched my arm and Guidry said, "He's on the fifth floor."

He steered me to the wall of elevator doors, and when one opened and vomited a gaggle of glassy-eyed people, we took their place. Some other people got on with us, and we all stood tensely silent as the elevator began its smooth upward glide. Guidry and I stood at the back, not speaking or touching as some people got off and other people got on at every floor.

Finally, Guidry said, "This is our floor."

He touched the small of my back with his fingertips, and I moved forward. A glass wall on our right showed a large waiting room where people were sitting staring straight ahead, each of them caught in a timeless worry.

I followed him down the hall to the ICU wing, where glassed cubicles were arranged in a circle around a busy nurses' station. A uniformed deputy sat in a straight wooden chair outside Phillip's cubicle. Phillip's bed was slightly elevated so his face was visible. It looked like a cut of raw meat. His eyes were swollen shut, his nose was bandaged, and his cheeks were wider than his head. A ventilator's blue accordion hose was taped inside his mouth, and an IV stand stood beside his bed. A couple of machines that looked like apartment-sized washer-dryer combinations stood behind him. Tubes snaked from them and disappeared under the sheet covering him.

I made a choking sound and covered my mouth.

"He looks a lot worse than he is," Guidry said. "He has some broken ribs and a broken nose, but his lungs weren't punctured and he only has a moderate concussion. He'll have a headache for a while, but nothing vital is damaged."

"His mother must be going crazy to see him like this."

"Actually, she hasn't tried to see him, and Carl Winnick keeps calling to warn us not to leak anything about the attack to the media. Says it's a liberal conspiracy to push an agenda of a perverted lifestyle and ruin his reputation."

I felt a little sick.

Guidry took my arm and said, "Let's go find a place where we can talk."

I got myself under control as we left the ICU unit and walked down the wide hall. Guidry tilted his chin toward a small waiting area where some overstuffed chairs were pulled around a coffee table. "Go sit down," he said. "I'll get us some coffee."

He went into the glassed room where a coffee urn had been set up for visitors, and I went to sit in the waiting area. In a minute, he came out carrying two Styrofoam cups with plastic stirrers jutting from them. He set them on the coffee table and pulled out a handful of sugar packets and tiny creamers from his pocket.

"I couldn't remember if you took anything in yours," he said.

I shook my head. "I drink it black."

He sat down in the chair opposite me. "This morning, a call came in a little after five o'clock from a man named Sam Grayson. He had been out walking his dog, headed toward Midnight Pass Road, and he had let the dog off his leash. The dog started

231

barking and then took off in the other direction, chasing a man running behind the houses, headed toward the bay. Mr. Grayson managed to call the dog off, but he called nine one one to report a prowler in the area."

"I know that dog."

"That doesn't surprise me. A deputy went out, but the man had disappeared and everything looked quiet. Then your call about the Winnick boy came in. More than likely, his attack was what the dog had been barking at. He may have saved the boy's life."

"Good old Rufus! Did Sam get a good look at the man?"

"No. It was dark, and the guy was half-hidden by trees. He thinks he was bald, but I don't know if he'd be able to identify him if he saw him again."

"Last night at the Crab House, a man with a bald head chased me in the parking lot. I barely got in my car before he got to me."

Guidry leaned back and looked hard at me, assessing me the way dogs do when they smell something new. "Was this before or after the Winnick boy told you about seeing a woman leave the Doerring house?"

"After. He tried to hit on me at the bar before I talked to Phillip. Sent me a drink and then got huffy when I refused it. I'd know him if I saw him again."

I put my coffee back on the table and leaned forward. "Phillip crawls out his bedroom window after his parents are asleep, and walks to the Crab House and plays piano until it closes at one. He probably goes home with somebody from there, but I don't know who, then he goes home and crawls back in the window again in the morning. My guess is that somebody drives him to that spot on Midnight Pass Road, and then he walks alongside the woods to his house. Whoever attacked him must have known his routine and waited for him."

Guidry was watching me closely, putting together all the pieces. "His parents know he's gay?"

"I don't think so. He doesn't think so, and he's scared to death they'll find out. When I got to him this morning, he said one thing before he passed out. He said, 'Please don't tell my mother.'"

"Shit. Poor kid."

"Yeah. He's leaving for Juilliard in August, and I suppose he's gotten more careless as the time grows nearer that he can be open."

"I'm not letting anybody talk to him until I can question him, and that includes his parents. I think I'd like you to be there when I ask him about the woman he saw. If he's up to it, I'd like to do it tomorrow morning."

I hesitated, wondering what Guidry's real reason was, but knowing that Phillip would be less nervous if I were there.

"Okay."

"Is there anything else?"

"What do you mean?"

"Do you know anything else you haven't told me?"

"Nothing except that I found Marilee's body this morning in the woods. I'm sure you already know that."

Guidry's eyes were calm and expectant. I had a momentary flash of what it would be like to be his kid. He would be the kind of father you couldn't lie to. You wouldn't even try, because you would know he could see right through you.

I said, "Marilee's grandmother lives at Bayfront Village. She's a sweet lady, and whoever tells her about Marilee needs to be very careful with her. She knows who Frazier is. She said he ruined Marilee's life, but she wouldn't say what she meant by that."

Guidry carefully put his coffee cup on the table. "When did you talk to the grandmother?"

"Yesterday. I went to see her because I thought she might know where Marilee was. She knew all about Frazier's murder from the news, but she wouldn't say what his relationship had been to Marilee."

"You talk to her very long?"

"A little while. We had tea and some fresh chocolate bread she'd just made. She uses a bread maker Marilee gave her fifteen years ago. Marilee bought her the apartment she lives in, too, and Cora said Marilee came by to visit real often."

For some reason, I wanted Guidry to know that Marilee hadn't been just a gold-digging bimbo who got herself murdered and thrown in the woods. She had also been a loving granddaughter who bought her grandmother a bread-making machine and a nice apartment.

He gave me a lifted eyebrow. "You get around, Dixie."

I thought about the letter I'd put in a folder in my desk — the letter Marilee had written to her daughter. I thought about the invoice for installing a wall safe in Marilee's house. I even opened my mouth to tell Guidry about them, but instead I shrugged.

"It's just that I find out things about people from taking care of their pets."

His expression changed, and I suddenly felt chilled.

He said, "Dixie, how did you know that Marilee's body was in the woods?"

20

My mouth went dry. I didn't need him to spell out his real question. He was asking me if I had anything to do with Marilee's murder.

"I got curious when I saw a strand of hair caught on a tree. I've always thought it was odd that she didn't take her hair dryer with her, and when I saw that hair, it reminded me of the hair in her brush. I just had a feeling I should look farther back in the woods."

"You didn't already know she was there?"

"Of course I didn't!"

"But you see how it could look, don't you? You had keys to the house where both murders were probably committed. You found Hamilton Frazier's body, and then you went straight to where Marilee Doerring's body had been dumped in the woods, even though she hadn't been declared missing. You talked to Phillip Winnick and he tells you that he walks home before dawn every morning, and that he saw a woman leave the Doerring woman's house the night Frazier was killed. The next morning, he's found badly beaten, possibly with the same blunt instrument used to kill both Hamilton Frazier and Marilee Doerring."

I felt dazed and confused, and at the same time intensely aware. The dark blue of Guidry's shirt seemed to brighten, and I could detect the musky fragrance of his aftershave. Guidry seemed on high alert, too. His gray eyes were wide and watchful as a hunting cat's. If he'd had cat whiskers, they would have been pointed forward and his ears would have been up.

My fingers were gripping my Styrofoam cup so tightly, the coffee was shivering. Just the thought of being a suspect caused a slick of hot guilt to coat my throat.

"Guidry, I never laid eyes on Hamilton Frazier before I found him dead."

"I believe you, Dixie, but you have to admit that logic would put you at the top of the list of suspects."

"Why do you believe me?"

"Motive, Dixie. You had opportunity, but I don't think you had reason to kill anybody."

He sounded like a professor lecturing a class of would-be homicide detectives. Or like somebody giving me a friendly hint of an effective defense to use in case I was arrested for murder.

Stiffly, I said, "This has been very interesting, Lieutenant, but I have to get back to work."

When I got to the elevator, Guidry caught up with me.

"Can I ask you a favor? Would you tell Cora Mathers that Marilee is dead?"

I stared at him, ready to tell him that I was a pet-sitter, dammit, not a member of the Sheriff's Department. But I knew why he wanted me to notify Cora. I had already made a connection with her, and she was more likely to give me information that might help the investigation.

"You owe me," I said.

"Big time. And you'll talk to her about Frazier's relationship with Marilee?"

"Sure, Guidry. I'll go tell a sweet old woman that her granddaughter's body has been lying in the woods with animals eating her, and then I'll ask her a lot of questions. Are you nuts?"

"I didn't mean it that way, Dixie."

The elevator doors opened and I stepped in. "I'll go see Cora," I said. "That's all I'm promising."

He put his hands in his pockets and stood

silently watching me until the elevator doors closed.

At the Sarasota Bayfront Village, the woman at the front desk called Cora's apartment and told me to go on up. In the elevator, I tried to find the right words to say what had to be said, but there is no right way to tell somebody about death.

Cora was standing outside her door again, waving at me like a little girl excited to have company. "Did you come back for some more of my chocolate bread? I don't have any fresh today, but yesterday's is still good. It doesn't have to be hot, you know. It's good cold, too. I keep it in the refrigerator and just heat it up in the toaster oven. Sometimes I don't even heat it, I just eat it cold."

"I have something to tell you, Cora."

"Well, come on in. You can tell me while we have some tea."

She scuttled ahead of me, talking a mile a minute. "I don't think there's anything that don't go down better with tea, do you? A lot of people here are drinking green tea. I never saw any green tea, did you? I just drink plain old brown tea. I don't think I'd like to drink something green. Would be like drinking hot lime Jell-O. Yuk. Here, you sit down while I make us some brown tea. I've always got the kettle on, you know."

I edged into one of the ice-cream chairs at her round table and watched her totter into the kitchen area. She turned up the heat under a steaming kettle and put teabags into a teapot, then clattered down cups and saucers while she continued to talk.

"A lot of people say they can't sleep at night if they drink tea after noon, but it never hurt me none. I drink tea all day long and I sleep just fine. If I don't, I get up and watch TV. Some of them shows are dirty, got people doing it right there in front of your face. You ask me, there's some things people ought not do in front of other people, and that's one of them. You ever see any of them dirty shows?"

I got up to get the tea tray and said, "I've seen some of them, but just for a few minutes. I don't much like watching other people having sex."

"Well, that's how I feel, too. What good does it do you to watch? If I'm not going to do it, I sure don't want to watch somebody else doing it. What did you want to tell me?"

She had caught me off guard, and when I looked at her, I realized she had been babbling because she was scared. I probably wore the same face that Sergeant Owens and Todd's lieutenant had been wearing three years ago when they came to tell me about Todd and Christy. They didn't have to say a word for me to know that my life was over.

I said, "I think you'd better sit down, Cora."

I've seen greyhounds who have been pulled from the track to be destroyed, and their eyes had the same defeated look as Cora's.

"Is it about Marilee?"

"Yes."

"Has something happened to her?"

"I'm afraid so."

"She's dead, isn't she?"

"I'm sorry, Cora. Yes, she is."

Her face imperceptibly crumpled, its thin skin suddenly cracking into an infinity of tiny lines. But her blue eyes remained blazingly dry, and she straightened up in her chair.

"How did he kill her?"

"I don't know, Cora. Her body was found this morning, but I don't know how she died. She was in the woods behind her house. I suppose she was killed about the same time Harrison Frazier was killed."

She closed her eyes at the image I had conjured, but mercifully didn't ask who had found Marilee's body or its condition. She was a sharp old lady, she probably knew the things that would happen to a body left lying in the woods for several days.

"I always knew he would be the end of her. I knew it from the first day."

"They don't know who killed her, Cora."

"I know. It was Harrison Frazier. I knew he would."

"Harrison Frazier was killed, too, Cora."

"I know that, and I'm glad. That's a terrible thing to say, isn't it, to be glad that another human being is dead, but I am. The world's a better place without him, if you ask me. But it's not a better place without Marilee."

The tears came now, spilling down her ravaged face. She didn't bow her head and she didn't wipe the tears away. She cried defiantly, as if her weeping were an accusation.

I reached across the table and took both her hands. "Cora, I'm so sorry."

"Oh, don't think this is the first time I've cried over what Harrison Frazier did to Marilee. This isn't the first time, and it won't be the last."

"What did Frazier do, Cora?"

"Turned chicken, that's what. His family thought Marilee wasn't good enough for him, and he didn't have the balls to stand up to them. That's what hurt her the most. The way he let them drag her through the mud."

"When did this happen, Cora?"

"Marilee was fifteen. I guess Harrison was just fifteen, too. Lord knows they weren't either of them old enough to take on a baby. I don't fault Harrison for that. But the way he acted later, that was the thing that just killed Marilee."

"Are you talking about Marilee's daughter?"

She sighed. "I'm not supposed to talk about her, but now I don't guess it matters. It wasn't right, what they did. I don't care how much money they paid Marilee, it wasn't right."

"What who did?"

"The Fraziers. They wanted Marilee to put the baby out for adoption, and that was all right with me. I didn't want Marilee to be tied down with a baby to raise and her just fifteen years old. I'd already been through that with her mother. If my daughter had given Marilee to some nice folks, Marilee might have been better off. I did the best I could for her, but I had all I could do to keep food on the table for us. If I had it to do over again, I'd have tried to get my daughter to let Marilee be adopted, and she wouldn't have ended up hanging herself, God rest her sweet soul."

My heart did a little slide. Cora Mathers

had lost more than any woman should have to endure.

"So Marilee's baby was adopted?"

"Bought is more like it. The Fraziers came up with the idea of their daughter taking the baby, and Harrison talked Marilee into it. His sister had been married a good while and I guess she couldn't have one of her own. You know how that goes. Them that wants them can't get pregnant, and them that can't handle them get pregnant if a man so much as looks at them. Anyway, Harrison told Marilee if she let his sister have the baby, they would always know she was being taken care of, and that after they married, they could get her back."

"He said they'd get married?"

"That's what he claimed. He said they'd finish school and then they'd get married. His family probably told him to say that, and Marilee believed him. She was just fifteen years old, she didn't know how men lie to you."

"You don't think he ever planned to marry her?"

"Not for a minute. They had Marilee sign a bunch of papers. She had to promise to stay away from the baby and never let on she was hers. They paid her to do that. If you're rich enough, you can pay somebody to do just about anything."

I poured her a cup of tea and waited while she took a shaky sip. I said, "The photograph on the refrigerator —"

"That's Lily. That's what they named her. She's nineteen now, and she got in touch with one of them places that find your real mother for you. I don't know for sure how it works, but they called Marilee and then she and Lily talked on the phone. Marilee thought since Lily had found her, it wasn't like she was breaking her promise to the Fraziers. They've been writing, and Lily sent her that picture. She looks exactly like Marilee. Marilee was so excited about meeting Lily. Now she never will."

"How old was Lily when Harrison's sister took her?"

"Oh, just hours. When the baby came, the Fraziers were right there with a lawyer and she signed papers and they took her."

"And Marilee thought one day she would get her back?"

"That's what Harrison told her. And he said it didn't make any difference what his folks said, he wasn't going to let Marilee go."

"But he did."

"Well, he did and he didn't. He didn't

marry her, if that's what you mean, but he never let her alone, neither. He was a fool for her, was what he was. Went crazy mean if she got mixed up with any other man. He told her one time he would kill her if he ever caught her with another man, and that's what he's done. Killed her."

"Wasn't he married?"

"Married and with kids. Marilee was just the woman he had on the side. He thought it was enough that he paid her. How do you think that made her feel? I tell you, all the money in the world won't make up for a man treating you like a whore. He ruined her life, and then he killed her."

"Did Harrison Frazier know that Marilee and Lily had found each other?"

"Oh my, no. She had promised, you know, and they'd paid her all that money. No, she couldn't let Harrison know."

Cora looked up at me and gave me a wry smile. "If I keep talking, this won't be true, you know? It'll all turn out to be just a bad dream."

"I know. Talking helps to let bad news settle in slowly instead of all at once."

"Well, I'll just tell you this, and you can pass it on to whoever it is that's looking into this. Harrison Frazier was the one who killed Marilee. Now I think I'd like you to leave me alone."

I understood. I had been like that, too, wanting to burrow into a hole and suffer by myself. I thought briefly about alerting somebody, but then decided to honor Cora's request to be left alone.

"Do you mind if I come by tomorrow?"

"That would be nice of you, Dixie. If it's not too much trouble, I'd like it if you'd stop by."

"Just one more thing, Cora. When the investigators are finished at Marilee's house, it will have to be cleaned. I need your permission to call the special cleaning people." I couldn't think of any other way to describe the professionals who clean and sterilize a house where blood and body fluids have been spilled.

She flinched a bit and then rallied. "You do whatever you need to do, hon."

I made fresh tea for Cora and left her sitting at the table warming her hands on a steaming cup.

Before I drove away, I called Guidry on my cell phone. He answered on the second ring with a clipped "Guidry here."

"Marilee had a baby when she was fifteen. Harrison Frazier was the father. His older sister adopted the baby, and his family paid

Marilee to stay away and keep it a secret. But Frazier kept seeing her on the sly, and he told her he would kill her if she ever had another man. Her grandmother thinks he murdered her."

For a moment, the line was silent, and then he took a deep breath. "Does the grandmother have any ideas about who killed Frazier?"

"No, but there's something else. The daughter is nineteen now, and she found Marilee. They've been corresponding and they were going to meet."

Okay, now I'd told him everything I knew. Well, almost everything.

21

I said, "If Frazier was insanely jealous like Cora says he was, maybe he killed Marilee when he caught her with another man."

"And what was the other man doing while Frazier was killing Marilee, standing by watching?"

"Frazier could have knocked him out first."

"And who took Marilee's body to the woods? Do you think Frazier did that while the second guy was unconscious and then went back to get himself killed? Damned co-operative of him if he did."

"Well, I don't know, Guidry. I'm just passing on what Cora told me, so don't give me attitude."

"I appreciate the information, Dixie. Like I said, you get around."

"Yeah. Now, when can I get a haz-mat crew in Marilee's house so I can bring Ghost home?"

"Who?"

"Marilee Doerring's cat. We talked about him, remember?"

"Dixie, the Doerring woman is dead. You can't bring a cat back to her house."

"What's the difference in her being dead and off on a trip?"

"A pulse, for starters."

"No, I mean what's the difference to a cat? The contract I had with Marilee Doerring gives me temporary custody of her cat, with the obligation to do whatever is necessary for his welfare in an emergency. This is an emergency. There's no reason why he can't stay in familiar surroundings while I look for a new home for him. He'd be a lot happier."

"That's what I live for, Dixie, to make a cat happy."

I batted away a floating cat hair and said, "Okay, that was snide, because I really do live to make a cat happy."

"Crime-scene tape should come down some time tomorrow. It's all yours after that."

"Just until I can find a home for Ghost. Would you and your wife like a nice cat? Absyssinians are usually good with kids. If you have some, that is."

There was another pause while my face got hot. I couldn't believe I'd just said what I'd said. He was going to think I was trying to find out if he was single, which was ridiculous. When he spoke, I could hear the grin in his voice. "I don't happen to have any kids, Dixie, never have. Don't have a wife, either, although I did once."

My lips were tingling like I'd had a shot of niacin. It was really stupid. I didn't care whether he was married or not. I said, "A cat would be good company for you, Guidry. Cats don't have to be taken for walks, and they don't bark and disturb the neighbors. They're really ideal pets. Research shows that people who have pets are healthier than people who don't. Did you know that?"

This time, he outright laughed. "I'll think about it, Dixie, but don't get your hopes up."

He clicked off and left me holding an empty phone.

I muttered, "Fuck you very much, Lieutenant," and started the Bronco.

Talking about Ghost had helped me get my priorities straight. I had to find a new home for Ghost, and I had to do it quickly. He was not only cramped in his private room at Marge's, but it was costing me forty dollars a day to leave him there.

I didn't want to leave him with just anybody, either. Pets are like surrogate children. Now that I knew how Marilee had been denied her own daughter, I understood a little better why she had lavished so much love and attention on Ghost. Unable to choose the most nutritious food for her child, she chose it for her cat. Forbidden to buy pretty clothes and toys and baubles for her daughter, she bought them for her cat. Even Ghost's collar with its silver hearts and keys was like a charm bracelet she might have given her daughter. I felt a new affinity for Marilee, a kind of mother-to-mother rapport. Marilee had entrusted me with her substitute child, and I wanted to carry out her wishes.

I was already late making my afternoon pet visits, but I turned the Bronco toward Roberts Point Road and Shuga Reasnor's house. I pulled up in front of Shuga's glass doors and slammed out of the car into the suspended heat peculiar to late afternoon on Siesta Key.

Shuga was home. I could see her through the glass doors. She was sitting on one of her rose linen sofas with a phone stuck to her ear and one long bronzed leg swinging like a nervous pendulum. She saw me when I got to the top step, and even that far away I could see her eyes widen. She got up and started toward the door, still talking on the phone. I put my fists on my hips and stood without ringing the bell while she ended her conversation and flipped the phone shut.

She pulled the door open and stood looking at me. At first, I thought she had two black eyes, but it was smeared mascara. She said, "I know she's dead. The detective called me."

"Can I come in?"

"What do you want?"

"You're the person Marilee authorized to make decisions about her cat."

"Oh, for God's sake!"

Rolling her eyes, Shuga stepped out of the way and pulled the door shut behind me. We walked silently to the living room and sat down across from each other.

"I just have a few minutes," she said. "I have to take care of things a lot more important than a damned cat."

"Things like calling Marilee's daughter and telling her that her mother's dead?"

Her leg stopped swinging, and she gave me a level look.

"Yeah, things like that."

"That's who you called, isn't it? That's where you thought Marilee was going when she left here."

"Okay. Is that a crime?"

"Why didn't you tell Lieutenant Guidry that you'd talked to her daughter? Why didn't you tell him you knew Harrison Frazier?"

Her head snapped up then and she jumped to her feet. "Get the hell out of my house, lady. My best friend just died, and I don't have time for this shit."

"Your best friend didn't die, she was murdered. Did you kill Marilee, Shuga? Were you involved with Frazier and got jealous because he had the hots for Marilee?"

She barked a loud laugh, then sat down and took a cigarette from the crystal holder on the coffee table. She stuck it in her mouth and talked around it while she lit it from the silver lighter on the table. "That's rich. Me involved with Harrison Frazier? I don't think so."

She sucked smoke deep into her chest and slumped back on the couch, looking at me the way a cobra looks at the man playing the flute, wondering whether to be nice or lunge for my throat.

I said, "Let me make it easier for you. I know that Harrison Frazier was the father of Marilee's daughter, and I know he's been seeing her for years. Did he come here to Siesta Key to see her?"

Through a fog of exhaled smoke, she said, "Oh, God no. Too close to Orlando. No, they met in other places. Every month or so, she would fly off and spend a few days with him. They always went to some out-of-the-way place where nobody would recognize them. Harrison would rent a cabin in some godforsaken spot in Louisiana or get a room in a mom-and-pop motel in Bumfuck, Nebraska, places like that. He could have taken her to the penthouse suite at the finest hotel in the world, but he took Marilee to dumb places like that. She was so crazy about him, she thought she had a good time. I think they spent all their time fucking, so I guess maybe she did."

"If they always met someplace else, what was he doing here when he was killed?"

"I don't know. That's why I got scared that something had happened to Marilee when you found him in her house."

"Marilee's grandmother thinks Harrison killed Marilee. Cora says he was crazy jealous and that he threatened to kill her if she got involved with another man."

"He was jealous. Marilee thought jealous meant he loved her, the dumb cluck. But he couldn't have killed her, he was dead. Somebody killed both of them."

"You said Dr. Coffey wouldn't kill her himself but that he might hire somebody to do it. Who else had reason to kill Marilee?"

"I don't know anybody who would kill her. I'm telling you the truth."

I wasn't sure I believed her, but I let it go.

"How did Marilee get involved with some-body like Harrison Frazier, anyway?"

"Cora was a cook at the grade-school cafeteria in Orlando. She barely made enough to scrape by, so she was always looking for ways to make money. The summer Marilee and I were fourteen, Cora got a job cooking at a ritzy camp for rich Baptist families outside Orlando. It was more of a resort than a camp, but it was supposed to be a way for families to have a clean, wholesome vacation with their kids and still give them a chance to swim and hike and hang out like normal kids. They let Cora bring Marilee and me with her, and we waited tables in the dining room. The rest of the time we were free to walk around the camp. If we were at the lake and one of the rich boys decided to come down and sit with us, we couldn't do anything to stop them."

"Harrison was one of those boys?"

"So far as Marilee was concerned, he was the only boy. She was nuts about him. If he'd asked her to drown herself in the lake, she would have jumped right in. She thought he was in love with her, the dumb dope, but I think he was more excited about the idea of easy sex. He was just fifteen, and she was probably his first. With all the things going on, it was easy for him to slip off to meet her, and neither of them knew jack shit about condoms or had any way to get any. By the time camp ended, Marilee was pregnant."

She shook her head and stared at the floor for a moment, lost in the memory. "Harrison hadn't even given her his address, but Cora tracked down his family and contacted them. She was smart enough to know they would pay for Marilee to go someplace and have the baby, but I don't think she ever expected them to want it. Poor dumb Marilee thought Harrison would marry her." She wiped away sudden moisture on her cheek and said, "What an idiot!"

"Did Harrison know how she felt?"

"Oh sure. Marilee never was good at keeping her feelings hidden, at least when it came to Harrison. She kept thinking one day he would leave his wife and marry her. Then their daughter turned eighteen, and Marilee got a letter from Harrison's attorney saying there wouldn't be any more money. It was like somebody had dropped a bomb on her."

"How much had they been paying her?"

She gave me a tight grin, exhaling a cloud of smoke and curling the tip of her tongue to touch her upper lip like a smirking dragon. "A quarter mil a year."

"Wow."

"Yeah, wow is right. They got her used to that kind of lifestyle, and then they expected her to go back to living in a trailer park?"

I had to agree that the idea of Marilee Doerring in a double-wide was a stretch of the imagination.

"She called Harrison when she got that letter. He said she'd had a free ride for eighteen years and now it was time she grew up."

I could almost hear Harrison Frazier's bitter voice speaking the words, the voice of a man who had been caught fooling around with trailer-park trash when he was fifteen and had been paying the price ever since, literally and figuratively.

"I heard she got some money from Dr. Coffey, too."

"Yeah, but every cent went to buying that place for Cora and setting up a fund that will take care of her if she ever needs a nursing home. Cora worked her ass off raising Marilee, and Marilee never forgot it."

"So when Frazier cut her off —"

"She went totally bonkers."

"Is that when she got in touch with her daughter?"

Shuga leaned forward and jabbed her cigarette out in the ashtray.

"She had a plan to get close to the girl and make the Fraziers squirm. Harrison has other kids, he wouldn't want them to know he had raped Marilee when she was fifteen and got her pregnant."

So much for the story Marilee had told Cora about her daughter finding her through an agency.

"She was going to say she was raped?"

Shuga nodded, her eyes bright with grim shrewdness. She wasn't disappointed in Marilee the way I was. She understood how Marilee's mind worked. She had pulled herself out of the same environment, told the same lies, created the same illusions, made the same place for herself in the world of money and possessions. She and Marilee had both played the hand nature had dealt them, the same way I had and everybody else does.

I stood up to go. "I have to find a home for Marilee's cat, and I need your approval of whatever I do."

"Hell, I don't care what you do. If you're thinking about sticking me with it, forget it."

Shuga didn't get up, and I didn't say good-bye. I felt her eyes boring into my back as I went out the glass doors and got in the Bronco.

I drove down Roberts Point Road, pulled

into a driveway, and dialed Guidry again. This time when he snapped "Guidry," I said, "Dixie Hemingway" just as crisply.

"What have you got, Dixie?"

"Shuga Reasnor says Marilee and Harrison Frazier went away for a few days almost every month for eighteen years. Marilee was in love with him and thought he loved her. Then she got a letter from his attorney saying the quarter of a million she had been getting every year was over. The lady was pissed. She got in touch with her daughter, whose name is Lily. She was going to pressure Frazier to keep paying. Her plan was to claim he raped her when she was fifteen."

"Interesting. Have the reporters got to you yet?"

"Reporters?"

"You know, the people who shove microphones in your face and yell questions at you."

"You think they'll do that?"

"Come on, they've already figured out that Marilee and Frazier had something going, and nothing sells like sex. Now that Marilee's dead, they'll really be licking their chops. You found both bodies and you take care of her cat. Hell, the *Today* show will probably want to interview you."

My throat closed up and for a moment I couldn't breathe.

"Dixie?"

I clicked off without saying good-bye. I knew Guidry was right. Just the fact that I was a pet-sitter who'd found the dead body of one of Florida's first families was enough to make me fodder for reporters, and somebody was bound to do a story about Marilee and her orphaned cat. While they were setting up that story, they'd probably dig up footage of me going crazy wild three years ago while cameras rolled. And the worst of it was that I wasn't sure I wouldn't do it again. Put me under enough stress and I could blow like Vesuvius.

22

Grimly, I pulled out of the driveway into traffic. I had to go on. Not just go on with my afternoon pet visits, but go on with my life. I couldn't let fear rule me, not even fear of myself.

My mouth still had the bitter taste of the hospital's coffee, and my mind jumped to the coconut cream pies that Tanisha makes at the Village Diner. Late as I was, I rationalized that except for a little bitty tub of yogurt, I hadn't eaten anything since breakfast. It would only take a few minutes to have pie and good coffee, and then I would be stronger and braver.

Judy was pouring coffee at a table near the front door when I walked in, and a look of surprise crossed her face when she saw me. I waved to her and plucked a Sunday *Herald-Tribune* from a thin stack by the cashier stand before I slid into a booth. Judy went to the back to get a coffee mug and setup for me, and I spread the paper on the table and scanned the article headings. The President had just issued a denial of something his opponents had accused him of, a CEO had just been indicted for cheating thousands of investors, some scientists had developed a way to alter another seed to make it sterile, and a question had been raised in Sarasota about the way the Sheriff's Department was handling the investigation of the murders of Hamilton Frazier and Marilee Doerring.

Judy plunked a mug on the table and poured coffee in it, but my eyes were locked on the article. It seemed that popular radio psychologist Dr. Win was claiming the Sheriff's Department was showing undue bias toward a former deputy by not arresting her. The woman in question was me. The article went on to say that I was known to have been dismissed from the department because of emotional instability following the tragic deaths of my husband and child, and that I had started taking care of pets after being declared unfit for law enforcement. The author of the article said he had interviewed Dr. Win but had not been able to locate me. Without coming right out and saying so, the implication was that I was hiding.

My heart was pounding hard. In a related article, other people had been interviewed for their opinions about me. As Marilee's ex-fiancé, Dr. Gerald Coffey said I had accosted him while he was eating breakfast on the morning of the murder, and that my behavior had been irrational and alarming. There were even quotes from a couple of people whose pets I had taken care of. They said they probably wouldn't hire me again because it was just too creepy the way I'd found two dead bodies, and how could they be sure I hadn't had something to do with them being dead. There were also several quotes from clients who said they thought the whole idea was ridiculous and that I was an excellent pet-sitter. But you could almost read a hint of doubt in their words.

Judy said, "You just now seeing that?"

I nodded, struck dumb with sick apprehension.

"Don't let it get to you. Stupid son of a bitch didn't have anything real to write about, so he made up a bunch of shit. Nobody'll pay it any mind."

"Yes, they will. Who wants to give their house key to somebody who's accused of murder?"

"You should sue that bastard," she said. "Sue him for slander and libel and defamation of character and loss of income and loss of reputation."

"Maybe I could sue him for my wrinkles while I'm at it."

"I'm serious," she said. "Don't let this go by without a fight, Dixie. This is your *name* we're talking about."

I swallowed the lump in my throat. "That wouldn't stop people from wondering about me."

"People who know you won't believe it, and that's all that matters. What do you want to eat?"

"I can't eat now."

"Yes you can, Dixie! Now you listen here, if you let that slimeball make you go crawling back in your shell, then he's killed you. You want to let him kill you?"

"No."

"Then hold your head up and go on about your business. That cop will find out who killed those people, and everybody will know you didn't have anything to do with it. Now I'm going to bring you some eggs and bacon, and you're gonna eat every bite of it, and you're gonna like it."

I looked up at her flushed face and had to laugh. "I don't want breakfast, I want some of Tanisha's coconut pie."

"That's more like it. If we let fuckers like that make us stop being normal people, then we might as well crawl in a hole and die."

She flounced off to get my pie, and I folded the paper and laid it on the seat beside me. My hands were shaking so bad I had trouble folding the paper. One thing kept running through my mind. While I had the greatest respect for the guys with the Sarasota Sheriff's Department, I wasn't so naïve that I didn't know they were under pressure to make an arrest. And if they decided to go with the obvious, it would be me. I had found Frazier's body, I had led them to Marilee's body, I had a key to Marilee's house, and I was known to be a mental case, no longer fit to wear a deputy's badge. If I had been conducting the investigation, I would have already arrested me as the prime suspect, and now Dr. Win had gone on the air demanding just that. If they arrested me, I didn't have a shred of an alibi. My only witness would be Rufus, and juries aren't known to pay much attention to what a dog has to say.

There were people who thought Carl Winnick walked on water. He was a pillar of the community, rich, educated, with plenty of well-placed contacts. I was a pet-sitter with two years of community college and a dubious medical leave of absence from the Sheriff's Department. An emotionally unstable woman who couldn't be trusted with a gun or with public safety. Which one of us would people believe, me or Winnick?

For a moment, I felt like going home and crawling in bed and pulling the covers over my head and hope it would all straighten itself out. But Judy was right. I had come too far to do that. I had faced things a lot tougher than Carl Winnick accusing me of being a killer.

Not a *lot* of things, maybe, but some.

One or two.

Okay, one. Losing people you love is harder than anything.

As Judy put my pie on the table, Tanisha moved her wide smiling face into the square opening between the dining room and the kitchen and waved at me, her jowls jiggling and her black eyes almost lost behind her round cheeks.

Judy said, "Tanisha says to tell that reporter to kiss your big fat ass."

It surprised me so that I laughed, a big belly laugh from deep inside. Tanisha winked at me and withdrew her head.

Judy said, "Why's she saying you've got a fat ass?"

"It's a private joke," I said. "We were in the ladies' room one day and big fat asses came up."

"Uh-huh. Well, she's got a big one, that's

for sure. You know, she cooks for somebody that lives around Marilee Doerring's house. I heard her telling somebody she was that close to the place where the woman was killed."

"Lucky them. She's good."

Judy splashed more coffee in my cup and left me making love to my pie. The crust was crisp and flaky, the filling rich and smooth, and the meringue was exactly right, not weepy or dry or too sugary, with flakes of fresh coconut making sweet little explosions in my mouth. I managed to eat almost a whole minute without thinking about the newspaper article. Instead, I thought about how a good cook like Tanisha could pick up big bucks cooking for parties or just making occasional meals for a family. I mentally ran down the houses near Marilee's, wondering where Tanisha cooked. I'd never seen her in Marilee's neighborhood, but most likely we were there at different times.

My cell phone beeped just as I downed the last pastry crumb. The ID readout showed Michael's number, so I answered.

He said, "Have you seen today's paper?"

"I saw it."

"Are you okay?"

"Yeah. I just had coconut pie. I'm at the diner."

"That asshole at the paper has been calling me, looking for you."

"I'm sorry, Michael."

"Not your fault. What does your detective say about it?"

"He's not my detective, and I haven't talked to him."

"Maybe you'd better. Tell him I'm going to stick my foot up that reporter's ass if he writes any more shit about you."

"It'll blow over, Michael. Any response from us will just give him something else to write about."

"You sound pretty cool about it."

There was a note of admiration in his voice. I took a deep breath and realized I *was* rather cool about it. No more hammering heart. No more fast, shallow breathing. No more fine hand tremors.

I gave a shaky laugh and said, "I guess I am. Who would have thought?"

"So when are you coming home?"

"I'll be late. I haven't even started my rounds yet. I had to talk to some people first."

"Well, be careful."

"Yeah, I love you, too."

I felt calmer after I hung up. I had a big brother who cared about me, and I had handled a lot of stress in one day with only a couple of minor breakdowns. I was making progress.

As I was leaving the diner, I saw Tanisha heading for the ladies' room, so I made a U-turn and followed her. She was already in a stall when I got there. I washed my hands and dried them while I waited. When she came out, she grinned shyly at me. I watched approvingly as she lathered her hands, then handed her some paper towels.

I said, "Judy said you did some cooking for somebody in Marilee Doerring's neighborhood — where that man was killed."

"Not no more I don't."

"Oh."

"Hunh-uh, I wouldn't set foot on that street again, no way, hunh-uh. Bunch of stupid people live on that street, and that man's the stupidest."

"What man?"

"You know, that one I told to kiss my ass, that's who."

"I didn't hear you say his name."

"I guess I didn't say it. Come to think of it, I don't believe I did."

"Tanisha, could you say it now?"

She laughed, but looked at me warily. "Why you want to know?"

I was stumped. I didn't know why I

wanted to know, I just did. I said, "I guess I'm just nosy. I work around there, too, and I'd just sort of like to know who to watch out for. I don't know what the guy did to piss you off so much, but you seem pretty easy to get along with, so whatever it was must have been something I wouldn't like, either."

She pushed out her lips and furled her brow while she considered my reason, and then nodded. "I guess you got a right to know if you work around there. He accused me of stealing something, like I gave a rat's ass about the stupid thing, and it wasn't even his."

"Why'd he do that?"

"He seen me getting this little piece of pipe out of the trash when I was on my way to the bus stop. Somebody had put it out at the curb, and I saw it. It's at the curb, it's the trash, it ain't stealing to take it, right? Somebody threw it away, it's for anybody to take that wants it. Short little piece of brass pipe about two feet long."

"That must have been the Graysons' house. They hung a carousel horse on some brass pipe."

"Uh-huh. I don't know whose house it was. It's on the other side of the woods where that man got killed. They just put the pipe out and I saw it and picked it up. I thought maybe I could make a towel rack or something out of it."

"And somebody accused you of stealing it?"

"Yeah, this little runt drove in the driveway and yelled at me like I was some kind of criminal. He said, 'What you doing with that, girl?' Called me *girl,* the old fool. I said I wasn't doing nothing with it and he come over and yanked it out of my hand. Took it *away* from me! Then he said, 'You go on home now, girl. You got no business here.' "

Tanisha's eyes were snapping with humiliation and anger. "I guess he thinks he lives on some kind of plantation and I'm one of his slaves. But them days are over, honey! Ain't nobody gonna talk to me like that. That's when I told him to kiss my big fat black ass, and I waggled it at him when I said it, too. I left and I ain't never going on that street again."

She threw her wadded paper towel in the bin and headed for the door. "I gotta get back to the kitchen or they're gonna send somebody looking for me."

"Who was he?"

She paused with one hand holding the door open. "I don't know who he was.

Never saw him before, and hope I don't never see him again, neither."

"Was he bald?"

"Bald? I don't think so. I didn't notice him bald."

"His car, was it a black Miata?"

She shrugged. "I don't know cars. It was black, one of them little low cars."

"When did that happen, Tanisha?"

She frowned. "Thursday night. Why're you so excited about it?"

"Because whoever killed the man in Marilee Doerring's house cracked his head with a blunt instrument. Like a piece of brass pipe. Somebody saw a black Miata around there that night, and later there was a bald-headed man acting suspicious."

Her eyes grew wide. "You think that little pig that hollered at me killed that man?"

"I don't know. Maybe. Would you recognize him if you saw him again?"

"Oh yeah, I won't never forget him."

We gave each other solemn stares just thinking of all the implications, then she moved on and let the door swing shut behind her enormous backside. After a few moments while I let it sink in, I followed her. Hot damn, maybe Tanisha and I had solved the murders.

23

As I went around the end of the diner's counter, I glanced toward the empty stool where Dr. Coffey had been sitting when I talked to him. Suddenly, a piece of our conversation fell into my brain as if it had been poised above my head, just waiting for me to return to the scene. I had said, "My client left town and didn't leave a number where she could be reached." I had said, "I was thinking you might have some idea where she might have gone. Like where her business takes her, or where her family lives."

When he jumped up and threatened to have me arrested, I had assumed he was jumpy about the possibility of getting involved in a murder investigation. But I hadn't mentioned a murder, and I had never used Marilee's name. All I'd said was that I was a pet-sitter. Surely Marilee Doerring wasn't the only woman he knew who owned a pet. I wasn't even sure the news of the murder had been on the news yet, and even if it had been, how could he have been so sure that's what I was talking about?

My hand was reaching for my cell to call Guidry and tell him all my brilliant deductions, when I caught sight of the wall clock behind the counter and changed my mind. I was over an hour late with my pet visits, and if I didn't get my mind back on my own business, I could lose it.

Like a robot on bunny batteries, I got in the Bronco and started my afternoon rounds, apologizing to each cat for being late and promising to make it up to them later. I left Billy Elliot's run for last, rapping on Tom's door to alert him that I was there and then using my key. Just as I stepped inside, a loud TV voice said my name. Tom and Billy Elliot were parked in front of the TV, and Carl Winnick's infuriated face filled the screen.

"The woman has a key to the house where at least one of these murders took place, and possibly both of them. She has a history of emotional instability that caused the Sheriff's Department to dismiss her, and is clearly the most obvious suspect. Yet the Sheriff's Department has not arrested her, and I want to know why."

Both Tom and Billy Elliot felt me behind them at the same moment and swung their heads. Tom grabbed his remote and clicked off the TV.

"Shit, Dixie, I didn't know you were here. I'm sorry you heard that."

I wasn't sure my voice would work, but it did, even though it came out a rusty croak. "Tom, do you believe what he said?"

"Good God, Dixie, of course I don't. Carl Winnick is an officious, self-righteous idiot."

"Then why were you watching his show?"

"That wasn't his show. That was the evening news with a clip of what Winnick is saying on his show."

My knees bent like Silly Putty. I sank onto a chair and stared at Tom. "So it's not just Dr. Win's usual fans who got that?"

"Don't let it get to you, Dixie."

I stared at him. Why did everybody keep telling me not to let it get to me? How could I not let it get to me that a talk-show celebrity was getting airtime to accuse me of murder?

He said, "Have the reporters found you yet?"

"Not yet."

"Would you like to hide out here until this blows over? Billy Elliot and I would be proud to have you as our guest."

I took a tremulous breath and stood up.

"Thanks, Tom. I appreciate the offer and the vote of confidence, but I'm not going to hide."

"Well, if you decide to just lay low for a while —"

"Okay."

I got Billy Elliot's leash and he and I went downstairs and ran as if it were a normal day. A casual observer wouldn't have known that I was beginning to be mad as hell. If Dr. Win had been there, I would have told him to kiss my big fat white ass.

It was a little after 8:30 when I got home. The sun had just set, dropping abruptly below the line of the sea as if it had been treading water and at the last minute had gone under. The sky was streaked with waving banners of cerise and turquoise and lavender, and a couple of brave stars were showing their faces. On the beach, the tide was spreading lacy ruffles on the sand like a lone flamenco dancer entertaining herself.

Michael was on the cypress deck with the hood of the smoker open, scenting the sea air with the aroma of smoking meat. He waved a long fork at me and yelled, "Your timing is perfect. Are you hungry?"

"Are you kidding? I'm starving."

Gingerly, he transferred a slab of brisket from the grill to a big platter and closed the smoker. "I've got potato salad and beans inside," he said.

I happily trotted ahead of him to hold open the kitchen door, then got down plates while he slid the hot brisket onto the butcher block. I opened the lid of a pot simmering on the stove and moaned like a cat in heat. Michael's pinto beans with hot peppers and garlic and tomato are good enough to make strong men weep with unabashed joy. I ladled some beans on each of our plates and added potato salad from a big bowl sitting on the counter. Michael's knife made thin diagonal slices across the tender brisket and transferred them to our plates, where they oozed their succulent juices.

I set our plates on the eating side of the counter and got silverware and napkins while Michael popped us both a beer. Then we both dug in, and for a while the only sound was my little whimpers of contentment.

We didn't talk until after we'd finished eating and got the leftovers put away. Then we took coffee out on the deck and sat in the redwood chairs our grandfather had built with his own hands — chairs so sturdy they'll be here long after Michael and I are gone. We waited awhile, letting the sea's breath cool our faces, before we talked.

"Dixie, I have to tell you something."

"What?"

"Somebody was in the house today while I was gone. There were tire prints in the drive, and more prints of somebody walking across the sand to your place, then to the back door here. Whoever it was broke the lock and went inside, there were footprints all over the place. I didn't find anything missing, but I guess something could be gone and I just don't know what to look for. I went inside your place, and it's the same. Nothing messed up, but sandy tracks on the floor."

I was sitting stiffly upright with the back of my neck tingling. Michael's house was old and the back door didn't fit well. My French doors would be child's play to an intruder.

"Did you call nine one one?"

A mosquito buzzed around Michael's head, and he waved at it in the reflexive way Floridians do, not really expecting to remove it but needing to show some resistance so the mosquito wouldn't think it had clear title to a particular piece of flesh.

"Yeah, they came out and dusted for prints, but I think they were just going through the motions to satisfy me."

"You think it could have been a reporter?"

"No reporter would stoop that low. Well, they might, but I doubt it was a reporter."

We sat silently for a few minutes. A muscle in Michael's jaw was working, and I knew he was forcing himself to stay calm for my sake.

He said, "I had left the brisket cooking. At least the bastard didn't take that."

I grinned at his forced joke. "What makes you think it was a man? It could have been a woman."

"Dixie, until they catch whoever killed those people, I want you to keep the hurricane shutters down when you're home by yourself. There are too many crazies out there, and with that son of a bitch Win splashing your name all over the news, somebody's liable to decide to come looking for you just for the hell of it."

I said, "Winnick hasn't even tried to see Phillip, and neither has his wife. He's afraid the media will find out what happened to him and hurt his reputation. His own son! Can you believe that?"

"I can believe most anything, Dixie. But my main concern is you. I want you to stay out of all this. Don't talk to anybody else. Don't listen to anybody else's sad story. Let the cops handle it by themselves."

"I haven't talked to anybody. Not really. Well, a little bit."

"Just promise me you'll back off, okay?"

"Okay. Come upstairs with me while I look around?"

He stood up and reached a hand to haul me to my feet, then put his arm around my shoulder and squeezed me to his side. "It'll be okay, Dixie. Just be careful."

Together, we went up the stairs to my apartment, but Michael had swept up all the sandy footprints, and nothing looked as if it had been disturbed. I stood on tiptoe to kiss his cheek, thanked him for dinner, and promised again that I'd stay out of the investigation.

When he left, I closed the hurricane shutters and hurried to the desk in my closet-office to see if the mail I'd taken from Marilee's house was still in the manila folder in the top drawer. It was, and I felt a little chagrined that I'd thought somebody had been looking for it. Meaning I had a guilty conscience. Not so guilty a conscience that I was ready to tell anybody about the letters, but guilty enough to be jittery about having them.

I put the folder back in the drawer and went in my bedroom and pulled my bed away from the wall. The bed is built on a wooden frame that has two storage drawers for linens on one side, but the side against the wall has another drawer that nobody knows about. It's not exactly a secret, it's just that nobody has ever asked and I've never mentioned it. When I pulled the drawer open, its contents were exactly as they had been when I put them there three years ago.

When a deputy quits or retires from the Sheriff's Department, she can either purchase her department-issued gun or let it go back to the department. Todd's 9-mm Sig Sauer went back when he was killed, and mine was turned in when I went on indefinite leave of absence. But almost every deputy qualifies for two or three personal backup guns as well as a department-issue weapon. Todd's primary personal was a Smith & Wesson .40, and mine was a .38. Both guns were fitted into a special case in the drawer on the dark side of my bed.

During the six months I trained at the Police Academy, they kept score of who put the most bullets in the head or heart region of the cardboard targets. The rule was that out of forty-eight shots, a minimum of thirty-eight had to hit dead center. The person who most consistently hit on target got a plaque at the end of the six months. It surprised a lot of people that I got that plaque. I still have it. They called it a "marksmanship award," but I was never able to forget that was a euphemism for "accurate killer." Most people don't know this, but it's against the law for a law-enforcement officer to shoot to maim or disable. By law, a law-enforcement officer is obligated to shoot to "eliminate the threat" — which means to kill. People who can't accept that shouldn't go into law enforcement.

It had been three years since I'd handled my .38, but it felt familiar and right in my hand. I sat at my kitchen bar and took my gun apart and cleaned and oiled it. When I was done, I popped a magazine in the butt and put two extra magazines in the pocket of the cargo shorts I would wear the next day. I laid the gun on the bathroom counter while I showered and brushed my teeth. When I went to bed, I put it on the bedside table where I could get it quickly.

Somebody had already killed two people and had tried to kill a third. I didn't intend to be next.

I drifted to sleep and dreamed that Marilee was clutching a cat exactly like Ghost to her voluptuous bosom, but his name was Phillip. She was pleading with me to save him. "You have the key, Dixie. All you have to do is use it."

When the alarm sounded, it took me a few

seconds to remember where I was. I went to the bathroom and stared at myself in the mirror. Was it possible that my dream had actually been a message? If not from Marilee's spirit, then from my own subconscious? Crazy as it seemed, I thought it was. Somehow, I had the key to solving the murders and to fingering the person who had attacked Phillip. I just didn't know what it was.

I brushed my teeth, splashed water on my face, and pulled my hair into a ponytail. I pulled on a knit top and the cargo shorts I'd laid out the night before, and stepped into my Keds. Holding my .38 ready, I raised the storm shutters. The porch was empty, and I slid the gun into the right pocket of my shorts, where it made a satisfying pressure on my thigh. I had no idea what I was going to meet, or if, in fact, I needed to take a gun with me, but I wasn't taking any chances.

By 4:15, I was halfway to my first stop, and the morning went smoothly. I didn't find a single dead body, nobody got beat up, no reporter accosted me, and none of the cats on my schedule had done anything naughty that I had to clean up.

While I fed cats and groomed cats and changed cats' litter boxes, my mind was on the strange message I'd gotten in my dream.

I take dreams seriously because they're the only way our subconscious can communicate with us. I went over the dream again and again — Marilee holding Ghost, except it wasn't Ghost, but a cat named Phillip. Was that because I saw Phillip as a pet? No, I really didn't. Was it because Phillip was similar to Ghost in some way? Maybe, but how? Ghost knew who the murderer was because he had been in the house when both murders happened. Did Phillip know, too? Had he recognized the woman he'd seen that morning and wasn't saying? What was the key that I was supposed to have to all this? A key is like a code breaker, something that unlocks secrets, but if I had such a key, I didn't know what it was.

At Kristin Lord's house, she greeted me coolly and left me alone while I groomed Fred. She didn't mention anything about Dr. Win's allegations, but I wondered if she had been on the phone trying to find another cat groomer.

Guidry called a little after nine o'clock, just as I was leaving Kristin Lord's house. "Can you be at the hospital in fifteen minutes? I'd like to talk to Phillip Winnick now."

I thought about my promise to Michael to end my involvement in this case. I thought about the two cats still on my morning schedule. I thought about how Guidry seemed to think that I had nothing to do except jump when he called. For all those reasons, I knew I should say no.

I said, "Okay."

24

When I got to the hospital, I stashed the gun and the spare magazines in the glove box after I parked. I stopped in the gift shop to get some reading material for Phillip, then took the elevator up to his floor. In the ICU unit, Guidry was outside Phillip's glassed cubicle, talking to a nurse. Beyond him, I could see Phillip. He no longer had the ventilator, but his swollen face was a mass of purple bruises.

Guidry didn't speak to me, just held his hand out and took my arm while he finished his conversation with the nurse.

He said, "Is he medicated?"

The nurse raised his eyebrows and gave Guidry a tight smile, the kind you'd give the village idiot. "Of course he's medicated. He's able to talk, but it will hurt. Try to keep it to a minimum."

The nurse followed my gaze toward Phillip and shook his head. "It's hard to take in, isn't it? You just never dream that somebody would deliberately do this much damage to a kid."

Guidry said, "Come on," and gave my arm a firm tug.

Phillip's eyes were closed, and when he heard us enter, he opened them with a hopeful look that quickly changed to polite disappointment. I felt like apologizing for not being the person he hoped to see.

I said, "Hey, Phil, good to see your eyes open. You look like hell. Blink twice if that's how you feel."

He managed a weak smile, winced at the pain it caused, and slowly blinked two times.

"I brought you some things to read," I said. "But they didn't have much of a selection. You have a choice of *Reader's Digest, House & Garden,* or *Sarasota Today.* When you've enjoyed as much of those as you can stand, I also got you a Carl Hiaasen book."

I was prattling to cover my dismay at how devastated he looked. Even without the ventilator down his throat, he looked pathetically vulnerable and ravaged. He closed his eyes, either from exhaustion or the effects of his medication, and I shut up. I knew he would recover from his injuries, but the sight of his sweet face so swollen and bruised made me want to go find the person who had done this to him and hurt him really, really bad.

I took one of his big hands and stroked it, wishing I could make all his pain go away just by rubbing him. The normal reaction to being beaten around the head and shoulders is to hold your hands over your head to protect your skull. I suddenly realized that Phillip must have tucked his hands under his armpits during his attack. Awed, I couldn't even imagine the incredible willpower it had taken to protect his hands and leave his head exposed.

I said, "Phillip, I know you didn't see the person who attacked you, but was there anything at all about the person that seemed familiar? Footsteps, scent, sound of his breathing, anything?"

His eyes opened, and for an instant the look he gave me seemed absurdly hostile, the way a drowning animal looks at its rescuers. He rolled his head side to side in slow denial, then closed his eyes again.

On the other side of the bed, Guidry cleared his throat meaningfully, and I took my cue. "Phillip, Lieutenant Guidry wants to hear about the woman you saw leaving Marilee Doerring's house. Just tell him about it in a few words, okay?"

He opened his eyes and gave Guidry a somber look. In a husky whisper, pausing to take shallow breaths, he said, "Black Miata came . . . woman got in . . . drove off. Top was up . . . couldn't see . . . driver."

Guidry said, "Was she carrying any luggage?"

Phillip's eyes widened. "No."

"You remember what she was wearing?"

Keeping his eyes fixed on Guidry, Phillip said, "Pants . . . light color."

"High heels? Low heels?"

"High . . . they . . . made a noise."

"What about her hair? Was it up or down?"

"Down, I think."

"Black hair?"

"Dark."

"You're sure it was a Miata? Couldn't have been an MGB or a Mercedes or a Toyota?"

"I'm sure."

"When the car door opened, did a light come on inside?"

Phillip's eyes grew wide again, and it seemed to me there was a flicker of fear in them. "I guess."

"But you didn't see the driver?"

"No."

"Do you think you could identify the woman you saw? Would you know her if you saw her again?"

"Didn't see her . . . that well."

"Where were you when you saw her?"

Phillip cut his eyes toward me and then swung back to meet Guidry's penetrating gaze. "My window."

"By your window, outside your house?"

"Yes."

"Did the woman see you?"

"I think so . . . she looked . . . over her shoulder . . . jerked . . . like she was . . . surprised."

Guidry's questions had come in rapid-fire sequence. Now he stepped back from the bed.

"Okay, Phillip, thanks. You've been a big help, and I won't make you talk anymore, at least not today."

This time, I was positive I saw fear in Phillip's eyes.

I squeezed his hand. "You just concentrate on healing. By the time you leave for Juilliard, you'll be fine."

He gave me a ghost of a smile, but the fear was still in his eyes.

Guidry was quiet as we walked down the hall toward the elevator. I didn't speak either. Something was bothering me about Phillip's account of what he'd seen that morning. Eyewitnesses are usually uncertain about a lot of details. They change what they say from one time to another, adding some elements and altering others. Phillip hadn't changed a thing. In fact, he had used almost the exact words that he'd used with me. That could either be because he had an unusually vivid recollection, or because he was repeating a rehearsed story.

I said, "It's probably a guy thing, but could you tell the difference between a Miata and some other sports car in the dark?"

"Sure. Why? Do you think the kid's lying?"

"I just wondered about the car."

He didn't answer me, and we got in an elevator full of people and went down without speaking again. In the lobby, he said, "Thanks, Dixie. It was easier for him with you there."

I gave him a half wave and went through the doors to the parking lot, half relieved and half annoyed that he hadn't mentioned the accusations Carl Winnick was making about me. The fact that he hadn't probably meant he hadn't been influenced by them, which was good. But he could have spoken a word of support.

Damn, now I was wanting Guidry to prop up my ego with nice words of encouragement.

I wrenched open the Bronco, flung myself in the seat, gripped the steering wheel, and gave myself a good talking-to. Mostly, that consisted of telling myself that the last thing I needed was to start caring what some man thought about me, and to get my head out of my butt and go take care of the other cats on my schedule.

It was 11:15 by the time I groomed the last cat, and I still hadn't checked on Cora. I was starving, but I knew I couldn't eat until I was sure she was okay. This time, the concierge at Bayfront Village recognized me and called Cora before I got to the desk. We both waited while the phone rang, the concierge counting the rings by little nods of her head while she smiled at me and rolled her eyes toward the ceiling in a show of amused patience. When Cora answered, the concierge said, "You have a visitor down here. Shall I send her up?"

She replaced the phone and said, "She's waiting for you."

From the casual way she acted, I gathered that reporters covering Marilee's murder hadn't yet discovered that Cora was her grandmother. I took the elevator up and found Cora's door open a crack.

I knocked and pushed the door open. "Cora?"

"I'm in here," she called.

I followed her voice, making a right turn

into a short hall that led to a large sunny bedroom. Cora was sitting upright in a bed that looked big enough to play hockey in. She wore a white pleated nightgown with a high collar and long sleeves, and her wispy white hair stuck out in all directions, like a newly hatched chick's.

"I'm sorry, Dixie, I just don't feel like getting up today."

"Well, of course you don't, Cora. Have you had anything to eat?"

"I'm not hungry, dear."

"I know, but you should eat anyway. I'll make you some tea."

I didn't give her a chance to argue, even though I remembered how she felt, throat closed tight with grief, stomach roiling in angry waves, lips compressed to keep from howling like an animal. I filled the teakettle, and while it came to a boil, I found bread and eggs in the refrigerator. I made buttered toast and a poached egg, poured a small glass of juice, and put together a breakfast tray that I carried into the bedroom.

"Oh, Dixie, honey, you didn't need to do that. And anyway, I don't want anything to eat."

I poured a cup of tea and paraphrased what Judy had said to me. "Cora, if you let the slimeball who killed Marilee make you stop living, then he's killed you, too. You need all your strength now to help put him behind bars, so eat the damned breakfast."

Her head jerked up at me, eyes blazing, and then she suddenly laughed. "You know, you're a lot like Marilee. She's bossy, too. Was."

She only picked at the egg, but she ate all the toast and drank the juice. When she was finished, I left the tea things on the tray and washed the dirty plate and glass in the kitchen.

Cora was out of bed when I went back into the bedroom, her bare toes peeking from under her nightie.

"Here," she said, "you can have these. I was saving them to leave to Marilee, but now that she's gone . . ."

She held out a pair of red glass earrings, the kind you see in a jumble of junk jewelry at a garage sale. My eyes misted as I took them. I wouldn't have worn them to a rat-turd exhibit, but I knew they held memories that made them beautiful to her.

"Thank you, Cora. Is there anything I can do for you before I go?"

"No, dear, I'm fine. I'll just rest for a couple of days and then I'll be ready for whatever comes next."

"I'll drop by tomorrow, if that's okay."

"That's fine, Dixie. You're a sweet girl."

I didn't feel so sweet when I drove away. I felt pretty sour, as a matter of fact. Both Phillip and Cora, two people I had come to care about, were going to have to face harsh realities in the coming days and weeks, and it wasn't fair.

It was noon, and I was starving. I don't do too well without food administered prior to 10:00 a.m., preferably with lots of black coffee. I took Tamiami Trail, passing slumbering boats in the marina and following the curve of the waterfront, where large sculptures were lined up like unexpected rib ticklers. I turned right on Osprey and took the north bridge to the key, going straight to Anna's Deli on Ocean Drive, where you can get the best sandwiches in the world.

Halfway to the take-out counter, I realized the couple ahead of me were Dr. Coffey and a young woman with frizzy blond hair hanging halfway to her butt. Her hand was raised to fiddle with a piece of hair at the back of her head, and a diamond the size of a doggy liver treat caught the light — a reminder to the rest of us that being a rich man's bimbo might not get much respect, but it paid well. I turned aside and pretended to study the menu on the blackboard on the side wall while Coffey paid for their sandwiches.

As they walked out, I looked over my shoulder at the woman. She turned full face toward me, and I could see what Judy had meant about her probably being a doper. Glazed eyes with pupils expanded so wide they looked like black holes you could get sucked into, skin slightly sallow under her salon tan, a general look of being lost in some private space. Coffey didn't see me, and he put a proprietary hand on the small of her back to propel her forward.

I went to the counter and ordered baked turkey with tarragon mayonnaise on a pumpernickel roll. "And a big dill pickle and two bags of chips," I said.

The woman at the counter laughed, showing a row of glistening white teeth that went well with her ginger skin and hazel eyes. "You sound like you're hungry."

"I went past hunger a long time ago. Give me a brownie, too. A big one."

"Coffee or tea?"

"Coffee. A triple, black."

She walked to a butcher-block counter in the back and turned in the order to a person of indeterminate sex who had dreadlocks and wore an oversized white shirt. She came back and rang up the sale while I watched the sandwich person slather tarragon mayonnaise on two thick pumpernickel halves.

Keeping my mouth firmly under control to keep from drooling, I handed over some bills and said, "You know that couple that just left?"

"Dr. Coffey? Yeah, he comes in here every week on his day off. Always gets the same thing, ham and Swiss on rye. I don't know how people eat the same thing all the time like that. I like a little variety in my life."

"You know her too?"

She made a mouth and counted out my change. "Not really. Don't want to, neither. Frankly, I don't know what he sees in her."

She leaned over and put her elbows on the counter, ready to get down to the nitty-gritty. "If you ask me, she's bad news for him. He seems like a pretty nice guy, but who wants to have a man cut open your chest and mess with your heart when he's dumb enough to hang out with a junkie like her?"

Personally, I didn't want anybody cutting open my chest and messing with my heart, no matter who they hung out with, but I could see her point.

I said, "That's funny, I've only heard about her two times, and both times people mentioned that she was a junkie."

"Well, you can tell just by looking at her, can't you?"

"You don't think he uses, too?"

"He don't seem the type, you know? That's why it's so weird that he's with her. You'd think he'd have better taste. I mean, that woman is pure trash."

The food-prep person had my sandwich assembled and was slicing it in half. He or she then wrapped it in that gray kind of waxed paper that you never see anyplace except in a deli, giving it a neat fold to keep all the goodies inside. The sandwich went in the bottom of a paper bag, with a dill pickle the size of a man's dick wrapped and placed on top of it. Two bags of chips went in last. I was ready to leap over the counter and snatch it up, but the counter woman must have had eyes in the back of her head, because the second a stack of napkins was thrown in and the bag was neatly folded down, she went and got it.

"Enjoy," she said.

I grabbed the giant-size coffee on the counter and headed for the door. "Thanks a lot," I said. "See you."

That's the nice thing about living on the key. It's small enough that when we say "See you," we really mean it.

25

I drove half a block to the Crescent Beach parking lot, parked under some live oak trees, and jogged to the steps leading to the main pavilion. Ask anybody who lives on Siesta Key and we'll proudly tell you that Crescent Beach was entered in the World Sand Challenge in 1987 and named the finest and whitest sand in the world. Heck, we'll tell you even if you don't ask. We'll also tell you the sand is made of ancient quartz crystal, and that even when the temperature is hot enough to make your brain boil, the sand on Crescent Beach is still cool to your feet. Some people claim the beach has healing properties, and that Siesta Key is one of the energy centers of the planet. I don't know if that's true, but if you live on the key, even if you have surf at your front door like I do, you get a compulsion every now and then to go to Crescent Beach and scuff your bare feet in the sand.

I climbed the steps with my precious deli sack in one hand and coffee in the other, bypassing the vending machines and snack bar and going to a picnic table under the shade of a soaring roof. I put my coffee and deli bag on the table, swung my legs over the bench, and took a seat facing the ocean. Down on the white sand, broiling tourists were laid out like meat on a grill. A few children were splashing around in the waves while their parents sat under umbrellas and watched them.

Except for a young man at a table about ten feet from me, I had the area to myself. He was swarthy and bearded, in dirty cut-offs and a floppy dress shirt with the cuffs suspiciously buttoned. With a faded bandanna tied over a mop of black curls and his eyes hidden behind dark reflective shades, he looked like a wanted poster for a Middle Eastern terrorist. He was staring out at the water and muttering to himself in the way of people who've stopping taking their medication, but he wasn't speaking English, and I couldn't tell if his foreign tongue was an actual language or one he'd invented for his personal world. A canvas bag sat on the pavement at his feet, most likely holding books or food or all his worldly possessions. Or a bomb.

I laid out my lunch like a priest preparing Communion. I unwrapped my sandwich and pickle and opened the chips, placing them at exactly the right spots. Placement of food is important. You don't want the important stuff to be over on the side. The main stuff should be in the upper middle, with accompaniments to the side or slightly below. I've been known to rearrange a plate several times before I get the order just right. Eating in the right order is important, too. First a bite of the main stuff, then one of each of the side things in turn. If you take two bites of something in a row, you'll screw up the whole rhythm. Not that I'm a control freak or anything.

I took a bite of sandwich and closed my eyes, making an *mmmmmmm* sound, like a baby nursing. There is nothing in the world as good as one of Anna's turkey and pumpernickel sandwiches with tarragon mayonnaise. If there were a sandwich hall of fame, it would be in it.

A faint breeze moved the shadowed air, and a couple of black gulls sailed in and landed a few feet away to look hopefully at me. Not to be selfish, I left two little corners of bread for the gulls, tossing it as far away from me as I could so they would move away. They went for it with a loud flutter of wings, and didn't even notice that I also had a brownie. The young man took no notice of me or of the gulls, but continued to look fixedly at the ocean. I was glad he was ignoring me. I much prefer being ignored.

Just as I took the last bite of brownie and was ready to take the last sip of coffee — I plan these things so they work out like that — there was a commotion over in the snack bar area. A security guard trotted past my table to see what was happening, and the young man at the adjoining table got up to walk a few steps away from his table and stare. I half-turned on the bench to look, too, and met the gaze of the bald-headed man who had tried to attack me in the Crab House parking lot. A crowd of people pushed between us, but I was positive it was the same man.

A woman separated herself from a group of passing tourists and walked briskly to the young man's table, where she swooped down and grabbed his canvas bag and walked away with it. The young man kept staring toward the dustup at the snack bar.

I jumped to my feet and yelled, "Hey!"

The woman broke into a run and disappeared down the steps to the parking lot. The security guard had been swallowed up by the crowd in the snack bar, so I stepped over the bench, ready to chase after the woman.

Without looking toward me, the young man stretched his arm out at shoulder level. His hand was clenched in a fist, with the first two fingers stabbing a stern V. Then he turned and walked rapidly away, going toward the beach.

I stopped and turned my gaze back to my own table. Trying to act as if nothing had happened, I gathered up my lunch refuse and carried it to a trash bin. The young man who seemed out of touch with reality was Paco, and he was telling me to butt the hell out. He had just made a drop in a drug sting, and I had almost ruined it.

Whatever had happened over in the snack bar area had apparently been resolved, and the crowd there began to drift away. The bald-headed man had disappeared, and I was left wondering if I had imagined him. Maybe the stress of everything that had happened was making me see danger where there wasn't any. Paco was moving along the edge of the shore, most likely headed toward one of the beach accesses where his Harley would be parked.

I walked to the steps leading to the parking lot and started down, my thoughts swirling with visions of Phillip's beaten face, the bald-headed thug, and the drug sting I'd just witnessed. I was tired. I wanted to go home and take a shower and crawl in bed and let this excess of reality recede a little bit.

On the way home, I swung onto Marilee's street. Jake Anderson, the trauma-scene cleanup guy I had called, was in the driveway next to his big white van with a bio-hazard icon on its side. He and a couple of other men in blue haz-mat suits were just loading their equipment into the truck. They had taken off their headgear but still wore vinyl gloves to their elbows.

I pulled up behind them and stuck my head out the window. Jake grinned and pulled his gloves off and tossed them into the back of the truck.

"All done, Dixie. It'll smell like cherry syrup for a while, but you can go in."

"Okay to take a cat in?"

"Sure."

"Thanks, Jake."

I backed out, knowing the house had been cleaned and sanitized the same way operating rooms are cleaned. Ghost might not like the lingering odor of ozone or the final deodorant fog, but he would be safe from any biological pathogens that are the natural aftereffects of a murder. I turned the corner onto Midnight Pass Road, and at the Graysons' street I saw Sam and Rufus out at their mailbox. I turned and drove to the curb beside them and parked. Sam looked up from a stack of mail with a questioning look, then smiled.

I got out and squatted beside Rufus and exchanged kisses while Sam looked on like an indulgent father.

When I stood up, I said, "Sam, I hope you and Libby haven't lost faith in me because of the things Carl Winnick has been saying."

"Oh good grief, Dixie, of course not! You know, Libby and I were just talking this morning about that, and we think he's off his rocker. His wife drinks, you know. She and Libby belong to the same Great Books club, where they talk about Virginia Woolf or somebody, and she says Olga Winnick has always had a nip or two before they meet. Her husband's on the radio yapping about how wholesome he is, and his wife's a lush."

"I guess you know about their son being attacked."

Sam shook his head. "It makes me sick that I didn't know the boy was lying out there when that man ran by. I thought he'd been trying to break in somebody's house. I never dreamed he had just attacked somebody."

307

"The detective told me Rufus may have saved Phillip's life."

Sam leaned to scratch Rufus behind the ears. "You hear that, boy? You're a hero."

Rufus wagged his tail and grinned modestly, basking in the pride Sam and I were lavishing on him.

I said, "Sam, before you and Libby left last week, did you put a piece of brass pipe at the curb for trash pickup?"

"Yeah, a piece left over after they got the carousel horse up. Why?"

"The cook at the Village Diner works part-time for somebody on this street, or at least she did until last week. She said that she picked up a piece of brass pipe in somebody's trash last Thursday night."

"There was a piece of galvanized steel, too, the pipe they used for lining the brass."

"She didn't mention that, but she said a man drove into the driveway and took the brass pipe away from her. He was pretty nasty about it, and she's hurt and angry. Do you have any idea who he might have been?"

"Drove in *this* driveway?"

"That's what she said. She said he drove a black sports car, but she didn't know who he was."

"I don't know anybody who would have done that, Dixie."

"Do you know anybody who drives a black Miata?"

"I don't think so. Can't think of anybody." Sam was standing like a soldier at attention. "Does this have anything to do with that killing? Do you think that's what the killer used? My brass pipe?"

"I don't know, Sam. It just seems odd for somebody to make a big scene over a piece of pipe that was left at the curb for trash pickup one night, and then the next morning a dead man is found in a neighbor's house with his head bashed in."

Sam winced. "God, that must have been awful for you, Dixie, finding that body."

Apparently, he didn't know I'd found Marilee, too.

I said, "Not as bad as finding Phillip beaten up. That was the worst."

I gave Rufus another hug and got back in the Bronco. "I'll see you, Sam."

He and Rufus watched me drive away, both of them with sad expressions on their faces.

At the meandering driveway to my place, I started to make the turn and then straightened the wheel and drove straight ahead. There was one more thing I had to do before I went home.

The Crab House doesn't open until five

o'clock, so there were only a few cars at the far end of the lot, probably belonging to cooks or staff. I parked by the front door and crunched over loose oyster shell. The door was locked, and when I rapped on it, a young Latino with liquid black eyes and a scraggly attempt at a goatee opened it a crack and peered out.

"We're not open," he said.

"I know, I'm here to see your manager. One of your employees has been badly hurt."

His eyes rounded and he looked uncertainly over his shoulder.

"I don't know," he said. I wasn't sure if he meant he didn't know what to do about me, or if he meant he hadn't understood what I'd said.

"I have to come in," I said.

He shrugged and opened the door wider, stepping aside with a shy smile as I passed him. A slight blond man in the waiters' uniform of black trousers and white shirt was putting little vases of flowers on the tables. He saw me and stopped what he was doing, looking at me with a question on his face.

"Can I help you?"

"Are you the manager?"

"He's not here right now. Did you want to apply for a job?"

"No, I wanted to tell him — you — something."

I walked closer to him and saw a name tag reading RAY. I said, "Ray, Phillip Winnick was beaten up Sunday morning on his way home."

"Who?"

"Phillip, the young man who plays piano."

"Oh my God! Phil?"

"I found him near his house early yesterday morning. He was in pretty bad shape. He's in the hospital now."

He sat down at a table and stared up at me, the implications of what I was telling him playing over his face.

I took a chair across from him and said, "Do you know who Phil leaves with when you close?"

His face tightened and he shook his head. "Nobody here would have done that. Nobody who knows Phil would have done that. Everybody who knows him likes him."

"I'm not suggesting that the person he leaves with was the one who beat him up. I'd just like to talk to him, find out if he saw anybody around when he dropped Phil off."

The door opened and the bartender from Saturday night walked in, going straight to the bar and beginning to set out bottles and glasses. He was a tall, bookish-looking man with rimless round glasses and a frieze of short beard around his cheeks and chin. Except for shirtsleeves that bulged with muscles, he reminded me of a chemistry teacher I'd had in high school setting out Bunsen burners and vials of smelly chemicals.

Ray got up and went over to the bar and spoke quietly to him. The bartender turned and looked at me with a frown, then recognized me. He put down the towel he was using to polish a wineglass and came over to shake my hand.

"I remember you," he said. "You're Phil's friend. I'm Dennis."

"Dixie Hemingway, Dennis. The reason I'm here is that Phil's been beaten up. I want to find out who did it."

26

Ray said, "I was just telling her nobody from here would have hurt Phil."

I said, "I think Phil leaves here with somebody who takes him home. I'd like to talk to whoever that is. He may have seen somebody in the area yesterday morning."

Dennis got the impassive look that people take on when they have information they don't want to divulge.

"Look," I said, "I'm not a cop. I'm not here in any official capacity. I'm just Phil's friend, and whatever this person told me would just be between him and me."

Dennis and the waiter exchanged a wary look. I completely understood their reluctance. Phillip and his unknown friend were gay. Phillip was still in the closet, and the other man might be, as well. To give me the man's name was not only to involve him in a crime, but to out him. Given the level of hysterical homophobia that still exists in this country, with its coy "Don't ask, don't tell" silliness, no ethical or responsible person would do that.

Dennis said, "Tell you what I'll do, if I see somebody I think might have given Phil a ride, I'll tell him you're looking for him. If he knows anything, he can give you a call. How's that?"

His voice was smooth and friendly, but I knew he would close me out if I pushed. That's all I was going to get.

I stood up and put my hand on his arm. "Thanks. I appreciate that Phil's a good kid, and I'm really upset about this."

Ray whipped out an order pad and I wrote my name and business phone number on the back of a slip.

I nodded good-bye to them and started for the door. Behind me, Dennis called out, "Hey, I just remembered something. You know that bald-headed guy that tried to hit on you the other night? He was back last night, and he asked about you."

I turned and stared at him. "About me?"

"Yeah. He wanted to know if you came here often. I told him I didn't know you."

"Did he know my name?"

Dennis grinned. "He just called you the blonde bitch."

"That guy's bad news. He chased me in the parking lot that night. I barely got in my car in time."

"You call the cops?"

"No. I just went home. I guess I should have."

"Damn right you should have. I'll pass the word about him."

I started to leave again, then turned back. "Does he come here often?"

"Never saw him before that night when you were here."

"When he came back, did he try to hit on any other woman?"

"Not that I noticed. He stayed at the bar by himself, left when we closed."

"Okay. I just wondered."

I went outside and got back in the Bronco, wondering why the man had picked me out to try to pick up. Or stalk.

I finally left the *whoosh* of traffic and drove under a blessed quiet canopy of green oak branches to my apartment. When I rounded the last curve, I saw Paco in front of the carport. Still in disguise, he was holding a man to the ground with one hand while he held a phone to his ear with the other.

I pulled into the carport and got out.

Paco snapped his phone closed and flashed a white grin up at me. "Got a friend of yours here, Dixie."

The man was facedown with his hands

cuffed behind him. His head was smooth and shiny as a dolphin's, and his piggy black eyes were spitting venom.

I said, "He's been following me. He chased me at the Crab House the other night and he was at the beach this morning."

Paco took one of the man's ears and twisted it. "How come you're following the lady, *pendejo?*"

"Fuck you, asshole!"

"Don't you wish."

Paco got to his feet and put one foot on the man's butt to hold him down. "I'll let you in on a little secret, amigo. The lady used to be a deputy, and she's still got a lot of friends in the department, and they're gonna be real mad when they find out you've been stalking her. They may decide to dump you in the surf and let the sand crabs crawl in your eyes."

Any other time, I would have enjoyed listening to Paco pretend to be a zonked-out bum who had no connection to law enforcement, but I hadn't had a shower all day and I knew company was coming.

I said, "Excuse me, I'll be right back."

I ran upstairs and took a two-minute shower. Just as I was pulling on underpants, I heard tires crunching the shelled driveway. I shimmied into a short skirt and T, stepped into sandals, ran lipstick over my mouth, and sprinted for the French doors.

Downstairs, Paco stood on one side of the downed man, and Lieutenant Guidry stood on the other. Guidry said, "Dixie, I'd like you to meet Bull Banks, a freelance thug who'll do anything for a buck. He was recently released from one of our penal hotels for beating up an elderly couple."

Paco said, "I was just asking him nicely to tell us who hired him to attack the kid."

Bull said, "I don't know what you're talking about. What kid?"

Guidry said, "Bull, it's not like it was when you started your career. Now we've got all kinds of technologies. When wc get DNA results from what we found on Phillip Winnick, I think we'll find that you're our man."

"Don't give me that shit. You gotta have hair or something for a DNA test."

"Oh, we can use lots of things. Little skin cells from your fists maybe."

"Fists! Ha, that's a good one."

"Oh yeah, we got good skin cells from your knuckles, Bull. Little knuckle cells were all over the kid's face."

"Didn't use my fists!"

Guidry and Paco exchanged looks and grinned. Just at the instant I realized they knew each other, Bull Banks realized he'd just made a tactical error.

"You can't prove a fucking thing! Anyway, the kid's a goddamn queer!"

My head exploded, and the next thing I knew, I was on top of Bull Banks like a rodeo cowgirl, using his ears to slam his face in the sand and yelling words at him that would have made my grandmother ground me for a year. I didn't know how long I'd been on him, but Bull was howling and sputtering and choking from all the sand in his mouth and nose and eyes. From the looks of his face, I'd been at him long enough to cause him some serious discomfort.

Paco pried my hands off Bull's ears, and Guidry hooked an arm under my waist and lifted me up. Guidry was grinning, and when they stood me on my feet, he kept one arm around me to keep me from falling on Bull again. I kicked Bull in the ribs and yelled, "Who paid you to beat him up? You tell me who, or so help me God, I'll kick your teeth down your throat!"

It felt so good to kick him that I kept doing it.

Bull yelled, "Stop it, bitch!"

Guidry said, "Now Bull, that's not a nice way to talk to a lady, especially when she's going to press charges against you for stalking her. When they add that to attacking the Winnick kid, you'll get the 'three times and you're out' life sentence. If you're nice to Ms. Hemingway, she might be persuaded to forget about the fact you've been stalking her."

Paco said, "The way you're protecting him, you must be a good friend of whoever hired you."

I turned at the sound of a marked squad car scrunching over the shell toward us. A uniformed deputy got out and took in the scene. When I turned my head back, Paco had disappeared.

Guidry spoke to the deputy. "This is Mr. Bull Banks. He needs to be Mirandized and taken in for the assault of Phillip Winnick."

The deputy nodded and hauled Bull to his feet. Guidry touched the small of my back with his fingertips and said, "Let's go upstairs and talk."

Feeling more surreal by the moment, I climbed the stairs ahead of Guidry. At the porch, he turned the umbrella in the table so it shaded us from the midday sun. "Sit down, and I'll get us something to drink."

I sat as if I were a guest and he was the one who lived in my apartment. He went inside as if he owned the place, and in a minute he came out carrying two bottles of water from my fridge. He sat down in the chair opposite me, unscrewed the cap on his water, and took a long drink. When he put the bottle on the table, his eyes were calm and expectant.

I said, "Do you think Bull killed Frazier and Marilee?"

"We'll look into where Bull was Thursday night, but I doubt he's our man. Not that Bull couldn't be bought to do it, I just don't think he did."

"He's the man who was at the Crab House Saturday night before I talked to Phillip, the one who chased me in the parking lot. This afternoon, he was watching me at the pavilion at Crescent Beach. He must have left about the same time I did, but I stopped by Marilee's house and the Graysons' on the way home, so he got here first. I think he was here yesterday, too. Somebody broke into my brother's house and then into my apartment upstairs. They left sandy footprints, and whoever it was drove a car down the drive."

"Any idea why he's stalking you?"

"He could have seen me talking to Phillip, I guess. I thought he'd left, but he could have come back without me seeing him. If the woman Phillip saw knew he was watching her, and if Bull had anything to do with killing Frazier and Marilee, he may have followed Phillip to the Crab House, intending to kill him. Then he saw Phillip talking to me and guessed he was telling me about the woman, so he decided he had to kill me, too."

"If he was going to kill you, why didn't he kill Phillip?"

"Because Rufus sensed what was going on and barked. That scared him away. Do you know what kind of car he drives? Is it a black Miata?"

"Bull might drive a *stolen* Miata, but he doesn't own a car."

"He must have had a car that night, because he probably waited in the Crab House parking lot and followed Phillip when he left. Then he followed him again when his lover drove him to that spot and let him out of the car."

Guidry rotated his water bottle on the table. "That's where your theory breaks down, Dixie. Bull's the type who would beat the kid up just because he's gay. It may not have anything at all to do with the murders."

"Then why was he after me?"

"You turned him down at the bar, and you chatted up a gay guy. In Bull's world, that's plenty of reason to hurt you."

"Guidry, you know Sam Grayson? The

man whose dog barked and scared Bull away when he was beating Phillip? The dog's name is Rufus. Well, Sam put a piece of brass pipe at the curb before he left town last Thursday night for the trash people to pick up Friday morning. A little piece about two feet long. Tanisha saw it when she was walking to the bus stop, and she picked it up."

"Tanisha?"

"The cook at the Village Diner. She'd been cooking for somebody on the Graysons' street, and she saw the pipe and got it. She said a man drove in the Graysons' driveway and took it away from her, sort of accusing her of stealing it. *And* he drove a black car that may have been a Miata."

For a second, Guidry looked like he needed to put his head between his knees and take deep breaths.

"And you think . . ."

"Maybe that was Bull. Maybe he used the pipe to kill Frazier and Marilee."

"He got inspired when he saw the pipe and decided to go kill somebody with it?"

"You have to admit it's a strange co-incidence."

"Somebody had to have a damn good reason for killing Harrison Frazier and Marilee Doerring, and unless we turn up some compelling evidence, I don't think Bull Banks had anything to gain by their deaths."

"Somebody could have hired him."

"Yeah, but who?"

"Shuga Reasnor said Gerald Coffey wouldn't kill them himself, but that he might hire somebody."

"That's just gossip, Dixie."

"Guidry, you didn't just meet Paco for the first time today, did you?"

"Who?"

"Paco, the guy downstairs, the one who called your private line when he caught Bull Banks."

"Is that his name? Nobody introduced us."

The guileless look he gave me would have fooled the most confirmed cynic, but it didn't fool me.

"Dixie, before you arrived at Marilee Doerring's house and found Harrison Frazier, where had you been?"

My heart skipped a beat. "Why are you asking me that? Do you believe that crap Winnick is saying?"

"That's irrelevant, Dixie. Where had you been?"

"I told you that before. I walked the Graysons' dog about four-thirty, and then

Billy Elliot, the greyhound at the Sea Breeze. After that, I went to a house to take care of a cat. Marilee's was my second cat of the morning."

My voice was tight and curt. I couldn't believe Guidry was asking me for an alibi.

He said, "Any humans see you? Anybody who can verify that you were where you say you were?"

I could feel my jaws clenching and my hands making fists. If there's anything I pride myself on, it's honesty. Having my honesty questioned was like jabbing me with a sharp stick to see how much pain I could take.

"That's the whole point of my work, Lieutenant. I wouldn't be going to those houses if people were home. Tom Hale was home, but he was still in bed."

"He lives where?"

"At the Sea Breeze, with Billy Elliot."

"The greyhound."

"Yeah."

"Besides Tom Hale, nobody else saw you that morning?"

"I don't know, Guidry, I guess somebody could have seen me, but I don't know who."

"Okay."

I stared at him a moment, feeling a confused mixture of anger that he'd asked me for an alibi, and a rational understanding that he was just doing his job.

I said, "This has been really fun, Lieutenant, but I need to take a nap so I'll be awake for my afternoon pet visits."

He stood and handed me his empty water bottle. "Thanks for the refreshments."

I watched him walk down my steps and then went inside and lowered the storm shutters against the glaring western sun. Amazingly, I was fairly calm. A year earlier, I might have curled up in a corner and sucked my thumb if in one ninety-six-hour period I'd found two murdered bodies, been accosted by a psycho in a parking lot, been vilified on radio by a radical hatemonger, stumbled on a kid I liked a lot who'd been badly beaten, and had a homicide detective question me as if I were a possible murder suspect. Now I was just pissed. A little jumpy, true, but mostly pissed.

It was true that I needed a nap, but first I went in my closet-office and checked my messages. One was from somebody named Ethan Crane, who claimed to be Marilee's lawyer but was probably a reporter trying to trick me.

"I need to speak to you about Miss Doerring's will," he said. "Please call me as soon as possible."

"Yeah, sure," I said. There was absolutely no reason why an attorney would need to talk to me about Marilee Doerring's will, and reporters will stoop to anything to get an interview.

I went in the bedroom, kicked off my Keds, and fell on the bed, lying with my toes pointed toward the ceiling like a body in rigor mortis. I wanted to be in the hammock on the porch, but now I didn't feel safe to sleep out there. Some creep like Bull Banks could sneak up the stairs and stand looking down at me sprawled out with my mouth open and drool running down my chin. A reporter could tiptoe upstairs and take photographs of me and run it with the caption "Is she a murderess being coddled by the Sheriff's Department?"

I got up and looked up the name Ethan Crane in the phone book. There really was an attorney by that name. The phone number was the same, too, but that didn't mean the call was legitimate.

I padded barefoot to the French doors and looked through the square glass panes. The sky was a clear and innocent blue. A young snowy egret stood one-legged on the porch railing, his yellow beak pointing upward and his raised foot invisible in his underfeathers. A soft breeze gently ruffled his fine feathers, and he seemed to be smiling. Why not? He didn't have to worry about reporters or public opinion or homicidal thugs.

I went back to my office-closet and dialed Ethan Crane's number. A receptionist answered in a nasal singsong: "Ethan Crane's office."

I gave my name and said, "I'm returning Mr. Crane's call."

She immediately put me through, which told me two things: She had been told to be on the lookout for my call and Ethan Crane wasn't very busy.

His voice was a smooth burr. "Ms. Hemingway, thanks for calling. I'm sure you're aware that Marilee Doerring is dead. We need to meet and discuss her will."

"Why?"

"That's what we need to discuss. I'd rather not get into it over the phone, but you are one of the principals named in the will."

I shook my head like a boxer taking one punch too many. "Mr. Crane, I hardly knew Marilee Doerring. I take care of her cat when she goes out of town, but that's my only involvement with her."

"Can you come to my office?"

Still dazed, I said, "When?"

"How about right now?"

I still felt like I was being set up for something, but I told him I'd be there in fifteen minutes. To make myself feel more like a grown-up, I put on a white linen skirt with a toast-colored cropped top. I put on high-heeled sandals, too. If you're going to match wits with a lawyer, you need to stand tall and stick your tits out.

27

Ethan Crane's office was in a narrow building on a side street in the cluttered business section of the key. The building was old and crumbling, set so close to the sidewalk that dark fingerprints and smudges from palms and shoulders spotted it. Down at ground level, chunks of stucco had flaked off like scabs from an old sore. The doorway was recessed in an alcove lined with wooden benches like church pews, on which a vagrant and a couple of tourists too tired to go on sat mutely staring at one another.

Old gilt paint on the glass door had faded so the words ETHAN CRANE ESQ., ATTORNEY AT LAW were barely discernable. Feeling like a character in a gothic novel, I pushed the door open and went up a flight of worn wooden steps rising from the linoleum-floored vestibule. Why in the ever-lovin' blue-eyed world would a woman like Marilee Doerring choose an attorney in a dump like this?

At the top of the stairs, a door stood open

at the far end of a wide oaken landing, with two closed doors on either side. A man sat at a desk watching my approach. He wore a white shirt with the sleeves rolled up, and a dark tie that had been loosened and thrown over one shoulder. He stood up, rearranging himself with amazing speed and grace, so that by the time he was fully erect, his tie was hanging true and knotted firmly under his collar, and his shirt cuffs were buttoned. He was fortyish, ruddy-complected, and extraordinarily good-looking. The reason for Marilee's choice of attorneys might not be so mysterious after all, I realized.

He said, "Ms. Hemingway?"

I nodded and we shook hands. He had a nice handshake, not the sweaty clasp I'd have expected from somebody in such a sleazy office. He was also a lot younger than the aged sign on the door had led me to expect. He gestured to a leather chair with a seat hollowed and darkened by decades of rear ends. I sat down and crossed my legs, giving the room's drab walls and musty bookshelves a quick once-over. I hadn't spoken yet, and that seemed to amuse him.

Before he sat down, he leaned forward to hand me a brown leather folder, and I caught a whiff of lime and musk and sweet cigar.

He said, "I think this will clear up some of your questions."

He leaned back in his chair with his hands clasped behind his head and watched me. Like a blind woman expecting Braille, I ran my fingertips over the folder before I opened it. It had a grainy texture like painted-over grit. Slowly, I opened it and read the heading on the first page: "The Marilee Doerring Living Trust."

The first few pages were standard explanations for a revocable living trust, and I skimmed through them quickly. Florida probate laws are so complicated and expensive that most Floridians have revocable living trusts instead of wills. A revocable living trust holds whatever assets a person chooses to put in it until the person either dies or revokes the trust. If it hasn't been revoked when the person dies, an assigned trustee carries out the wishes expressed in the trust without having to pay probate fees or being under the constraint of a court's supervision.

After the explanatory section, there was a quitclaim deed to Marilee's house, and then four more pages of legal explanation. On page five, under a section headed "Trust Income and Principal Distribution," were instructions for the trustee in the event of

Marilee's death. Mainly, the instructions specified that all listed assets were under the control of the trustee, to sell or maintain as the trustee saw fit, for the benefit of the named beneficiary. Listed assets were Marilee's house, her car, and all personal possessions within the house.

I was named trustee.

The beneficiary was Ghost.

At Ghost's death, any remaining assets would go to me.

I looked up at the attorney and caught his amused look.

"This can't be right," I said. "What about Marilee's grandmother?"

"Ms. Doerring had a separate irrevocable trust set up for her grandmother," he said, "fully funded with enough to take care of her for the rest of her life. The revocable trust for the cat will hold up, don't worry."

"I'm not worried! I don't want it. I don't want Ghost, and I don't want the responsibility of handling all that money."

He shrugged. "Sorry. You've got it anyway. The cat and the money."

"Can she just do that? Without asking me?"

"Can and did," he said.

"Can I refuse it?"

"Yes. If you refuse, everything in the trust reverts to the state."

"Including the cat?"

"Including the cat."

I shuddered. That was pretty much the same thing as saying the cat would be euthanized.

"When did you draw this up?"

He pointed at the folder. "It's dated there. I didn't draw it up, my grandfather did. He passed away a few months ago, and I've taken over his practice. I never met Ms. Doerring."

I flipped some pages to find the date the trust had been signed. It had been a little over a year before, shortly after I'd begun taking care of Ghost when Marilee went out of town, when Ghost had been still a kitten.

"You're not Ethan Crane?"

"I am, but not the same Ethan Crane who drew up that document."

He really was a handsome man, and it annoyed me that I was aware of that, especially when I was seeing my life pass before my eyes like somebody going down for the third time.

He leaned across the desk and clasped his palms together. "Look, it's not as bad as it sounds. There are no bank accounts involved, no stocks or bonds or cash other than what's in the house. You've got complete power of attorney, so you can do whatever you want to with the house, the car, the jewelry, whatever her personal possessions were. If you want to, you can move into the house with the cat and use the car and everything else as if it's your own. If you don't want to do that, put the house on the market and let an estate-liquidation company sell the rest of it. So long as you see that the cat's well cared for until it dies a natural death, you can do whatever you want to with the assets in the trust. It's a pretty sweet deal."

I could feel my lower lip creeping out like a sulky four-year-old's, and I felt like throwing myself on the floor and kicking and screaming. A healthy, happy, active cat can live twenty years or more, and Ghost was less than two. The last thing I wanted was to complicate my life for the next twenty years with a dependent. I didn't want Ghost for my own. When Michael and I were growing up, we'd always had pets, but I didn't want a pet now. Owning a pet requires a commitment. It forces you to have a close relationship with a living being with needs and feelings. I didn't want to make that kind of commitment. I didn't want a close relationship with anybody, no matter how many legs he had.

I stood up. "What do I do now?"

He rose to his feet and held out his hand. "Whatever you want to do. That's the beauty of a living trust. You're the trustee, and that's that. Get a death certificate from the Sheriff's Department, and then all you need is the power of attorney in that folder."

His hand felt so warm that I knew my own must be frigid. I tucked the folder under my arm and walked out of his office like a condemned woman on her way to the execution chamber. I could feel him watching me, and for a humiliating moment I hoped my butt looked good.

In a bemused daze, I drove home. Michael's car was still gone, but Paco's Harley was under the carport. More than likely, he was in bed catching up on lost sleep from whatever job he'd been doing — a job that had involved a drug sting at Crescent Beach. I might never know what had been in the canvas bag I'd seen a woman pick up because Paco's life could depend on my not knowing. I accepted that the same way I had accepted department secrets that Todd hadn't told me. It comes with having detectives and undercover cops in the family.

What I didn't accept was what I'd just learned from Ethan Crane.

I kicked off the heels and changed clothes again, pulling on a clean pair of shorts and a sleeveless T. My brain was screaming for sleep, but I was too disturbed to lie down and shut my eyes. I stripped my bed and threw the sheets in the washer with some towels and dirty clothes. While the washer chugged away my body's cells and scents, I attacked the bathroom like an avenging Fury until every square inch sparkled and smelled of bleach. I love the smell of chlorine bleach. Breathing it makes me feel I'm cleaning my brain of old gunk while I'm destroying germs and stains. By the time I put the last polishing rub on the sink's water spigot, I felt cleaner inside, as if all the images of violence and ugliness of the last few days had been polished away.

I padded barefoot to the office-closet and read the living trust again. It still said the same thing. I was now Ghost's legal keeper, and I had complete control over Marilee's house, her car, and eveything in her house.

Boy-howdy.

Whoop-de-do.

Shit.

My office phone rang and I froze, waiting for the answering machine to click on. It was a man, and not a voice I recognized. This one was sure to be a reporter. He said, "I called before. I'd like to talk to you, Miss Hemingway."

I made a face at the phone and said, "I'll just bet you would!"

Then he said, "I got your name from Ray at the Crab House," and I snagged the phone before he could hang up.

"Hello, this is Dixie."

"I'm calling about Phil. Do you know how he is?"

"He's going to be all right, I think. He has some broken ribs and a broken nose, but he's not terribly hurt."

"His hands?"

"His hands weren't hurt. I think he must have tucked them under his arms to protect them."

"Oh God."

"Yeah. His head was totally uncovered. But it could have been a lot worse. A dog started barking and the attacker ran away."

"I've called the hospital several times, but they wouldn't tell me anything."

I said, "Did you drive Phil home yesterday morning?"

I could hear a quick intake of air, and for a moment I was afraid he wasn't going to answer.

He said, "Phil told me about you. He likes

you. He said you weren't going to out him to his folks."

"I wouldn't have either."

"Do they know yet?"

"I really don't know what they know. Look, could we meet and talk someplace?"

There was another long pause and then he sighed. "Do you think it would help Phil?"

"I don't know. It might, and it certainly won't hurt him."

"Where would you like to meet?"

"How about Bayfront Park in twenty minutes?"

"How will I know you?"

"I'll be the blonde sitting on a bench facing the waterfront. You can't miss me."

"Okay."

Almost exactly twenty minutes later, I drove under the arched entrance to Bayfront Park, a hiccup of land jutting into Sarasota Bay. I parked in a space facing the bay and followed the sidewalk that curves around the park. Bayfront Park had been Christy's favorite place in the whole world. She and I had spent a lot of time at the Steigerwaldt-Jockey Children's Fountain, her favorite, and we'd both loved the wonderful flying dolphins on the Dolphin Fountain.

Benches line the walkway, and on any day people are sitting on them, mesmerized by the view of Sarasota Bay. I found an empty one and plunked myself down and waited. A thin young man in chinos and a white knit shirt turned from where he'd been standing looking out at the moored boats, then looked around to see if anybody was with me. After a minute or two, he walked toward me. He was younger than I'd expected, twenty-two maybe, and had pale skin that wasn't well acquainted with sunshine. His hair was sandy brown above dark sunglasses that I suspected were worn more to hide his eyes than to shield them from the sun.

He stopped in front of me and said, "Miss Hemingway?"

"It's Dixie," I said, and put out my hand.

He had a nice handshake, firm and dry. He sat down beside me and said, "I'm Greg."

I nodded, wondering if it was his real name.

"Greg, I appreciate your meeting with me. I'm just trying to help find out who hurt Phil."

He took a deep breath, the way people do when they've been holding their breath, and gave a shaky laugh. "I don't know why I'm so nervous."

"You don't know me from Adam," I said. "Of course you're nervous."

He grinned and nodded. "I guess you'd like to know how I know Phil."

"If you don't mind telling me."

"We met at summer music camp a couple of years ago. I was a counselor, and Phil and I just hit it off. When I graduated from Juilliard, I got a job with the Sarasota Symphony Orchestra and looked Phil up. I'm a violist."

"Do all you musicians go to Juilliard?"

He smiled. "No, just some of us."

"Juilliard's very important to Phillip's mother."

"I know. I think that's the main reason he's going there. He says she's had her heart set on Juilliard for him since he first started playing piano."

"You think he's just going to please her?"

"Not completely. But he'd like to do something that would make her happier. He feels protective toward her. From what he says, she's pretty depressed. Phil's her whole life."

"I'd been thinking you two might have met at the Crab House."

He laughed. "No, that place is too noisy for me."

"But you do go there and pick Phillip up when he's through playing?"

He colored. "We have a late supper and spend some time together, then I take him home. Well, not home exactly. I take him to that spot where you found him there on Midnight Pass Road. He walks the rest of the way home."

"Had you ever noticed anybody there at that time? An early jogger maybe, or somebody walking a dog?"

"Never. There's never a soul out at that hour."

"Somebody was there yesterday. Did you see anybody then?"

He shook his head. "He must have been hiding in the trees and grabbed Phil after I left."

"Did you see a car parked on the side of the street? Anything?"

"Nothing. Absolutely nothing."

"Greg, do you know anybody who drives a black Miata?"

"I don't think so."

"When you go to pick Phil up at the Crab House, have you ever seen a bald-headed man hanging out in the parking lot?"

He frowned and took off his glasses. He had intelligent green eyes, and without his glasses, he looked no older than Phillip.

"You know, I *have* seen a man like that. I noticed him the first time because he was standing next to a car, looking into it like he might be thinking about breaking into it. When I drove up, he walked off and went around the corner to the side of the building. Then I saw him again a couple of nights later. He was just leaning against the wall near the front door like he was waiting for something. Not like he was waiting for some*body,* but for some*thing,* like something to happen. Why? Was that who beat Phil up?"

"It might be. Somebody in the neighborhood saw a bald-headed man running along beside the woods right after Phillip was attacked."

"Do you think he was hanging around the Crab House to watch for Phil?"

"I think he might have been, yes."

"But why?"

"Greg, has Phillip talked to you about the murder that happened in the house next door to him?"

"A little."

"He saw a woman come out of the house on the morning the murder was committed. I think somebody wants to make sure he doesn't tell who the woman was. Do you have any idea who it might have been?"

He looked shocked. "He hasn't said a word about it."

His surprise seemed genuine, and so was mine. I thought Phillip would have confided that secret.

Greg said, "You know, he's been awfully quiet since that happened. Maybe that's why."

"Quiet?"

"Withdrawn, not himself. I was afraid it was something to do with us, but maybe it was because of the murder."

"Did he mention seeing a black Miata next door?"

He shook his head. "I can't remember anything about a Miata ever coming up. All he said about the murder was that you'd found a dead man in the next-door neighbor's house and took the woman's cat over to his house to stay for a while. He said his mother was annoyed because she not only hates the woman, she hates cats. That's when I understood what a cold woman his mother must be. I know some people like dogs better than cats, but to *hate* cats?"

I studied him for a minute. He had a kind, intelligent face that I liked. "You have a cat?"

"Not anymore. I left her with my mother when I went off to school, and now they've bonded and Mom won't let me move her. Actually, she was supposed to be the family cat when we got her, but she sort of adopted me, and after awhile the whole family thought of her as my cat. She got really depressed when I left for college, but my mother spent a lot of time with her and she got over it. We got her when I was eight, so she's pretty old now."

"Maybe it's time for you to get another cat, one that's all your own."

"I've thought about it, but I'll have to wait until I can afford one. You know, the vet bills and the food and all. I still have a school loan to pay, so it may be a few years before I can take on that kind of responsibility."

The more I knew about this young man, the better I liked him.

"Greg, if Phillip knows who the killer is, his life is in danger. I don't want to alarm you, but if the killer has seen you and Phillip together, he may think Phillip told you what he knows. Until this whole thing is over, make sure you're not alone in a secluded spot."

He gave me a wide-eyed stare. "I can't believe all this is happening."

"It should be over soon. Just be careful."

28

Greg and I promised to stay in touch, and I left him staring out at Sarasota Bay. For the next couple of hours, I was too busy with my afternoon pet visits to think about everything that had happened. To tell the truth, I was on sensory overload. I couldn't take in much more. The wonder was that I had been able to withstand as much as I had. I took it as a good sign. I must have gotten stronger without even knowing it.

It was almost sunset when I got to Tom Hale's apartment and ran with Billy Elliot. When we got back upstairs and I took his leash off, I went into the kitchen and sat down at the table where Tom was pushing buttons on a calculator and writing numbers on a form of some kind. He gave me a puzzled look over his glasses, and then laid down his pen.

"What's wrong, Dixie?"

"Tom, did you know that Marilee Doerring had a living trust that left her house to her cat?"

He did one of those blinking head jerks that people do when they hear something shocking, and then he laughed.

"I didn't know it, but I'm not surprised. She had a kind heart."

"You were her CPA. How come you didn't know that?"

"Because it had nothing to do with how she paid taxes."

I picked up a pencil on the table and studied it intently. Nice point. No teeth marks.

I said, "She made me trustee."

"Why is it that I don't think you're happy about that?"

"Because it sucks, that's why. I don't want that responsibility, Tom. I don't want the house, I don't want the car, I don't want the cat. I don't think it's fair that she could just dump it on me without my permission."

I sounded a lot like Shuga Reasnor, but it was how I felt.

"Being trustee doesn't mean you have to take care of the cat personally. You can hire somebody else to do it. There must be a thousand people right here in Sarasota who would jump at the chance to move into that house and take care of the cat for you. Hell, if I didn't think Billy Elliot would be jealous, I'd do it."

Hearing that affected my brain like I'd just had a slug of double-caffeine coffee.

"Are you sure?"

"Absolutely. You're only responsible for seeing that her wishes are carried out. You don't have to take on each responsibility personally."

"Will you take care of all the financial stuff for me?"

"Sure. You decide what you want to do and how you want it done, and I'll take care of it. I'll pay myself a fee from the estate. I'd recommend that you sell that Ferrari right away. I can handle that for you."

I was feeling better and better. Maybe Marilee hadn't played a dirty trick on me after all. Except that a lot of people would consider having the trust a huge bonanza for me. A lot of people might also think I had known about the trust all along. A lot of people might consider it a motive for murder.

When I left Tom, I drove to Bayfront Village. The woman at the front desk saw me when I came in the door and immediately picked up the phone to call Cora. Cora must have answered on the first ring, because the woman waved me on before I got to her desk.

"She's waiting for you," she chirped, as if

my visit were a magnificent gift. I suppose in a retirement home, all visitors are considered a magnificent gift.

Cora had opened her door a crack again, and I rapped on it with my knuckles and pushed it open. No lights were burning, and the apartment had the dreary look of space where sunlight had recently withdrawn its warmth. Cora was sitting in a wing-back chair by the glass doors to the sunporch, still in her nightgown, her wispy white hair sticking up in the gloom like apparitional floss. I switched on a lamp and sat down in a chair at an angle to her. Neither of us said anything for several minutes, just sat there in the half-lit room and breathed in and out.

After awhile, Cora sighed. "They say God never gives us more than we can handle, but sometimes I think God has overestimated what I can take."

I said, "Have you eaten anything since this morning?"

She looked startled, as if the idea itself was foreign. "Well, hon, I don't remember if I did or not."

I got up and went in the little kitchen, switching on fluorescent lights that made harsh reflections on the white countertops. I found a can of vegetable soup, and while it heated, I made a pot of tea and got out cups and saucers for two. I poured the soup into a pretty blue pottery bowl, added crackers and butter, and carried the supper tray to the living room.

Cora eyed the tray with a flicker of interest. "There's a TV tray behind the sofa there," she said. I put the tray down on a lamp table and looked behind the sofa, where a wooden TV tray was folded flat. I pulled it out and set it up in front of Cora's chair, put a napkin in her lap, and arranged her meager meal.

"You'd make a good waitress," she said.

I poured myself a cup of tea and sat down and watched her take a few tentative spoonfuls.

"It's good," she said. "I didn't think I was hungry, but I guess I am."

For a few minutes, the only sound was the click of spoon against bowl and Cora's faint slurping noises. She ate the entire bowl of soup and several buttered crackers before she pronounced herself full.

I removed the TV tray and poured us both another cup of tea. Her color was better now and her eyes had lost some of their stunned dullness.

I said, "Cora, do you know an attorney named Ethan Crane?"

"Well, I did, Dixie, but Ethan's been gone now for a good while, a year maybe. Did you know him, too?"

"No, but his grandson called me today and asked me to stop by his office. It seems he has taken over Mr. Crane's practice. His name is also Ethan Crane. Do you know the grandson?"

"No, I can't say as I do. He's taken over Ethan's practice?"

"That's what he said. He had a living trust that his grandfather had drawn up for Marilee. Do you know about that?"

She frowned. "A living what?"

"A trust. It's a kind of will. According to the younger Mr. Crane, Marilee had two trusts, one for you and this other one that he talked to me about. Do you know about the trust she set up for you?"

"Oh my, yes, I know all about it. I have a copy of it. It's personal, dear, so I won't tell you what's in it, but I won't ever have to worry about running out of money."

Her face crumpled and she sobbed quietly with her hands over her face. I waited, knowing that tears would come like that for a while, just spring out when she least expected them, as if there were a well of tears inside her that had to pour out on their own time. When she was cried out, I got up and got Kleenex for her from the bathroom and sat back down.

"Cora, the trust that Mr. Crane wanted to talk to me about was different from the one Marilee had for you. This one was for her cat."

Cora stared at me wide-eyed. "Her cat?"

"The cat that I take care of when Marilee leaves town. His name is Ghost. She made this trust about a year ago, right after I started taking care of him. I didn't know anything about it until Mr. Crane told me, but she put her house and car and everything in her house in this trust."

Cora looked as if she was about to smile. "For her cat?"

I nodded. "For her cat. And she named me the trustee."

Cora put her head back against the chair and laughed. Then she looked at me. "This is the truth? Marilee left her house and car to her cat?"

"It's the truth."

She laughed again, a girlish laugh of pure delight. "That's Marilee," she said. "Lord, that girl was always dragging home every stray cat she saw. She wanted to give a home to all of them, and some of them didn't even want a home, they'd rather be roaming the alleys. But no, she couldn't stand it, she had to take care of all of them."

"It's an awful lot of money, Cora."

"Well, don't worry about it, hon. Marilee must have trusted you to take good care of her cat or she wouldn't have named you that whatchacallit."

"Under the terms of the trust, when the cat dies, all the money that's left goes to me."

"And it should. Cats live a long time. You ought to get paid for all that time."

"But I don't want it, and I'll get somebody else to take care of Ghost."

She smiled at me with a new sparkle in her eyes. "Well, you'll have plenty of time to figure out what to do with it when the time comes. And by that time, you might want it."

"This doesn't bother you?"

"Land no, it don't bother me one bit. It tickles me, is what it does. You know, Marilee was a good girl. Lots of people might look at her with all the money she made and think she was something else, but she was a good girl, and her leaving all that to her cat just proves that she was. Now when I think of my baby, I won't be thinking of how she ended her last minutes on this earth, I'll be thinking that up to the very end, she was a little girl wanting to take care of all the cats in the world. A generous, loving little girl. That was my Marilee."

I leaned over and patted her veined hand. "The apple doesn't fall far from the tree, Cora."

"I guess that's true. We never had much, but I always gave what I had."

Carefully, I said, "For such a young woman, Marilee acquired quite a lot."

She nodded proudly. "She did, that's a fact. Marilee always had a head for figures. When she started getting the money from the Fraziers, she wasn't old enough to take care of it herself, and Lord knows I didn't know how to handle that much money. We wanted to get away from the Fraziers, so we moved here and she went all by herself to Ethan Crane and got herself declared a grown-up. I don't remember what he called it, but I signed some papers and he had her something or other removed through the court."

"Disabilities of nonage."

"I guess so. Anyway, after that she could handle all that money by herself, and she did right well. She bought us a house first off, a nice little frame house in Bradenton, and then we went out and bought everything new. New refrigerator and new stove and new beds and mattresses. Oh my, we had a time doing that. First time either one of us had ever had a whole houseful of new things. She spent over half of the first money she got on the house and furniture and a new car for herself and one for me. But the money was going to keep coming in, every year, you know, so Marilee would sit up every night studying about how to invest it."

I did a bit of fast calculation of what half of a quarter of a million dollars invested twenty years ago would be worth today at 10 percent compounded interest, and my head got swimmy. If the same amount was invested every year for twenty years, the total value would be more than I could count. Even accounting for Marilee's expensive lifestyle, she had made herself an extremely wealthy woman.

Cora was watching me figure it out. "When I die," she said, "all the money she made goes to help other poor girls get an education or start their own businesses. Ethan Crane set it up that way for her."

"I never realized," I said.

"Well, you wouldn't, would you? Marilee never forgot where she came from, or how hard it was for us before the money. I kept working for a couple of years, but she wouldn't hear of it, and so I finally quit. It was about time, too, my ankles were going real bad. I haven't worked a lick since, and Marilee's always taken good care of me. She was a good girl."

Feeling chastened and slightly guilty, I got up and washed the supper dishes. I wondered if I would have been half as responsible as Marilee had been if I had started getting a quarter of a million dollars every year when I was sixteen. Marilee continued to surprise me.

On my way home, I turned on impulse and drove around the curve to Marilee's house. A white Jaguar sat in her driveway, and I pulled up behind it and got out. When I rounded the corner of the garage, I saw Shuga Reasnor at the front door, trying to unlock it. She looked around at me with a dark expression of frustration and resentment.

"Have you had the damn locks changed?"

I shook my head, all innocence. "Doesn't your key work?"

"I don't know what's wrong with it! You must have a key, let me in. I need to get some of my things."

"I'm not authorized to let anybody in, Miss Reasnor."

"Oh, bullshit! Who's going to authorize you? Cora? The police? I have a right to go in and get my personal property before they send in some estate liquidator to haul everything off."

"I'd have to make a list of everything you took and you'd have to sign a statement saying you took it. Otherwise, I can't let you in."

"Oh, for God's sake! What difference does it make to you? It's not your house."

It didn't seem the time to tell her the house now belonged to a cat.

I said, "I'm responsible for it, though, at least for the time being."

She stretched her mouth into a semblance of a smile. "Look, it's worth a couple of hundred dollars to me to get my things now. What do you say?"

"I say you'd better leave."

"What's the problem? You said Marilee left my name to call in an emergency."

"An emergency involving her cat, not something you left in her house."

"I'll call Cora. She'll let me in."

"If Cora gives me permission to let you in, that's fine. I just can't do it on my own."

She turned away from the door and clumped past me on her high heels. "Of all the stupid, idiotic, ignorant . . ."

I waited until she was in her Jag before I ambled past her to the Bronco and pulled out, backing up by the curb to let her exit the driveway and drive off in front of me. She gave me a murderous glare as she spun out and away. We both knew that she would come back, but only she knew why.

I waited until she'd had time to get onto Midnight Pass Road before I pulled back into the driveway. Marilee's yard was freshly edged and the walk and driveway blown clean. Even after death, yards get maintained and pools get cleaned on Siesta Key. The Winnicks' house was blank-faced and silent. I imagined Olga Winnick inside grieving the loss of innocence — either her son's or her own.

Shuga obviously hadn't known that Marilee's locks had been changed, and that was surprising. If she'd always had a key to Marilee's house, why hadn't Marilee given her a new key when she had her locks changed? And why hadn't she known about the change? That's the kind of things that women tell their friends, but Marilee hadn't told Shuga. Maybe Shuga had been the reason she'd had them changed. Maybe it was Shuga she didn't want goming in her house while she was gone. But why? And why now, after being friends for so long?

Whatever it was that Shuga had hoped to get was something very important to her, and it seemed strange that she hadn't said what it was, the way one woman would tell another. "I loaned her my best shirt and I want it back." Or "I took a bracelet off the last time I was here and forgot it." Instead, she had looked pinched and grim when I told her she'd have to reveal what she took and sign a statement listing everything. Shuga didn't want anybody to know what she was taking from Marilee's house. I wondered if this was the first time she had come looking for it, or if she had been the person who'd ransacked Marilee's bedroom and closet.

Phillip had said the woman he'd seen had dark hair, but in the dark Shuga's hair might have looked dark. Maybe Shuga had entered through the lanai and killed Frazier and Marilee, searched for whatever it was she wanted, and then left in a black Miata driven by an accomplice. But who was the accomplice? And who took Marilee's body to the woods? Marilee was small, but Shuga didn't seem muscular enough to carry her body that far.

I finally got out of the car and used my key to go inside. I flipped the switch to bathe the foyer in muted light, and sniffed at the cherry-scented air. I made a tour of the house, ending up in the kitchen, where I stayed clear of the spot where Frazier's body had lain. It was the first time I'd ever been the first person in a house after the crime-scene cleaners, and I found the experience more disquieting than finding the dead body. Crime-scene cleaners remove not only spilled blood and body fluids but every living microbe, which leaves a house strangely absent of life. I had never realized before how invisible agents in our homes are constantly throwing off subtle scents and energies that create the essence of our interiors. Without them, a house is as impersonal as a tray of surgical instruments.

I went to the garage, where Marilee's Ferrari took up half the space. The other half held a plastic garbage can, empty red and blue recycle bins, a stepladder, some stacked paint cans, and a few folding chairs propped against the wall. I knew the investigating team had thoroughly checked the car, but I opened the passenger door anyway. The Ferrari had creamy leather seats, so soft you could have made underwear from them. I ran my hand inside the storage pocket and under the seat. I opened the glove box and took out the sole content, a thin leather folder which held registration and insurance information. Otherwise, there was nothing. No maps, no sunglasses, no boxes of Kleenex or breath mints or left-over napkins from a fast-food drive-through. Not even a CD in the CD holder.

I opened the trunk and shined my penlight inside. As far as I could tell, there wasn't a speck of dust in it. I hadn't learned a thing except that Marilee had been an extremely tidy woman who'd kept her car as fastidiously neat and clean as she'd kept her house and person. The remote control for the garage door was clipped to the sun visor, and I slipped it into my pocket. Before I went back in the house, I positioned the recycle bins and garbage can against the garage wall, next to the folding chairs and stepladder.

29

When I got home, I saw Michael's car, but neither he nor Paco was outside, and their house was dark. It was close to nine o'clock and I'd been up seventeen hours. It seemed like a week since I'd eaten my turkey sandwich at the beach.

Forlornly, I went upstairs and cleaned up a bit, then went back down to go someplace for dinner. Paco called to me from the cypress deck, and I made a detour to where he was sitting in the waning light nursing a beer. He had removed his bushy beard and mop of unruly hair, and only a redness along his jawline betrayed the spirit gum that had held his beard firm. Nobody would dream this smooth-shaven guy with short-cropped hair and John Lennon eyeglasses was the same person as the scruffy beach bum he'd been at noon.

I went inside and got a beer and some cheese and crackers and joined him. We sat watching the light fading on the horizon while baby wavelets sucked at the shoreline.

Paco broke the silence. "Are you okay?"

I took a bite of cheese and chewed it morosely. I was way hungrier than cheese.

"I guess. I haven't done anything too outrageous, so I guess I'm cool."

"You want to talk about it?"

"Talk about what? The thing at the beach or the thing here?"

"The thing at the beach didn't happen. The thing here did."

"How did you catch him? Did you know he was coming here?"

"I noticed him watching you at the beach, and I thought I recognized him. After the thing that didn't happen was over, I got the Harley and left. Later, when I was driving home, he pulled out of a parking lot in front of me. I followed him, and when he turned into our drive, I went on past and then doubled back and walked down the lane. He had pulled his car into the trees, but he was an easy mark. He's not the brightest bulb in the string, believe me. He was looking around trying to figure out where to hide when I rushed him."

"If you hadn't come home when you did —"

"Dumb luck."

"I don't think so. I think somebody was watching over me."

He gave me a searching look, knowing I meant Todd. "Okay."

"What will happen to Bull Banks now?"

"Unless they can hold him on something more than beating up a gay kid, he'll be out on bail in no time. With luck, he'll get sent up as a three-time loser, but in the meantime he'll be out, without a whole lot to lose. Which is why I want you to be extra careful, Dixie. Bull Banks wouldn't be following you just because you're a hot babe, somebody's paying him."

"You think I'm a hot babe?"

He gave me an exaggerated leer. "Hon, if I was straight, I'd jump your bones in a minute."

"Do you think I should be scared?"

"You think I'm in danger of becoming straight?"

"No, I mean should I be scared of Bull Banks."

"Damn right you should. Dixie, can you find someplace else to stay for a while? Until this whole thing is cleared up?"

I started to tell him about Marilee's trust, then decided to wait and tell him and Michael at the same time.

"Paco, where is Michael?"

"In bed with a headache. Too much sun today. He's sort of lobster-colored."

"Tom Hale invited me to stay at his place for a while."

"He's the guy at the Sea Breeze? That's a fairly secure place. Do it. I'm leaving in a little while and I don't want you here alone. Especially with Michael out like a light."

I got up and gathered our empty bottles. "I'll get my things together."

"Dixie? It'll just be for a couple of days."

I heard the concern in his voice and smiled back at him.

"I know. I'll be fine."

It took me less than fifteen minutes to throw some clothes in a duffel bag and copy Marilee's Social Security number and birth date from her tax return. Then I drove straight to Marilee's house. I used Marilee's remote control to open the garage door, and pulled the Bronco inside. Funny how things have a way of working out the way you intended all along.

My heart was jumping like crazy against my ribs. If Guidry knew what I was doing, he would have my head on a platter. If Michael and Paco knew what I was doing, they would have my whole self on a platter. I intended to find Marilee's new wall safe, and I intended to open it. Call it intuition, a hunch, or an informed guess, but I was convinced that whatever was in that safe was the reason Harrison Frazier and Marilee had been murdered.

A little voice sitting on my shoulder yelled that the killer had trashed Marilee's bedroom, looking for whatever was in the safe, and might come back to try again. I could imagine newspaper headlines screaming "Curiosity Killed the Cat Sitter!" But I had been cowering from danger too long, protecting myself from ugly reality like I was a delicate flower that would wither at a breath of hot air. If I went on like that, I might never get back my courage or my ability to live in the real world. Besides, I kept seeing the words Marilee had written to her daughter, and imagining how awful it must have been to miss seeing her daughter grow up. This was something between Marilee and me — mothers banded together against everything and everybody who would take our children away from us.

My bet was that the code to open the safe would be one of the numbers I had copied, and that the safe would be hidden somewhere in Marilee's closet. Women always keep valuables in places that feel intimate and inviolate to them, places like their underwear drawer or under their mattress. The killer had looked in those obvious places, but he — or she — hadn't known about the wall safe. I, on the other hand, not only knew about the safe but was a pro. If a safe had been hidden behind a baseboard or in the floor or in a wall, I would find it.

Two hours later, hot and sweaty from crawling around Marilee's closet, I gave up. I hadn't found a thing. So much for being a pro.

I showered in Marilee's guest bath and crawled into bed in her guest room, first sliding my .38 under the pillow. My stomach was gnawing on itself, my knees hurt from thumping around on the Mexican tile, and my head ached from hunger and anxiety. It was after midnight when I finally fell into exhausted sleep. It didn't seem that I'd been asleep five minutes when a scream rang out in the darkness, and it took me a full minute to realize I had made it. I lay with my heart pounding, trying to get oriented.

Okay, I was at Marilee's house, in Marilee's bed, and something — a sound of somebody breaking in the house or a nightmare I couldn't remember — had caused me to scream. The red numbers on the bedside clock read 3:34. I got my gun from under the pillow and slid out of bed. Holding the gun in the stiff-armed position and hugging the wall as much as possible, I

moved to the open bedroom door. If somebody had broken in, my scream had already
clued him that I was on the alert. It had also
told him exactly where I was located. Arms
stiffly extended, I flattened myself against
the wall beside the door, ready to take out
anybody who entered.

For a terrible second, I remembered an
exercise at the Police Academy that tested
our physical and emotional reflexes — not
to mention our gag reflexes — by having us
handle the aftermath of a mock terrorist attack. We had to pick up body parts and lead
hysterical survivors away from the severed
heads of their loved ones. Even though we
all knew the body parts were plastic covered
in fake blood, they felt and looked real
enough to make us feel horrified sympathy
for the actors who played their roles so con-
vincingly. I had nightmares about that exercise for months, which was the whole point
of it. Life is precious, and the obscenity of
willful destruction of human bodies is an af-
front to the soul. We should never forget
that, no matter who we are. People in law
enforcement, with the legal *obligation* to
blow people away if they're a threat, need to
have it indelibly seared on their brains.

I wasn't a deputy anymore, so I didn't
have the sworn duty to kill a person threat-

ening me. I could legally clip them in the leg or arm just to stop them. But my police training told me that doing that would almost surely get me killed. Criminals have a way of shooting back even when they're wounded. They have a way of playing dead and then turning their guns on you when your guard is down. So would I shoot to kill, or would I shoot to maim?

The truth was that I didn't know.

Minutes passed without a sound, and then the alarm sounded and made me jump a foot in the air. I flipped on the light and padded down the hall, holding the gun ready but now acutely conscious that I was naked except for underpants. Turning on lights as I went, I checked the entire house, feeling more foolish with every closet door I opened. All the doors and windows were secure, and I didn't find any evidence of a break-in. I probably had just scared myself with a bad dream.

I finally went to the bathroom and got ready for the day. Now I would be late getting started because I'd let fear get in the way. I drove the short distance across Midnight Pass Road to Tom Hale's condo, where Billy Elliot was pacing behind the door, waiting for me. We ran for about fifteen minutes and I took him back upstairs.

He wanted more, but I didn't have the stamina. All the cats on my schedule got the same short shrift. I was too wasted to give them what they deserved. I promised I would make it up to them in the afternoon, and as soon as time came for the diner to open, I sped there like a winter bird to a feeder.

The diner was moist with biscuit heat and coffee steam. I waved to Tanisha behind the cook's window and took a stool at the bar. Judy raised her eyebrows at me from across the room and I nodded. She stopped at the cook's window and put my order in before she came with a mug and the coffeepot.

She said, "Everything okay?"

I said it was, because that wasn't the time or place to tell her everything that had happened since we last talked. Besides, if I told her about Phillip, I would probably break down and blubber all over the counter.

"The regular?"

"With two biscuits. And bacon."

She said, "Baaay-connn," as if I'd had some kind of epiphany, and went off to turn the order in.

I pulled my cell phone out of my backpack and looked at it. I knew I should use it to call Guidry and tell him where I was staying and why. Knew I should tell him about the safe, and about the trust. I put the cell phone back in my backpack and drank coffee instead. I couldn't talk to Guidry until I'd had food.

When Judy plunked down my breakfast, I went about eating it with serious efficiency. Tanisha's biscuits are like her piecrusts — light, flaky, and delicious. I ate one with my eggs and bacon and saved the other to eat with jelly, like a dessert. I was just about to eat the jelly one when a man slid onto the bar stool next to me and spread a *Herald-Tribune* on the space in front of him. His hands were pale and bloodless, with stiff black hairs between his knuckles. I saw Judy do a double take, and I looked sideways to see who it was. Dr. Gerald Coffey was so intent on an article he was reading that he didn't notice who was beside him.

Judy did the same quick question and answer routine with him that she'd done with me, then brought him coffee and topped mine off. She gave me a hard look while she poured mine, like she would pound me into the floor if I caused him to leave again. She needn't have worried. I wasn't up for another confrontation with him. I just wanted to eat my biscuit and drink my third cup of coffee and go back to Marilee's house.

I was eating the last crumb when Judy brought his scrambled whites and dry rye. I carefully kept my gaze straight ahead while she set it down, and shook my head when she asked if I wanted anything more.

For a minute or two, Coffey ate silently. Then he cleared his throat. "I think I owe you an apology, Miss Hemingway."

I still didn't look at him, and for a moment I couldn't think of anything to say.

He said, "I don't blame you for being angry. I was pretty unreasonable when you spoke to me before."

I turned my head then. "Marilee's dead, you know."

His face reddened and for a second his eyes shone with unshed tears. "Look, could we go someplace more private and talk?"

I nodded and slid off the stool. He followed me, and we both left bills with the cashier and went out the front door. I pointed to the Bronco and said, "We can talk in my car."

I beeped it unlocked and got in the driver's seat. After a momentary hesitation, he opened the passenger door and got in. We both sat staring straight ahead at people going in and out of the diner. I was too wiped out to do anything except wait for whatever he planned to say.

"I loved Marilee," he said softly. "You probably don't believe that, but I did."

"Why wouldn't I believe it?"

"You've talked to Shuga Reasnor, haven't you? I'm sure she's told you that I hated Marilee. She's told everybody that, but it isn't true."

"Dr. Coffey, I don't really give a gnat's ass whether you loved Marilee or not. What I'd like to know is how you knew I was talking about Marilee when I told you I was a pet-sitter. I didn't mention her name, and nothing had been on the news yet about the murders. Not hers and not Frazier's. So how did you know I was talking about Marilee's cat?"

"You think I killed her, don't you?"

"I think it's a definite possibility."

He gave a laugh that sounded more like a sob, and pounded his fist against his khaki knee several times to get himself under control.

"I think it was her skin that I loved most," he said. "She has the most fantastic skin, so smooth, you just want to —"

He broke off and blushed, caught in the act of reliving how Marilee's skin had felt under his hands. "I'm sure I seem pathetic to you," he said. "Hell, I seem pathetic to myself. She was like a disease I'd caught, you know? I didn't intend to start anything with her, it just happened."

I said, "I'm not making any judgments."

"Oh, of course you are. And I don't blame you. I'll tell you something I've never told another soul. I used to look in her windows at night to see if she was with somebody. I would actually hide in the bushes and spy on her." He shook his head sadly, as if he were watching himself doing that shameful thing and couldn't get over how dumb it was.

"Love makes people do crazy things," I said.

"The craziest thing was that even when I saw other men go into her house, I'd still believe her when she told me they didn't mean anything to her. That I was her only one."

"Were you watching her when Harrison Frazier went in? Did you go in and bludgeon them both?"

He raised trembling hands in front of his face and looked at them. "Just telling about this makes me shake. But all this was two years ago. If I'd been going to kill her, I'd have done it then."

"Maybe you waited so nobody would suspect you, and then hired somebody to do it for you."

"No."

"You still haven't explained how you knew it was Marilee I was working for."

"I recognized the cat's collar on your wrist. I was with Marilee when she bought it. We got it in New Orleans from a silversmith. It's one of a kind, I'd know it anywhere."

"So why did you go apeshit just because you knew I was taking care of Marilee's cat? You said, 'I know nothing about this!' What was it you knew nothing about?"

His Adam's apple did a nervous bobble, and I got a whiff of sour breath. "Marilee and Shuga sometimes got involved in moneymaking schemes that turned out to be bogus. I guess I thought they were doing something shady again, and that you thought I was involved in it, too. Because I'd been involved with Marilee."

I turned the key and started the Bronco. "Dr. Coffey, that's about the lamest lie I've ever heard in my life. Now if you'll excuse me, I have work to do."

He gave me a long-searching look, then opened his door. "I didn't kill her," he said. "I really did love her."

I didn't answer, and he shut the door softly and walked across the parking lot. I watched carefully, but his car wasn't black. It was a red Porsche that fairly screamed *man with little dick.* Dr. Coffey might have been telling the truth about being with Marilee when she bought Ghost's collar. He might even have been telling the truth about recognizing it on my wrist. But he sure as hell wasn't telling the truth about why he'd jumped up and threatened to call the police when I spoke to him. He'd had some other fear in mind.

30

I still had two more cats to see, and then I drove to the hospital to visit Phillip. I took the elevator to his floor and followed the arrows to the ICU. Even before I got there, I could hear the beeps of heart monitors and the occasional squeal of an IV or blood bag that had emptied. Doctors were making rounds, and the head nurse darted from cubicle to cubicle as private duty nurses stood aside like penitents at Mass while the doctors leaned over their patients. Fluorescent lights gave everybody a washed-out look. I turned toward Phillip's cubicle, hoping he'd look better than he had before.

He wasn't there. His entire room had been stripped, even to the wall cabinet unit that had held medical supplies.

I must have looked stricken, because the head nurse jogged over and put his hand on my shoulder.

"It's all right," he said. "He went home."

"I was afraid he had —"

"I know. It's this place. It makes you expect the worst. To tell the truth, I don't know why they put him here. His injuries weren't that critical."

"It was for the extra security. I'm surprised the doctor dismissed him so soon."

He looked uncomfortable. "Well, she didn't. His father came and took him against the doctor's advice. He said he could recuperate at home just as well as here, and he took him. We couldn't legally keep him."

I could feel myself going pale. I felt as if I'd just heard Phillip had been shipped off to hell.

The nurse read my face and shrugged. "We did all we could to change his mind, but once the Sheriff's Department removed him from protective custody, we were helpless."

"Did anybody contact Lieutenant Guidry?"

An alarm sounded in one of the cubicles, and he skittered backward a few steps with an apologetic smile. "I'm not sure. We're so busy."

He ran to help somebody whose condition was truly critical, and I retraced my steps down the hall, dialing Guidry as I walked. He wasn't in, so I left a message on his voice mail, telling him that Phillip wasn't safely tucked away in the hospital any longer, but with his parents.

Morosely, I drove to Bayfront Village, where I found Cora up and dressed. She looked worn, but a lot stronger.

"I decided to go downstairs and have a bite in the dining room," she said. "I guess I've been in this room by myself long enough."

"That's good, Cora. Is there anything I can do for you while I'm here?"

"No, dear, I'm all right for now. You've been very sweet to look in on me, Dixie. You're a good girl."

We went into the hall, and as I helped her lock her door, I said, "Cora, what do you know about Dr. Coffey?"

She smiled. "Oh, he's a strange man, dear. I don't go to him anymore, not since he and Marilee split up. They were engaged, you know."

We started walking toward the elevator, Cora taking teensy steps and me slowing down to such a slow pace that I felt off balance.

I said, "I talked to him this morning and he said he had been so jealous of Marilee that he would hide in the bushes and watch her house. I'm wondering if he kept doing that even after they broke off their engagement."

"You're wondering if he killed Harrison and Marilee?"

"I've thought about that, yes."

"Dixie, I told you before, Harrison Frazier killed Marilee. Now I don't know who killed Harrison, and I can't say that I care a whole lot. That's awful, I know, but it's the truth."

"Was Dr. Coffey always your doctor?"

"Not my regular doctor. He just does hearts, I think. No, I had some chest pain and nothing would do Marilee but that I see a heart specialist. She took me to him, and he did some tests. At first, he thought I needed one of those operations where they take a detour around your heart. I don't know how they do that exactly, but people get it done all the time. But then he decided I didn't need that after all, and I just went back a few times. Him and Marilee were pretty hot and heavy there for a while, but then she got mad at him about something, I never did know what, and quit him."

Ahead of us, the elevator doors opened and two elderly women got off and looked around like migrating geese after a landing. One of them said, "Oh, this is the wrong floor," and they giggled like girls. They turned back to the elevator and pushed the button.

Cora and I continued our snail walk toward them. I said, "I heard she and Dr. Coffey were actually in the church about to get married when Marilee called it off."

Cora laughed. "It wasn't that bad, but almost. They were supposed to have a rehearsal for the wedding and she told him before they went. But they weren't in the church, they were at her house. I thought it was just wedding jitters, you know, but she was serious."

The elevator doors opened and the two women hopped inside. They didn't even ask if they should hold it for us. We were moving so slowly, they could have taken several trips before we got to it.

"I also heard a rumor that Dr. Coffey gave Marilee a million dollars just before she called off the wedding. Was that an exaggeration, too?"

"Well, I can't rightly say about that. He may have, I don't know. He's pretty rich, you know, I guess he could have given her some without missing it."

Her voice had taken on a serenely hard edge, and I remembered that Shuga had said it was Cora who had demanded money from the Fraziers when Marilee was pregnant. She apparently found it wholly appropriate that Dr. Coffey might have given

Marilee a million dollars, just because he had it to spare. I didn't ask her anything else, and we finally reached the elevator and went downstairs. I declined an invitation to have brunch with her and hugged her good-bye outside the dining room.

The doorman had left my Bronco parked near the front door with the keys in it, so I didn't have to wait for him to get it. I waved to let him know I was the one taking it, then headed toward Marge Preston's Kitty Haven. The time had finally come that I could bring Ghost home, only now the home he was going to was truly *his,* not just where he lived with his owner.

I paid Marge for the time Ghost had been with her, and carried him out in one of my cardboard cases. I could see through the air holes that he was hunkered down in a de-pressed rabbit pose. Neither of us was holding up well.

At Marilee's house, no reporters lurked in the bushes, and Bull Banks's ugly face wasn't anywhere in sight, but I slowed down when I saw Carl Winnick's black Mercedes in the driveway next door. I could imagine the kind of conversation going on in that house, and it made me sick. Carl Winnick would be spouting his twisted hate for homosexuals, and Olga would be bleating about Phillip's future musical career.

I wanted to call Guidry and yell at him for allowing Phillip to leave the hospital, but I knew he had no reason to hold him there. And if I told him that Phillip shouldn't be with his god-awful parents, he would tell me they had the legal right to take him home. I told myself Phillip's parents loved him. I told myself they wouldn't hurt him any more than he was already hurt, but I didn't believe myself for one minute.

I opened the garage door and pulled inside. When the door shuddered down behind me, I took a deep breath — either of relief or apprehension, I wasn't sure. I got the .38 out of the glove box and put it in my pocket, then carried Ghost into the house through the kitchen door. When I opened the carrying case, he bounded out like a demented gazelle and made several mad careering turns through the house.

When he was run out, he began aggressively sniffing at the walls and making the peculiar face that cats do when they smell certain chemicals. It's called "doing flehmen" — stretching the mouth in a tight little smile, front teeth covered by upper lip. The purpose is to expose pores in the upper gum and palate, where a cat's vomeronasal organ is located — the organ that gives cats a sixth sense, along with the five that humans have. All cats have it, from lions and tigers in the wild to the tamest domestic pussycat. The more they hate a scent, the more pronounced they'll do flehmen. Sometimes it's the only warning an animal or person gets before they're attacked. Tigers, for example, will attack somebody with alcohol on his breath and rip them to shreds.

I never wear any kind of fragrance when I'm working with pets, but watching Ghost's reaction to the odor of chemicals on the walls made me remind myself to be extra careful with scents for a while. Ghost was going to be supersensitive until he got used to all the changes in his life. That made two of us.

I got down an ordinary ceramic bowl — Ghost's silver bowl being not only impounded by the Sheriff's Department but forever rendered too gross to drink from — and put out fresh water for him. He brushed his cheeks and rubbed his ass against all the cabinet doors to leave his scent and reclaim his territory from the haz-mat crew.

I knew he hadn't been eating much at the Kitty Haven, so even though he had already had breakfast, I got out his food dish. Ordinarily, I preach a daily diet of dried organic food, because it contains all the nutrients a cat needs to stay sleek and healthy. But a constant healthy diet gets pretty boring, even for cats, so an occasional dish of canned stuff is okay as a special treat. Ghost loved sliced beef in gravy the way I loved bacon, and after all he'd been through, I thought he needed sliced beef. I wouldn't have minded some myself.

Marilee kept a ten-pound bag of dried cat food in the pantry, along with stacks of canned food. I opened the pantry door and did a double take.

"Huh," I said. When you're all by yourself with a cat, you can make an intelligent comment like that without having to explain yourself.

The pantry was L-shaped, with the short end at the left of the door. In the past, the sack of dried food had sat on the floor under the long shelves, and stacks of canned food, jars of catnip, boxes of special treats, and some kitty toys had taken up a long shelf facing the door. Now they took up two shelves on the short end. Marilee had apparently rearranged the pantry since I'd last seen it.

As I moved cans of veal and lamb and chicken around on the short shelves, looking for sliced beef, I realized the shelves were now only half as deep as they used to be. Marilee hadn't just rearranged her shelves, she had remodeled them.

"Huh," I said again, my repertoire of intelligent exclamations being somewhat limited by then.

I got out a can of sliced beef and opened it for Ghost. He began to swoon with ecstasy even before I put the bowl on the floor. Then I went back to the pantry and removed everything on the newly foreshortened shelves so I could get a better look at the back wall.

It looked like all the other wallboard unless you looked closely, then you could see it was freshly painted hardwood. I got a knife and slid it in the crack on the left. I moved the knife up and down without hitting any resistance. I did the same thing on the right side, and hit resistance at the top, middle, and bottom.

"Bingo," I whispered. The back of the shelf was a hinged door.

Right then, I should have got on the phone and called Guidry. I should have confessed that I had an invoice to a wall safe in a folder in my desk drawer. Should have admitted that I had opened Marilee's mail and found the invoice. I should also have told him I had been keeping this information from him, and that I had no earthly reason for doing so except that Marilee had lost her daughter, too. Even I knew that was an irrational reason to hide evidence, but it seemed logical at the time. If I could protect her secrets, she and I wouldn't be so vulnerable.

I tried prying the door open with the knife, but it didn't budge. Thinking it must have a pressure-sensitive latch, I pushed my fingers all along the top edge of the door. When I got to the left side, I heard a click, and the door swung open.

"Oh gosh," I whispered, because a cream-colored safe was set flush inside the wall.

"Oh hell," I muttered, because the safe had both a combination and a keyed lock.

To open this sucker, you not only had to get inside Marilee's mind and figure out her code, you also had to have a key.

My cell phone rang and I froze. Only two or three people in the world had my cell number, and I wasn't looking forward to talking to any of them. It was Michael, calling from the fire station.

He said, "Are you okay?"

"Yeah, I really am."

"You're at Tom Hale's, right?"

I twisted the toe of one of my Keds into the floor, exactly the way I used to do when we were kids and Michael quizzed me about something we both knew I'd done and I was denying. I took a deep breath and straightened my back. I was thirty-two years old and I could do anything I wanted.

"Actually, I'm at Marilee's house. I'm going to spend a few days here. I'll explain about it later. It's a long story."

He said, "Are you crazy?"

"I think that's still to be decided."

"Aw shit, Dixie, I don't like this one bit. That asshole Dr. Win is right next door. He'll have every reporter in town over there."

"I don't think so. I think this is the last place anybody would think to look for me. I'll be back in a day or two. After this blows over."

He warned me about a hundred times to call if I needed anything, and I promised I would.

He said, "I don't like it, but I guess it's okay."

"I love you."

"Love you, too, Dix."

That's my big brother, the gentle giant.

Ghost was still hunkered over his sliced beef, blissfully chewing with his eyes half-closed. I went back to the pantry and fingered the safe's keyhole. I hadn't expected to need a key. People usually select a birth date or address or Social Security number for a numerical code, so I had thought I had everything I would need to open the safe when I found it. Needing a key was a major problem.

I looked around the kitchen. If Marilee had chosen the pantry to hide the safe, maybe she had hidden the key in the kitchen, too. But before I started searching, I needed to take care of my primary business of pet-sitting. I sat at the kitchen bar and used my cell phone to check phone messages at my apartment. A few more reporters had called, and one client had called all the way from North Carolina to say she had heard the news about me and didn't want me going back in her house. She had called another sitter, she said, and she would never hire me again.

That really hurt my feelings. I felt like a little kid whose best friend had just told her she didn't like her anymore.

The last call was from Phillip Winnick. His words were slurred, but more intelligible than they'd been the day before. It wasn't how he talked that alarmed me, it was what he said.

"Um, Miz Hemingway . . . I mean Dixie . . . this is Phillip . . . If I don't see you again . . . I just want to say . . . thank you . . . That's all. Oh, and . . . I'm sorry I lied."

I played the message several times, and every time he sounded terrified and desperate. Something was going on, and whatever it was had made Phillip think he might not see me again. I put the phone down with a chill running down my spine.

31

Feeling leaden and dull, I took a shower and changed clothes. No matter how hard I tried to convince myself that the Winnicks loved Phillip, I couldn't shake a feeling of impending doom. Phillip was about as scared and miserable as a kid could get, and it sounded as if he was feeling guilt for not being honest about being gay. I knew his family wasn't likely to give him the love and support he needed. If anything, they were more likely to add to his despondency. Phillip needed a friend, and right now I might be the only one he had.

I finally couldn't stand it any longer, so I marched out the front door and down the street to the Winnicks' house.

I could hear voices shouting even before I got to the front door. Olga Winnick shrill and pleading, Carl Winnick harsh and threatening. Under their harangue, a tortured undertone that was Phillip. It was exactly what my worst fears had been, and maybe even worse. I didn't care if Phillip was their son, I was going to take him out of there. He was over eighteen, they couldn't keep him if he wanted to leave.

I jabbed the doorbell and then banged on the door for good measure. Once I could have yelled, "Sheriff's Department, open up!" but I couldn't do that anymore. Anyway, I wasn't there in any official capacity. I was there as a friend, which takes precedence over all other reasons.

The door didn't open, and the yelling continued. I rang the bell again and banged harder on the door. Olga screamed, a long wail that brought fine bumps to my skin. Carl Winnick shouted something that sounded like "What the hell are you doing?"

Faintly, I heard Phillip reply, but I couldn't make out the words.

Something was terribly wrong. I grabbed the handle on the door and tried the thumb latch. The door wasn't locked. I rapped on it one more time and pushed it open, calling out as I did.

"Hello? Phillip?"

Olga and Carl Winnick stood in the shadowy living room with their backs to me, their postures strained and stiff and angry. Phillip stood beyond them in front of the closed drapes. I couldn't see him very well in the murky light, but he seemed to be in dark pajamas almost the same shade as the bruises on his face.

Olga whirled and shrieked, "Get out of my house!"

I didn't try any pretense. I said, "I've come to get Phillip."

Olga came at me like an avenging Fury, actually running with her arm held out stiff and her fist closed like a battering ram. The woman was nuts if she thought she could scare me with that fist.

I grabbed her wrist and twisted it, then got her other wrist and locked it behind her back. The woman was wiry, and stronger than I'd expected, but I knew I could have her on the floor in a second. She seemed to know that, too, because she didn't kick at me, just twisted her stiff neck and panted like a tethered dragon, sending out hot air and the odor of liquor.

Carl Winnick ran past us toward the kitchen. Without his executive suit jacket, his barrel chest and short legs made him look almost pathetically misshapen.

Olga said, "This is all your fault! You and people like you, filling his head with filthy ideas!"

I called to Phillip over her head. "Phillip, you're a good, decent, talented young man, and you don't have to stay here. Come with me."

He shook his head. "It won't . . . make any difference."

"It will! Of course it will. You're hurt now, but you'll heal and everything will be okay. You don't have to live a lie anymore."

"Just . . . live with my parents hating me."

"They don't really hate you. They just don't know you. They'll change, you'll see."

Carl ran from the kitchen and jammed his red face close to mine. "I've called the police, girl, so you'd best leave before they come and arrest you."

I stared at him, and something clicked into place in my brain.

Phillip took a couple of steps forward and said, "Leave her alone, Dad."

That's when I saw the gun. The barrel was dark, like his pajamas, and he carried it with the muzzle pointed down by his thigh. In his large hand, the stock was almost invisible. But I could see the telltale red pinprick that showed the safety was off. I should have known. In addition to teaching his son to open doors for ladies, Carl Winnick had taught his son how to handle a semiautomatic.

I said, "Phillip, what are you doing with a gun?"

Too calmly, he said, "I'm going to kill myself with it."

Most of the time when people threaten to kill themselves, you can hear in their voice a silent plea to talk them out of it. To bargain with them. To promise them that things will change, that their lives will get easier, that some injustice to them will be righted, that somebody will listen to them and actually hear what they're saying. Phillip wasn't doing any of those things. He was stating a cool intention, one that he'd already worked out in his head, one for which he could see no alternative.

Carl said, "Didn't you learn anything when you got beaten up?"

"I learned how ashamed I make you. I learned I'll never be the son you want."

Slowly, Phillip's arm raised so the gun's barrel was at the side of his head. I heard a silent whimpering inside my own head, and a sick metallic taste coated my mouth. I had to stop him somehow, but every idea carried the possibility of making him pull the trigger.

Even Carl seemed to understand that something had to be said that would change Phillip's mind.

"I'm not an unforgiving man, son, you know that. You can make me proud of you again!"

Phillip's voice took on a new irony. "Sure, all I have to do is kill myself."

"Do you have any idea what that would do to me and your mother? Do you want to heap more shame on us?"

I lost hope then. Just completely lost the last thread of thin hope I'd been clinging to.

So did Phillip. Wearily, he said, "There's more than one way to kill myself. With a bullet, or living the way you want me to live. Either way, I'll be dead."

I had loosened my hold on Olga, and she suddenly twisted free.

"Phillip, we're going to send you to a hospital! They'll cure you! When you're yourself again, you can still go to Juilliard!"

Phillip barked a hoarse laugh that jerked his head backward, and the gun sounded with a roaring blast. He crumpled to the floor with blood spilling around his head in a bright pool. Olga screamed and covered her face with both hands. Carl gripped the door frame and stared goggle-eyed and frozen. I tried to push past them, my cell phone in hand, already dialing 911.

I didn't realize I was sobbing until Deputy Jesse Morgan gently shoved me aside.

"Somebody already called," he said.

He had his own phone out, calling for an

ambulance, then he rushed to Phillip and blocked my view.

The thin wail of an ambulance's siren was already cutting through the midmorning heat, and I knew that several more cars from the Sheriff's Department would soon arrive. I walked back to Marilee's house and closed the door.

I didn't want to see them take Phillip's body out in a bag. I was afraid I might kill Carl Winnick if I did.

Back in Marilee's guest room, I crawled into bed. With the wooden blinds closed, the room was dark as a cave, and the stucco walls were thick enough to muffle sounds from outside. If I covered my head with a pillow, I couldn't hear any noise at all from the Winnicks' house.

I knew how to do this. I knew how to numb myself from horror. I knew how to withdraw into myself so the sharp edges of reality wouldn't scrape me and jab me and cut me. I had thought I could face life, but I couldn't. I didn't even want to.

Ghost slithered under the covers and pushed himself into the crook of my body, sending his body heat into my stomach. Instinctively, I cupped my hands around him and felt his heart beating. His rough tongue lapped at my wrist, and he began to purr.

Dumb animal to dumb animal, he was sending me love in the only way he knew how, and gradually it crept into my cold veins and to my anguished heart.

I finally had to admit to myself that it wasn't the world I was retreating from, but my own rage. I truly and sincerely might take my .38 in hand and go over and fill Carl Winnick with bullets. I truly and sincerely might go over and pistol-whip Olga Winnick to death. I had it in me to do that, and I knew it and was terrified by it. I also knew there's nothing so paralyzing as unexpressed fury.

My cell phone rang in my pocket and sent Ghost scrambling out of bed. I checked the ID and groaned. It was Guidry.

Without any preambles, he said, "Dixie, the Winnick boy is alive. He's on his way to St. Petc's trauma center. I don't know how badly he's hurt, but he's alive."

I sat up and wiped at the tears on my face with the edge of the sheet. "Carl Winnick was the man who took the pipe away from Tanisha. He either clubbed Phillip himself or he hired Bull Banks to do it for him."

"How do you know that?"

"I just know. He used the same words to me that he used to Tanisha, called us both *'girl.'* I know it was him."

"Deputy Morgan says you were at the door

when Phillip shot himself. The Winnicks say they don't know why he did it. Do you?"

"Sure. He told them why. They didn't want the son they had, and he couldn't live with that. His mother's response was that they were going to send him to a hospital to 'cure' him."

"Jesus. Poor kid."

"You'll go after Carl Winnick, right? Because if you don't, I will."

"No you won't."

The phone went dead, and I slammed it against the covers.

"Son of a bitch! Egotistical bastard! Shithead!"

Yelling is always good when you feel totally helpless.

But Phillip wasn't dead. Maybe a miracle would happen and he would be okay.

I got out of bed.

My cell rang again, this time Michael calling from the firehouse. "Dixie, I just heard about the Winnick boy."

I collapsed right where I stood, crumpling to the floor and sobbing into the phone. "Oh Michael, that sweet, gentle boy! His beautiful face!"

"I know, Dixie. I know."

"It's not fair!"

"No, it's not."

Huddled on the floor, I clutched the phone to my chest and cried so hard it seemed I was stripping out the lining of my throat. I cried for the horror of what had happened to Phillip, for what had happened to Todd and Christy, and for every other senseless tragedy that destroys the light of the shining young. I don't know how long I cried, but when I was able to hear again, I lifted the phone to my ear and Michael was still there, still holding me from his end of the line.

I said, "I'm okay."

"If you need me, I can take a sick day and be with you."

"No, I'm fine, really."

"Call me in a couple of hours, okay?"

I wiped my wet face and nodded at the phone. "I will, but don't worry. I really am okay. Or at least as okay as anybody would be after . . . you know."

"Yeah. I'm not worried, but call me anyway."

I got up and washed my face. What I'd told Michael had been true. Anybody would be disturbed by watching a boy shoot himself in the head, and the fact that I wasn't any more upset than the average neurotic was encouraging.

Ghost trotted after me and patted at my

ankles. I knelt to stroke his silvery fur, and he nosed his head into my hand and arched his back, insistent as a needy baby. I went to the Bronco and got my grooming kit out and took Ghost to the lanai. Pulling my slicker brush through his hair until his coat was smooth and shiny calmed us both down.

As I brushed him, I looked toward the Winnicks' house. I could see a back window that was probably in Phillip's room. He had been outside that window when he saw a woman get into a car in Marilee's driveway. I had been sure that was the reason he had been beaten up, but I had been wrong. Phillip had been beaten because Carl Winnick had hired somebody to scare him straight, to punish him for being gay, to destroy his burgeoning self-esteem . . . who knew what Winnick's sick reasons were?

I don't often use the word *evil.* It smacks too much of wild-eyed fanatics eager to control the world by imposing their skewed ideas of right and wrong. But when I thought about the kind of mind that would hire a thug to beat up his own son because the kid was gay, the only word that came to mind was *evil.* Carl Winnick was truly an evil man, and the fact that he presented himself to the world as the voice of morality made him all the worse.

When Ghost was combed and feeling sleek again, I left my grooming supplies on the lanai table and carried Ghost through the slider before I pulled it closed. I've learned not to try to coax any cat through a door, because they will always get halfway in and decide to contemplate the secrets of life while you stand there like an idiot telling them to please get a move on. Instead, I carry them over the threshold like brides.

It took two hands to securely lock the slider, so I put Ghost back on the floor before I locked it. Then with Ghost trotting by my side, I went back in the kitchen and made a cup of tea. I drank it sitting at the snack bar while I imagined what was happening to Phillip at the trauma center. Doctors would be fighting for his life. There might be surgery, blood transfusions, ventilators, and all the other modern techniques that exist to preserve life. But no matter how many devices I could envision working for him, I couldn't escape the reality of what a bullet does when it explodes inside a skull.

I washed Ghost's food bowl and my teacup while Ghost twined in and out between my ankles, arching his back and rubbing against me with his tail held high. I was touched. Cats have tiny scent glands on their faces and at the roots of their tails. When they rub against you, it's their way of mixing their scent with yours. You can't get any closer to a living being than sharing odors, and Ghost was telling me that he and I were now bonded as one. He was signing on as my closest friend, my confidant, and my protector.

Even domestic cats can be vicious, and Ghost was also letting me know that if he and I went hunting together in the wild, he would pounce on a rodent, stick his daggerlike eyeteeth in it, and sever its spine for me. He would shred its flesh into bite-size chunks and share them with me. Since we weren't in the wild, he would have to content himself with bringing me the occasional unlucky lizard caught on the lanai. All that bonding behavior made it even more imperative that I find a new owner for Ghost before he became too attached to me. He had already lost one person he loved, I didn't want him to lose another one.

I left our dishes draining on the counter and went back to the pantry and looked at the safe again. It didn't seem so important anymore, but I had to get my mind off what was happening to Phillip. I fingered the keyhole again. It was small, so the key would be small, too, and easily concealed. Just the thought of looking in all the possible places Marilee could have hidden it was mind-numbing. Guessing the numbers for the code would be a lot easier.

I got the numbers I'd copied from Marilee's ruined tax return and went back to the safe to demonstrate my savvy knowledge of how people use their birth dates or Social Security numbers or house numbers for codes they commit to memory. Easy for them to remember, but also easy for a burglar to figure out. Not that I was a burglar. I was more of a protector.

Ghost watched intently while I tried the first six digits of Marilee's Social Security number. I tried the last six digits. I tried them both backward. I tried her birth date, first by month and year, then by day, month, and year. I tried them backward, too. I tried her house address and her zip code and various parts of her phone number. Nothing worked.

I closed the wooden door over the safe, replaced the cat food on the shelf, and crawled back in bed. Ghost joined me, staying politely down by my feet but close enough to warm me. Immediately, visions of Phillip shooting himself swam before my eyes. I hadn't seen Phillip's injury before Deputy Morgan pulled me aside, but I had seen the gun and I knew what an exploding bullet does.

In the trauma center at St. Pete, doctors were working to save Phillip's life. But if they succeeded, would he be Phillip or a pitiful shell without a mind? Without consciousness of his surroundings, without the ability to think or create, without the ability to live with any degree of joy? To me, such a life was not a life, but a breathing death.

I hadn't been on speaking terms with God since Todd and Christy were killed, but now I had a little talk with him. Or her, as the case may be. I said, I'm still mad at you for taking Todd and Christy, but maybe you did that because they were hurt so badly that they wouldn't have been *them* if they'd lived. They would have hated that, so I guess you did the right thing. Now Phillip has been hurt, and he would hate having to live not as himself. He would hate not being able to play the piano, not being able to have fun, not being able to love and be loved. So I just want you to know that if you decide to take Phillip, I'll understand. I won't like it, but I'll understand. Not that you need me to okay what you do. But if he can have a good life in spite of what happened, then I ask you to help the doctors save him. That's all. Amen.

It probably wasn't much of a prayer by most people's standards, but it was the best I could do and it made me feel better.

I slept for a little while, and when I woke, I was ready to take care of the cats and dogs on my schedule. Ghost was sunning himself on a window ledge when I left, and he blinked a couple of I love you's when I said good-bye. We were making progress.

32

Tom Hale was hovering near the door waiting for me when I got to his condo. He had heard about Phillip's suicide attempt on the news, and he was determined to find out everything I knew. I gave him the short version, but it was still a lot to condense. When I told him what I suspected about Carl Winnick, he shook his head in disgust.

"That's always the way," he said. "Those sanctimonious holier-than-thou types are always covering up something rotten. I hope they roast his balls over an open flame."

"First, they'll have to prove he did it."

"The boy, how bad is he?"

"It was to his head, Tom."

Tom looked down at his ruined legs. "It would be better for the kid if he doesn't make it. Not if it's to the head."

I felt tears coming, so I stood up and got Billy Elliot's leash and snapped it on his collar. Tom rolled his chair toward me and fixed me with a stern look.

"Dixie, don't try too hard to make sense

of any of this. Life doesn't make any sense. Like they say, bad things happen to good people. It's like chaos theory. You know chaos theory?"

I considered my options. If I was honest and said I didn't know diddly about chaos theory, Tom would tell me everything about it twice, and I'd never get away. If I lied and said chaos theory and I were old friends, he'd catch me in my ignorance and I'd still end up hearing all about it.

I sighed. "Tom, I really have to go. I've got a million things happening at once and none of them make any sense, and so far as I can tell, they're all impossible."

He smiled and gave me a thumbs-up. "You've got it, Dixie! That's chaos theory!"

When I got back to Marilee's house, a green-and-white vehicle from the Community Policing Unit was in the Winnicks' driveway — either to gather information or to offer the services of the Victim Assistance Unit.

I laid my .38 on the kitchen bar, and sat on a bar stool to use Marilee's phone to call the trauma center at St. Pete. A woman told me she could not provide any information about any patient, period.

I said, "I just want to know if he's still alive."

"I'm sorry. I can't tell you anything."

I had known before I called that I wouldn't get anywhere. To the woman answering the phone, I could be a ghoulish reporter following up a lead on a kid who'd committed suicide, or I could be the person who had pulled the trigger, checking to see if I'd been successful.

I called Guidry to see if he knew anything, but he didn't answer his cell, so I left a message.

I fed Ghost, showered, and changed clothes, then went out to the lanai to get the grooming supplies I'd left on the table when I combed him. Phillip's window was dark. I walked to the side screened door to look at it, as if the window held some secret that might help Phillip live. Phillip's phone message now made perfect sense. He had already decided to kill himself when he called. He had wanted to thank me and to apologize for lying before he died. He should have known he didn't need to apologize to me, especially not for lying about being gay.

A coil of surprise moved at the base of my skull, and I looked at Phillip's window again. Drought-tolerant Bahia grass grew from Marilee's lanai to the wooden fence that marked the back boundary at the woods, with a bed of low junipers separating her yard from the Winnicks'. I opened the lanai's screened side door, stepped out onto the grass, and went to stand at Phillip's window. From that spot, I looked toward Marilee's driveway. It was completely hidden from view by the corner of her house. Even the street in front of her house was invisible from Phillip's window. I walked down the side of his house until I came to a spot where I could see Marilee's driveway and the walk from her front door. It was at the very front of the Winnicks' house, next to their garage. If Phillip had seen a Miata pull into Marilee's driveway, it hadn't been from his window.

With my mind whirling, I went back to Marilee's lanai and picked up my grooming supplies. As I was going through the glass door, my cell phone started beeping from the kitchen bar and I hurriedly pulled the slider closed and sprinted to answer it. It was Michael, his voice anxious because I hadn't answered promptly. I told him I was absolutely jim-dandy and not to worry. I still hadn't told him about the safe, but now didn't seem the time. I also didn't tell him that I'd just discovered that Phillip had lied to me.

I put my grooming supplies in the Bronco and went back to the kitchen. I was hungry, but there was still the danger of being caught out by a reporter or by Bull Banks out on bail, so I toasted some waffles from Marilee's freezer and ate them dry while I thought about Phillip's lie. He had lied either about where he'd been when he saw a woman leave Marilee's house or about what he'd seen. I tried to put myself in the shoes of an eighteen-year-old kid who had seen something connected with a murder. Could he have heard a woman's footsteps and a car's engine and then exaggerated, saying he'd seen a woman walking and a black Miata pulling in the driveway? Maybe. Or maybe the Miata pulled back far enough for him to see it in the street when it drove away. It made me too sad when I thought that Phillip might not live to explain what he'd lied about, so I wrenched my mind away from the lie and focused on the combination to Marilee's safe.

I hadn't given up on the expectation that it would involve numbers most familiar to Marilee, but I had already tried the obvious ones. I got a bottle of water from the refrigerator and leaned on the bar to drink it, staring blindly at the phone on the counter. Ghost came and wound sinuously around my legs, rubbing his silky hair against my bare skin. Marilee had probably stood in exactly this spot a million times, talking on the phone while he rubbed against her ankles.

Marilee had loved Ghost. She had chosen a strange name for him, but I supposed it had meaning to her. Thinking about that made the hairs on the back of my neck rise to attention. What if Marilee hadn't been thinking of numbers when she chose a combination for the safe? What if she had been thinking of a word? I grabbed a pen and wrote *Ghost.* Then I looked at the phone's keypad and put the corresponding number under each letter.

I went to the safe and punched in 1 1 6 7 8. A satisfying click told me I had guessed right. The combination to the safe was the name Ghost. Now that I had figured it out, it made perfect sense. All I had to do now was find the key to open the second lock.

I toasted some more waffles and tried to think where I would hide a key if I were Marilee. The killer had ransacked her closet and the drawers in her bedroom and bathroom. I had assumed he'd been searching for the safe, but maybe he'd known where the safe was and had been searching for the key. If that were true, maybe he'd had reason to search where he did.

I got a black plastic garbage bag and went

into Marilee's bathroom. Ghost sat on the countertop and watched me empty bottles of lotions and boxes of powder, throwing the empties in the trash. I checked for a key inside every bottle and jar in the medicine chest and tossed them, too. Except for some aspirin and several bottles of vaginal gel guaranteed to feel like natural secretions, Marilee's medicine cabinet was as innocent as a twelve-year-old girl's. No prescription painkillers, no tranquilizers or antidepressants, no stimulants or hormones. Except for an occasional headache or dry vagina, Marilee had apparently been bloomingly healthy.

I gathered up some unopened bottles of perfume and cologne and bath oil to take to Cora along with a bunch of scented candles with virgin wicks. The rest went in the trash bag, including half a dozen sticks of mascara and enough lipsticks to paint the lips of every woman in Sarasota and still have some left over for Bradenton. Ghost followed me when I hauled the bag out to the garage and stashed it in the garbage can. I made a mental note to remember to put the can out at the curb Thursday night, then went back into the kitchen.

Getting rid of the bathroom trash had made me feel more organized. I hadn't found the key, but at least I was doing something constructive.

I stood in the middle of the kitchen and looked around. Get focused, I told myself. Think.

I put a colander in the sink. Then I went through all the cupboards and got out every sack of flour and sugar and cornmeal, every box of cereal, every jar of spices, every opened package of anything. Ghost sat on the counter, intently watching my every move, his head turning like somebody watching a tennis match while I sifted everything through the colander. I ended up with a sinkful of dry stuff that would probably stop up the drains.

I looked at Ghost. "I should have done this over the wastebasket, shouldn't I?"

He looked at me and let the vertical aperture in his eyes widen, but not in a judgmental way.

I scooped the mess into a big bowl and dumped it into a garbage can under the sink, but I hadn't given up yet. I got out all the jars in the refrigerator and lined them up next to the sink. I stuck my hand inside jars of jelly and jam and pickle relish and mayonnaise and mustard. All I got for my trouble was yucky fingers and gross condiments which I then tossed in the trash.

Ghost's whiskers wavered and he scooted back from the sink's edge, disgust written all over his face.

Pointedly, he got to his feet and arched his back and yawned. I knew what he was saying: It was bedtime, and I was wasting my time. But I couldn't stop. I searched the refrigerator's vegetable drawer and meat drawer. I got out every opened bag of frozen vegetables and dumped them in the colander, running hot water on them in case the key was frozen inside a solid mass of peas or carrots. At least I could get rid of the ruined vegetables by pushing them down the disposal.

Ghost left me when I turned on the disposal. He had been loyal, but even an Abyssinian's loyalty has its limits.

I sat down at the bar and glumly considered my options. If I told Guidry about the safe, he could have somebody from the department crack it. But that would mean I'd have to tell him about the invoice I'd found in Marilee's mail. And then I'd have to come up with a good explanation for not telling him before. And what if the safe held a wad of cash or valuable jewels? Common sense told me I was still a possible suspect. The same common sense told me that nobody considered me a strong suspect, because I'd had nothing to gain by the murders. But if there was a chunk of money in the safe, Guidry might think I'd known about it all along.

See how the mind works when you have an overactive conscience? Not to mention a guilty secret.

In my dream, Marilee had said, "You have the key." I had thought she meant it in a metaphorical way, but maybe I was trying too hard to read symbols into something that was literal. Like Freud said, sometimes a cigar is just a cigar. Maybe she meant a real key. Maybe I had the key to the safe in my possession and my subconscious was trying to remind me of that.

Thinking of the dream brought back the image of Marilee holding Ghost. Maybe that was the dream's message — the key had something to do with Ghost. Marilee had chosen Ghost's name as the numerical code for the safe, so maybe the key was hidden with something of Ghost's, too. With a burst of inspiration, I sprinted to the pantry and grabbed the bag of dried cat food and dumped it into the sink. I searched through it, stirring it and turning it with both hands, but I didn't find a key. Guiltily, I put it back into the bag handful by careful handful. Ghost came back in the kitchen and jumped on the counter while I did that, giving me a look that suggested he would eat food that had been roiled around in the sink when hell froze over.

I went back to the bar and drank some more water. Ghost hopped down from the counter and meowed up at me. In the bright kitchen light, his shiny fur gleamed like silver. I knelt and stroked his head and neck.

"I wish you could talk. You probably know where the key is."

He gave me a couple of I love you blinks, and in the next instant, I was racing for my backpack. I rummaged inside and pulled out Ghost's velvet collar with its little silver hearts and keys. A silly, frivolous thing for a cat to wear, a one-of-a-kind item made by a silversmith in New Orleans and bought on a trip Marilee had made with Dr. Coffey. I turned it around, examining each silver key, and then found the one that was heavier and thicker than the others.

"Hot damn," I whispered.

It was a real key, not just a charm, and I had been carrying it around all week in my backpack. I cut it off with Marilee's kitchen shears, and went back to the safe. The key glided into the lock like a hot knife into butter. I wiped my hands on my shorts and pulled the door open. Inside the safe was a stack of manila envelopes.

Carrying the stack with both hands, I went to the bar and put it down as gingerly as I would lay a ticking bomb. The stack tipped over and envelopes fanned out beside my gun and cell phone. I took a deep breath and moved the gun and phone over a bit. A thin thread of warning spiraled across my cortex like a figure skater making frantic figure eights, but I ignored it. If the contents of the envelopes held information vital to the murder investigation, I would most certainly call Guidry and turn them over to him. But if these were records having to do with Marilee's daughter and her relationship with Harrison Frazier, I would protect them. For Marilee's sake. For Lily's sake. For Cora's sake. Maybe for my own sake.

The envelopes were the kind that have a metal clasp to hold the flap down, and my fingers trembled a little when I pulled up the prongs on the first one and opened the flap. I upended the envelope and let its contents slide out onto the bar. They were photographs, all turned facedown. Expecting a photograph of Lily in her formative years, I turned over the one on top. It wasn't Lily. It was definitely not Lily.

It was a view of a large naked man laid out

on a messy bed. His arms were spread across the rumpled sheet and his hairy legs were open. Incongruously, he wore black dress socks. A black-headed woman lay prone between his legs with her face shoved into his crotch. A blond woman hovered above him with her breasts dangling above his head, and his lips had a firm hold on one of her nipples. Neither woman's face was clear, both being shrouded by long hair, but the man's face was clearly visible. He could not have looked any sillier.

All the other photographs were of the same man, and some of the poses made the first one seem innocent. The man had been caught in every conceivable obscene position with two hookers. He had not only made a complete and total fool of himself, he had exposed himself to eighteen kinds of blackmail, loss of respect, ridicule, and perhaps loss of his loved ones. Each photograph bore the date and time, as if the photographer wanted them to have every possible stamp of validity. A ruled sheet of paper was folded with the photographs. In her rounded handwriting, Marilee had recorded a column of dates, with numbers beside each date. The dates went back over five years, regular as a calendar every month. The amounts were regular, too. Five thousand, five thousand, five thousand. There were no dollar signs, but I assumed the numbers referred to money received.

I put the photos back in the envelope and washed my hands at the sink. Before I went back to the other envelopes, I drank a glass of water. Revulsion really dries up the mouth. The next envelope held almost identical photos, but the man was different. This one was a squat, round man with a receding hairline. He looked vaguely familiar, but I couldn't place him. The two women were the same blonde and brunette, and the man's look of mindless bliss was also the same. Another ruled sheet of paper with a column of dates and figures, but this one had started only two years ago. The numbers were greater, though. Eight thousand every month. Next to the dates and amounts, Marilee had noted where the money had gone, always distributed in amounts of one or two thousand dollars to several mutual funds. Marilee had apparently believed in diversity. Cora had been right, Marilee *had* been good with numbers. Big numbers. She had also had a savvy sense of how to invest small amounts of cash without attracting attention.

I had to wash my hands again before I opened the other envelopes. It wasn't that I found the graphic sexual images so shocking, it was the reason for the photographs being taken that made me feel like I'd been dipped in a vat of congealed chicken fat. The reason was obviously blackmail. And while the two women were always careful to keep their faces hidden from the camera, I was almost positive they were Marilee and Shuga. At least one mystery was solved. Now I knew how two women without any marketable skills could make an indecent amount of money. Literally.

I went through the other envelopes with increasing horror, revulsion, and reluctant admiration.

The photographs of Dr. Gerald Coffey were in the fourth envelope, and they confirmed my first mental image of his hairy back. The pose that exposed it was a special one, involving the insertion of a large dildo into his equally hairy backside while he knelt on all fours and apparently howled like a wolf. It was not the sort of pose that would inspire confidence and trust in heart-surgery patients. Which was no doubt why the column listing his payments culminated in the number one, followed by six zeros. The million he had paid Marilee before she jilted him at the altar had been hush money, not the love money he claimed. Wondering briefly why she had ever considered marrying him in the first place, I moved on to the other envelopes.

33

The photographs seemed almost common-
place now, all of naked men made hopelessly vulnerable by lust and stupidity. Some
of the faces looked faintly familiar, and I assumed they were in the public eye in one
way or another. Each of them had been
paying Marilee between five and ten thousand dollars a month for years. Even split-
ting the take with Shuga, she would have
been raking in a considerable amount of
money. With the quarter million she got
every year from Harrison Frazier's family,
she surely had never worried about paying
the rent.

The vulnerable fifteen-year-old girl who
had been tricked into giving her baby to
Harrison Frazier's sister had grown up to be
a woman who extorted money from a lot of
men for the sheer pleasure of it. The money
the Fraziers had given her had been more
than enough for her and Cora to have a
good life. It had been enough to live well in
the present and also invest for the future.

But it hadn't been enough to fill the need Marilee had nurtured, the need to have control over men and to make them pay. And she had been aided and abetted by her friend Shuga, the poor girl who wouldn't have had enough to eat if Marilee's grandmother hadn't fed her. I wondered if all the money they'd taken had ever made up for what they thought they'd missed out on.

Now I knew what Shuga had come to get, and why she had been so frightened. If Marilee had the only copy of the photographs, Shuga's blackmail income was now up shit creek. From what Cora had said, Marilee had always been the cleverer of the two, the one who had led the way. It made sense that she would have controlled not only the money but the photographs. I wondered if Marilee and Shuga had had a dispute that made Marilee change her locks to keep Shuga out. If Marilee had decided to cut Shuga out of her share of the blackmail income, Shuga might have come for the photographs, gotten into a fight with Marilee, and killed her. But where did Harrison Frazier fit into that scenario? Had he simply stumbled into a situation by accident and been killed because he knew who killed Marilee?

I spilled out another photograph and my

heart jumped crazily. I should have known he would be included, but I was still shocked. It was Carl Winnick, apparently photographed so recently that there were no payments listed yet.

There were still some unopened envelopes, but I had a question that interested me more than seeing the rest of them. Who had been taking the pictures? Who was the third party to this blackmail ring? I shuffled through another collection, this time searching for clues to the place where they'd been taken. In every photo, the camera had been positioned so nothing was visible inside the frame except the sheets on the mattress, the two women, and the victim. Such consistency suggested a tripod holding the camera, but surely none of these wealthy men would have cavorted in front of a camera he could see.

I left the photos on the bar and went down the hall to Marilee's bedroom, flipping lights on as I went. It was past midnight now, and I should have been in bed two hours ago, but I was wide-awake and curious. When I flipped the switch in Marilee's bedroom, the bedside lamp on the far side of the bed lighted up, and Ghost lifted his sleepy head from his spot in the middle of the bed and gave me an annoyed look.

The armoire faced the foot of the bed, and I supposed they could have left the doors ajar and positioned a camera on one of its shelves. I opened both doors and looked for a spot where a camera might have been placed, but the shelves were filled with a large-screen TV, a VCR, a DVD and a CD player, not to mention speakers, along with filed videos and CDs neatly organized according to musical category and artist. Somehow, the idea of Marilee disturbing the neat order of her entertainment center for a smut-capturing camera didn't fit. And even if she'd been willing to lower her neatness standards to accommodate her lack of moral standards, it would have been too risky. Even with all their blood pooled in their penises, the men would have noticed the open doors to the armoire and gotten suspicious.

I looked toward the top of the armoire. It was a perfect place to hide a camera, using one of the remote controls in Marilee's night table to turn it on. I dragged a high-backed Spanish Colonial armchair from the corner of the room over to the armoire and climbed on it. From that height, I could see a camera mounted behind a perfectly round lens-size hole drilled in the carved cornice. I felt a tug of reluctant admiration for the way

Marilee had gone about the business of blackmail. She had been resourceful, efficient, and organized, all marks of the true professional.

Ghost suddenly sat upright with his ears and whiskers pointed toward the door. At the same moment, I smelled the reek of alcohol behind me and whirled to see Olga Winnick in the doorway, her eyes blood-red with fury and despair, her mouth a rectangular gash of malicious rage. She held a butcher knife in her raised hand, with an unmistakable intention to kill me with it.

Suddenly, it seemed inevitable that she was the one. I said, "I should have known it was you."

She swallowed with a convulsive movement of her neck, which made me think of pythons swallowing mice. "I will do anything to protect my family. Anything!"

"Let me guess. You thought Marilee Doerring was after your husband, so you killed her."

"Don't be stupid! I would not dirty my hands on that woman."

For a woman who must have consumed a lot of alcohol before she came, she spoke with amazing control and clarity. The only thing that betrayed how much she'd had to drink were her red eyes and the odor she radiated.

She took a step forward and Ghost sailed over my head to the top of the armoire. She flinched and looked up at him, interrupted for the moment. Ghost crouched at the edge of the armoire and peered down at her, his mouth making the peculiar little smile of a cat smelling something highly offensive, every muscle in his body quivering, his whiskers pointed forward and his ears on alert. With all the chemical odors in the house, the alcohol she radiated was too much for him to stand.

My mind was scrambling, screaming at my body to *do something,* but I was paralyzed. My gun and phone lay on the kitchen counter with the photographs, and she had me cornered. Marilee's big bed blocked me on one side and the bedroom wall was at my right. The only possible weapon was the nearest lamp. The lamps were tall and made of what appeared to be heavy cast iron. If I could grab the closest one and unplug it before Olga Winnick stabbed me, I might be able to stun her with it and run.

As I edged a half step toward the table, she looked back at me.

In that split second, I understood why she was there. I said, "You're protecting your family right now, aren't you? You're here to stop me from telling the truth about who killed Marilee Doerring and Hamilton Frazier. It wasn't you, it was your husband."

Tears filled her eyes and spilled unheeded down her cheeks. "She lured him into her perversions! She was an evil, evil woman."

I thought of the photographs on the kitchen counter. "She did lure him and trick him and use him. How did you find out?"

She wiped at her eyes with her free hand. "A wife always knows. He would leave our bed and come here, he was obsessed. Night after night, I saw him go through her lanai to her. She was here waiting for him, here with all her filthy practices."

Her voice broke and she shut her eyes for a second to compose herself. I took the opportunity to scoot a few steps closer to the lamp. If I could keep her talking, I had a chance.

She opened her eyes and looked at me with renewed determination.

I said, "He came here Thursday night, didn't he? And found Harrison Frazier with Marilee. That must have been a shock to him."

She shook her head, quick to support her husband's intelligence. "He already knew. He saw him when he arrived. He kept watching the house, pacing back and forth, acting as if I wasn't even there, didn't see, didn't understand. Men can be so blind where predatory women are concerned."

I nodded sympathetically, thought about saying "Ain't it the truth," then decided against it. Instead, I said, "Did you know when he came here Thursday night?"

"Oh yes, I knew. Carl didn't know I was awake, but I knew when he got out of bed and left the house. I stood in my kitchen window and watched him go to her lanai just as he always did, saw him disappear into her house just as I'd watched him many times before. He carried a weapon in his hand, a piece of pipe he must have had in the garage. My heart was breaking, but I could not stop him, you see, because it would have led to a scene that might have wakened Phillip. I did not want him to know what his father was doing. A boy should look up to his father as a role model."

"So you stood at the window and waited and watched."

Her breath shuddered, sending out more intense waves of alcohol. "Yes."

"And what did you see, Mrs. Winnick?"

"I saw my husband come out of this house with something in his arms. He carried it across the backyard and walked along the fence beside the woods, and then he disappeared from my view. I didn't know what it was that he carried. Then he came back here to the house again. In a little while, he went out to the driveway and got into that man's car and drove away."

I pushed my foot a few inches to the left and said, "What time was this?"

Wearily, she said, "It was exactly five minutes past one. I know because I looked at the clock on the microwave after he left."

I pulled my right foot alongside the left one, trying to make it look as if I were just adjusting my posture, and said, "You must have been extremely concerned. I mean, it didn't look good for your family, did it?"

"I had to do something. A woman like you can't understand what it is to be a good wife and mother. You can't know how a real woman will go to any length to save her family."

For a minute there, I'd been feeling sorry for her, but that brought me back to reality. "What did you do, Mrs. Winnick? How did you save your family?"

"I came over here and saw what had happened. Saw the mess here. The shower was still running, that naked man hanging out of the tub and blood on the floor. That piece of pipe next to him. It was awful. I turned off the shower and put the man on the floor while I cleaned everything. I went out the side door and put the pipe in the garbage can at the street. Then I went back home."

Above her head, Ghost had gone into a stalking crouch on the armoire, neck stretched forward and down, legs bent and quivering, tail swishing side to side. I had seen cats go into that pose just before sinking their fangs into a snake's body and flinging it side to side until it died. Olga Winnick and her alcohol fumes had become an enemy, prey to be pounced upon and crushed.

The shrill *beep-beep-beep* of my cell phone sounded from the kitchen, and all three of us went rigid. Distracted, Ghost's head twisted nervously toward the sound.

I said, "I really should answer that."

She grimaced. "You underestimate my intelligence, Miss Hemingway."

"Not true, Mrs. Winnick. I think you've been brilliant. I'm really impressed. But you left out the part about dressing the man and taping his head to the cat's water bowl."

She sighed again and gave me an irritated glare. "That wasn't until later. Carl was home when I got back. He had driven the man's car to the Landings and parked it there, then he took a taxi to the Sea Breeze and walked home. He was shaken and humble. We had a long talk. He begged me for forgiveness and I forgave him for what he'd done. It was one of the best talks we've ever had."

"How nice for you."

"Yes. Then he told me he thought there were photographs the police might find, and I came back to look for them. While I was looking, the man made a sound. He wasn't dead after all, you see. I knew he could identify Carl, so I dressed him and dragged him into the kitchen and taped his head to the water bowl. I would have put him in the tub, but he was too heavy and I didn't want to ask Carl to help. He was far too upset by then to be of much use anyway."

"It was a little after four o'clock when you left here, wasn't it?"

Her eyes narrowed into suspicious slits. "How did you know that?"

"Because Phillip saw you. I guess he's more like you than I realized, because he made up a big lie to save you."

"That's not true! Phillip was asleep."

"Phillip had been playing piano at the Crab House, Mrs. Winnick. He had just climbed back in his window when he saw you leave Marilee's lanai."

A tremor played over her face, as if her

nerve endings were readjusting themselves, and the hand with the knife raised an inch.

Okay, if I was dead anyway, I might as well say what would hurt her the most.

"Phillip knew what you did. He loved you so much that he didn't tell, but he knew. He killed himself keeping your terrible secret."

"I don't want to hear any more!"

She charged toward me with the knife held high, enveloped in a miasma of alcohol and revenge. I lunged for the lamp and jerked it forward, pulling the cord out of the wall and plunging the room into darkness. But the thing was incredibly heavy and too thick to wrap my hand around. In the darkness, I could see her silhouette flying toward me.

I did the only thing that seemed halfway logical. I dived for her legs, hoping to knock her down before her knife plunged into my back.

As I hit her, she screamed and flailed the air. I scrabbled behind her and straightened up, ready to grab her knife hand. Something soft brushed across my face, and she screamed again. I realized it was a scream of pain and that it was Ghost's tail I had felt. Ghost was on her head, raking his claws across her face and shoulders.

I sprinted to the kitchen and grabbed my

gun. I was halfway down the hall with it when I doubled back to get my cell phone. As I left the kitchen, I heard the thud of footsteps running down the hall toward the bedroom. I knew who it was. I also knew Ghost would be killed if I didn't get to him in time.

With my gun held in both hands, I rounded the bedroom door. The overhead light was on, and Olga was on her knees, thrashing her head and howling in agony. Ghost was still on her head with his claws embedded in her skull. Her face was shredded, with so much blood spilling from it that her features had disappeared. Carl Winnick stood beside her with a gun trained on Ghost, probably the same gun Phillip had used to shoot himself.

"Be still!" he shouted to Olga. "Stop moving!"

I yelled, "Drop the gun, Winnick!"

He turned his head toward me, wide-eyed and ashen, then swung the gun in my direction.

A shot rang out and his throat burst in a flare of red blood. Ghost screamed and jumped from Olga's head and streaked from the room. Winnick crumpled to the floor beside Olga, and a geyser of blood shot toward the ceiling. Covered with her own blood and his, Olga leaned over him and shrieked a sound so full of grief and rage that it will live in my head forever.

Suddenly, the room was filled with people running past me. In a daze, I turned toward the doorway where Guidry was holstering his Sig Sauer.

"Your brother called us," he said. "When you didn't answer your cell, he knew you were in trouble."

His gray eyes were calm, watching me closely.

"I had it under control," I said, but my voice warbled.

"You had it under superb control, Dixie."

The next thing I knew, my face was buried in his chest, and his arms were holding me close. Except for Michael and Paco, I hadn't felt a man's arms around me since Todd died. I hadn't thought I wanted a man's arms around me, but this felt very familiar and comforting.

34

Sunlight glittered on the sailboats rocking at anchor in Sarasota Bay. A few seagulls strolled along the sidewalk, hoping for handouts. Phillip and I sat quietly, the way people do when there's too much to say to trust yourself to speak. Phillip's forehead still bore an ugly channel from the bullet he fired with the intention of killing himself. If he hadn't jerked his head back just before he pulled the trigger, he would have hit the frontal lobe of his brain. If he'd jerked it forward instead of backward, he would have hit the cortex. As it was, he was physically and neurologically intact. Psychologically, he had a lot of healing to do.

A bold seagull stepped forward and pecked at Phillip's shoelace. Phillip waggled his foot and the gull fluttered its wings in a show of sassiness and then took flight, sailing out over the boats in a graceful swoop.

I said, "How do you like living with Ghost?"

The corners of his mouth twitched in something close to a smile. "He's funny. He curls up in Greg's violin case while he practices. I never was around a cat before, but I think I'll actually miss him when I leave."

"Did you get things squared away with Juilliard?"

"They said I could enroll next year."

"That's good. You'll be completely healed by then."

"Yeah."

We both heard the lie in our voices and fell silent. Plastic surgeons were going to try to smooth the deep groove in his forehead, but he would always bear the emotional scars of his parents' actions.

Do any of us ever escape those scars?

About the Author

Blaize Clement is a writer living in Sarasota, Florida.